C000225184

The Missing Brides

THE LADY MORTICIAN'S VISIONS SERIES

HELEN GOLTZ

The Missing Brides – The Lady Mortician's Vision Series, book 1.

Copyright © 2023 Helen Goltz. All rights reserved.

This book is a work of fiction. Names, characters, places, and incidents are either the product of the author's imagination or are used fictitiously. Any resemblance to actual persons, living or dead, or actual events or locales is entirely coincidental. No part of this book may be reproduced in any form or by any electronic or mechanical means, including information storage and retrieval systems, without the written permission from the author or the publisher, except for the use of brief quotations for review purposes.

Published by Atlas Productions, 2023.

Beta Reader: Mary Fuxa

Proofreader: Crystal L. Wren, COL Proofreading Service and Penny Clarkson.

Cover designer: Karri Klawiter, Art by Karri.

Helen Goltz - https://helengoltz.com/

PLEASE NOTE: This book is written in British-Australian English.

Chapter 1

*B*RISBANE, AUSTRALIA. MONDAY 7TH *April, 1890.*
Mostly fine to cloudy, 27 degrees.

Miss Phoebe Astin stood back and admired her work. She circled the table once, studying her subject from all angles, and then, with a smile and a nod to herself she declared the job finished.

'I think I can say with some confidence, Rose, that you are ready,' she professed happily as if she were assisting a dear friend dress for a dance, rather than preparing the poor deceased Mrs Rose Beatty for viewing and burial. Phoebe was correct, however. Mrs Beatty looked a great deal better now than when her body arrived at *The Economic Undertaker* and was left in the care of Phoebe to 'do something, anything, to make her less offensive to the family', as the relative – clearly not a close one – requested.

In preparation for her next client, Phoebe dusted the powder off her hands, straightened her apron and ran her hands down her loose dress – a style favoured by the aesthetic movement with its flowing fabric and uncorseted waistline, and somewhat unconventional. She neatened her hair which also flouted convention being tied loosely with a ribbon at the back and not worn up or curled in the traditional fashion.

The hurried pace of footfalls on the steps warned Phoebe her brother was on his way, and without turning she knew it to be Ambrose. He was not one for sitting still, not like Julius – her eldest and very restrained brother whom often she barely knew was in attendance.

'You may take Rose,' Phoebe said with a glance over her shoulder at Ambrose. She turned back to the lady on the table in front of her as her brother bellowed up the stairs. 'Grandpa, need a hand here,' he yelled making Phoebe wince and roll her eyes.

'You will wake the dead,' she scolded him.

'Hasn't happened yet,' he said with a chuckle and moved to Phoebe's side. 'My, you have done a fine job on this lady; she was quite a fright when she came in.'

'Thank you, I like to think I've restored her to her best.'

'You have. She looks good... open casket good,' he said using a measure only applied by those in the industry.

Phoebe dropped her voice as if she did not want the dead to overhear. 'The detective believes she died at the hands of a man, most likely her husband.'

'She had the bruises to show for it,' Ambrose agreed and looked up to beckon his grandfather over to help him carry the small lady on the hand stretcher to the waiting wagon for transportation.

'I wonder if Lilly might do a small story on Rose in her births, marriages and deaths column in *The Courier*; it would be nice to acknowledge Rose's life, as short as it was,' she said.

'That's a fine idea, Phoebe. It can't be easy for Miss Lewis to find regular feature stories but I am sure the family would appreciate the tribute,' her beloved grandfather and the business's front man, Randolph Astin said joining Ambrose to collect Mrs Rose Beatty.

Phoebe touched the lady's shoulder. 'I hope the next life will be kinder to you, Rose.'

She covered Rose and then stood back. Phoebe favoured her routines and as she had done many times in the past, she watched as her grandfather and Ambrose removed the body, staying still and silent until the deceased was out of sight. As Phoebe could not go to every funeral to pay her respects, this was her personal tribute and farewell. Sighing, Phoebe turned to see Mr William Walker sitting in the corner.

'Mr Walker!' She brightened. 'Thank you for your patience, although I suspect you were not in a great hurry,' she teased.

'That is the truth, young lady. Your day starts where mine ends,' he said with a wink, 'and I believe I have come to the end. But I am pleased it is my turn, at last, you have been very busy.'

'I have clients dying to see me,' Phoebe jested, using her well-worn line which always got a laugh, and Mr Walker did not disappoint.

She moved to another table where a body lay under a cloth and lowered it to waist length, it revealed the man with whom she was speaking; he was in his forties, handsome and distinguished. His body smelled of dampness. Mr Walker sat in the corner without saying a word as she looked over his body. There was a lot to be said for a good death; unfortunately, William Walker did not have one.

As she studied him, Phoebe thought how she would miss William; he had been good company for the short time they shared her workroom. He had waited patiently to be prepared for his final departure to the grave which would be his body's last resting place, and he'd shared a little of his life journey. Perhaps he might visit again – some did, one welcome guest in particular often dropped in – but Phoebe preferred they moved on and found solace.

'I am sorry for my appearance, Miss Astin. I am not one to boast, but I believe I was much better looking in life than in death.'

'There is no need to apologise at all, Mr Walker, but I thank you for it. Being immersed in water does tend to make one blue and bloated. But, I can tell from your spirit appearance that you are a most handsome man indeed.'

He chuckled, delighted.

'Besides, I am no stranger to seeing people in the last throes of life, and I have seen many startling sights. You are not one.'

'Thank you, my dear,' he whispered in a low voice. Had he been alive he would have been humbled by her kindness.

Phoebe noted the coroner had removed everything he needed, and now she bathed the body with great respect. Mr Walker was not perturbed. He watched and waited, allowing Phoebe to do her work. On completion, she covered him once more with the cloth to his shoulders, leaving only his head bare, and combed Mr Walker's hair covering as best she could the wound to his scalp.

'Is that how you wore your hair, parted to the side?' Phoebe asked. It was hard to tell with the top hat he wore.

'Exactly so,' he agreed.

'Now, let me see.' Phoebe moved her mortician kit closer. Mr Walker was not normally pale she imagined, but water immersion can alter the skin's colouring to a blueish-grey. His skin was now very thin as a result of his immersion, and she selected a powder – Royal Bond's *Life-Glo Tint* and brushed it on.

'That has me looking better,' Mr Walker said pleased.

'I'll put some colour in your cheeks too.'

After a few moments, Mr Walker said, 'Miss Astin may I speak freely on a delicate subject?'

'Please do,' she invited the ghost. 'If not now, when?'

He chuckled. 'Yes, fair point. It's just that I am not ready to move on as yet, my work is not done.'

'Of course,' Phoebe said. She had heard the same said from many a person who chose to talk with her. Though, not all of her clients lingered; many were happy to go to the next life without as much as an introduction to her.

'No, it's not what you might think. I am not that attached to my daily toil,' he assured her. 'It is just that there are people to protect and I would like to see justice done... for my murder.'

Chapter 2

MOVING THE HEAVY CURTAIN aside, Ambrose Astin stood by the window in *The Economic Undertaker* reception waiting for his brother, Julius, to conclude his business so they could head to Mrs Rose Beatty's burial at 10 o'clock. They also had another body to collect from the hospital to take for burial and Ambrose was keen to get the day started so it did not interfere with his evening plans. He shifted impatiently as he watched Julius sign cheques for his grandfather for payments required this business day.

'Oh dear, she's back,' Ambrose said and Julius looked up alarmed. He rushed to his brother's side as Ambrose moved away laughing. 'Just seeing how quick-footed you are brother.'

Julius looked less than amused at his brother's antics. 'Very droll, Ambrose. Since you are impatient to leave, I suggest you do not delay me with your silly games. Besides,' narrowing his eyes as he stared down the street, 'it appears Miss Primrose Carter is on her way, no doubt to see you,' he said with a smile.

Ambrose's eyes widened with alarm and he returned to his brother's side.

'My mistake, it was just a lady who looked like her,' Julius said and moving away from the window, he grabbed his hat, grinned at his grandfather and headed down the hallway to the back door.

'Oh, very amusing, Julius.' Ambrose grumbled and grabbed his own hat, following behind his brother.

'Take care, boys,' Randolph called after them.

On exiting, they thanked their stable hand and took charge of the horse-drawn hearse. There was no need for plumes or a caparison – a regal blanket draped over the horses that some families received in their package – as neither of the families had chosen the top package for their deceased one's funeral. Nevertheless, Julius used a few trimmings to ensure the hearse looked dignified, and he chose the hearse that subtly bore the business name to keep it top of mind for the living.

'Shrouds, coins, rope,' he said checking each item was on hand in the box under his seat. Occasionally they required the coins to rest on the eyes of the deceased, and rope for the tying of the hands and ankles although most bodies were well and truly stiffened by the time they arrived on the scene.

But not every family laid the body out as they should and there was a growing expectation that the service be provided by the undertaker. Julius was not averse to doing so, and fully expected to provide the shrouds, but the rest came at a price. On some occasions, the living did not know what to do – bereaved young widows, husbands at a loss – and in these cases, Julius happily stepped in and took charge, with no additional expenses added to the bill. Death was complicated, he knew that more than most.

'Mrs Beatty is definitely loaded?' Julius asked glancing to the back of the hearse before taking his seat.

'On board and ready for dispatch,' Ambrose confirmed climbing up into the cabin beside Julius and affixing his top hat. As they pulled out of the year, Ambrose asked, 'Do you remember Mrs Grace?'

'Who could forget? If only everyone was as prepared for death,' Julius said with a smile.

'We are not that prepared and we work in the industry.' Ambrose laughed and reflected on the lady who had her shroud made by her dressmaker, and kept it in her trousseau from the day she married in the event of her death that came sixty years later.

'Do you have a favourite client?' Ambrose asked as they started along the street.

Julius glanced at him and then back to the horses as he held the reins and guided their journey. He preferred to take the reins as Ambrose tended to move along too fast which was undignified for a hearse. After all, the dead were in no rush.

He reflected on his brother's question. 'A favourite... no, is that not a bit odd?'

'I bet you do,' Ambrose said and grinned.

'That implies that you do. Who might it be?' Julius asked amused by his brother's antics.

'Anyone who comes to us prepared and ready for burial, and I can count only half a dozen of those so far this year,' he said, with a frown.

'Soon I imagine we will be doing the entire death practice; I believe that is happening overseas. We will pick up the deceased at the moment of their death and prepare them for showing and for burial.'

'Like Phoebe does now for those with few family members to tend them or if the hospital pays us to do so,' Ambrose mused.

'Yes. Inevitable I would say.'

Julius nodded his thanks to several ladies who stopped their amble across the street to let them pass. The hearse had a way of stopping people in their tracks. 'Have you the next of kin's names?' He had of course noted it but liked to make his brother earn his keep.

'Yes,' Ambrose said, fishing in his pocket for a piece of paper his grandfather had pressed into his hand and recited the names as they moved down the wide street to meet with the waiting mourners. The day was warm and the heat dictated they did not dally. 'Grandfather had a client this morning requesting a cedar coffin.'

'Did he tell them cedar is very hard to get at the moment and hence dearer? Hoop pine will serve their purposes just as well.' Julius shook his head in frustration. It wasted their time to chase whims that were best suited to the undertakers serving the loftier ends of the market.

'Grandfather said they insisted and will pay. Cousin is finding the timber and will make it.'

'As they wish,' Julius said releasing his annoyance with a small shrug of indifference. Perhaps they wanted a cheaper funeral to afford a better coffin. They were *The Economic Undertaker* after all and very few of their clients chose that which was uneconomical, happy to go with the packages on offer at a time when grief disabled their ability to make sound decisions.

'What are we expecting at the first collection?' Ambrose asked, shuffling uncomfortably in his dark suit in the heat of the day as Julius turned the hearse at the end of the street to come up on the right side near their destination.

Julius sighed. 'If you read the booking or asked Grandpa you would know.'

'But I know you do so I don't have to,' he said and nudged his brother.

Julius gave him a well-worn look of exasperation, 'We are meeting Mrs Beatty's family outside the Chardon Hotel and her mourners will join the cortège en route to the South Brisbane cemetery.'

'So, we can't bring the horses to a gallop then?' Ambrose joked.

'Wait until we size them up and see if they could keep up,' Julius joined in his brother's good humour for the morning. Julius identified the small crowd as they approached which was not difficult given their black attire.

Both men went into their professional roles – sober, competent, in charge when all seemed lost – and in no time, they were moving off slowly.

'A reasonable-sized group,' Ambrose said with a glance back at the mourners following the hearse. Should I be so popular,' he joked.

'I am sure we can lash out and give you our top-of-the-line funeral plan,' Julius said in jest. 'We could even persuade a crowd to attend if I pay for drinks at the wake.'

Ambrose chuckled as quietly as he could beside his brother. 'After that comment, you'd best hope I die first.' Ambrose glanced behind. 'There's a couple of very attractive young ladies in the procession, they are most becoming in black. I'm sure I could cheer them up to no end.'

'You're incorrigible.'

An hour later and getting weary in the warmth of the mid-morning sun, the young men ventured to the next location for a smaller and quicker burial service.

'And what am I to expect at this one?' Ambrose asked stifling a yawn.

'The deceased died in hospital, so the mourners will gather there to follow us to the grave, a short journey only.'

'Excellent. What are your plans for this evening? I am off to a gallery opening, do you wish to come?' Ambrose asked.

'I am meeting Tavish at the club,' Julius said referring to his friend, the coroner. 'You are welcome to join us.'

'I might do so later if I do not catch the eye of a lovely lady.'

Julius hid a smile. Smiling was not encouraged while driving the hearse. 'Would you like to swing back by the South Brisbane cemetery on the way home and collect a couple of those ladies you thought most lovely at the last funeral?'

Ambrose clapped his brother on the back. 'An excellent idea,' he teased, and then they sobered to collect the last body for the day. A small party of no more than six mourners in black awaited them. After taking the body on board and pulling away slowly to allow the mourners to follow, Julius reignited the conversation.

'Is there no one in your acquaintance that you could form a genuine attachment to?' Surprised by his questioning, Ambrose hesitated. 'Ah, there is.' Julius smiled.

Ambrose looked away.

'She does not return your affection,' Julius said in a low voice.

'She does not know of my affection,' Ambrose said with a shake of his head as if dismissing the thought of love. He lifted his chin. 'We are very serious this morning; the day is too nice for maudlin subjects even if we have the dead on-board.'

'So, love is a maudlin subject now? It is acceptable for you to have some serious thoughts now and then, Ambrose,' Julius teased his brother, giving him a glance that spoke of brotherly affection and concern.

'I believe her affection lies with another.'

'Can she not be persuaded to care for you in time?'

Ambrose frowned and looked displeased with the turn of the conversation. 'You cannot fix everything, Julius, as much as you have in the past and as much as you would like to make mine and Phoebe's life a happy one. We must have our share of life's experiences and that includes the good and the bad.'

Julius turned the hearse into the grounds of the cemetery.

'Would that I could keep the bad from you both,' he spoke quietly, and stopping the hearse, they alighted to bury the deceased.

Chapter 3

'OH BOTHER,' LILLY LEWIS said, as she caught her skirt on the edge of the desk once again on her way to the editor's office. If only she could wear trousers like the men, life would be so much simpler. She saw a few of her male colleagues hiding smiles at her expense and gave them all a stern look.

'You look lovely today, Lilly, very pretty. When are you going to let me take you to dinner?' Lawrence Hulmes – the feature writer, a confirmed bachelor closer to forty than thirty and with a keen eye for the ladies – offered. He enjoyed the ribbing of his colleagues for his constant attempts to woo the attractive Miss Lewis who once conquered was bound to be less interesting to him. Lawrence was a womaniser of the first degree and Lilly was determined, regardless of his charms

– and he was charming – that she would not be one of his successes.

Turning her blue eyes to him, Lilly adopted her most supercilious expression. 'Thank you, Lawrence.' She was on a first-name basis with all her colleagues, in the same manner as the men in the office were with each other. She added with a smile, 'if I am ever faced with the choice of starving or your dinner invitation, I'll give it some serious thought.' Her retort earned a cheer from the boys.

Truth be known she quite enjoyed the teasing of her male colleagues and gave back as good as she got. Lilly was regarded as a 'good sport' amongst the men and in a male-dominated office, who could ask for more? Clearing her skirt from the corner of the desk and departing her colleagues, she tapped lightly on the editor's door, even though she had been summoned. At two-and-twenty and all of five-feet-six, she stood tall in front of his desk, bracing herself for his usual tirade that he freely gave to men and women without discriminating.

Lilly had grand ambitions to be a serious journalist on *The Courier,* but for now, she had to bide her time on what the editor affectionately termed 'the hatches, matches and dispatches' – births, marriages and deaths column. It was better than being the agony aunt, she consoled herself and she did get to select her own feature to write from any one of the

17

notices. The death notices were that much more interesting than the births and marriages, but she had to mix them up just to ensure she did not come across as maudlin.

Lilly was also getting quite a following according to the editor and if she could continue to put a little bit of scandal, gossip or mystery into her columns, the readership of the paper would definitely benefit, he had told her last time she was summoned.

'Lewis.' He addressed her by her surname as he would the men.

'Mr Cowan,' she said and nothing more. The editor studied her, blowing puffs of cigar smoke in Lilly's direction.

'Nothing to say for yourself?' he asked.

'You summoned me, Sir. Besides I believe that while speech is silver, silence is golden.'

The editor laughed a hearty laugh.

'Where did you learn that then, Lewis?'

'I have five brothers, Mr Cowan.'

'Good Lord,' he exclaimed. 'It will be a brave man who seeks your hand in marriage. I like your last article, very good. Keep it up,' he said and waved a hand to indicate dismissal.

'Thank you, Mr Cowan,' she said and started to depart.

'One more thing...'

Lilly grimaced and turned to face her editor. 'Sir?'

'The hatch stories are boring, matches not much better,' he said referring to her birth and marriage short stories, 'but I know you need to mix them up.' He stopped, studied her again and blew out a large puff of cigar smoke before continuing. 'See if you can find a good match and dispatch story all in one!' he said, giving her a challenge. 'You can partner with Hulmes if you find something decent and make it a special feature, illustrations and all.'

'Yes, Sir, I'm onto it.' Lilly tried to sound enthusiastic, which she was, until the editor mentioned partnering with Lawrence who asked her to dinner every chance he could, five minutes ago being his last attempt.

'Good, good,' he said, dismissing her again and this time she made it to the door and out of the office without being called back.

Lilly returned to her desk.

'Still got your job?' Fergus Griffiths, the shipping news writer asked with a wink.

'I live to tell more tales, and lucky you. It would be awful to break in a new neighbour who might not like your leftovers lying around,' she teased indicating his messy desk, a full ashtray and several cups. He lifted a folded paper packet on his desk and looked inside. 'You'll like these... the wife's peanut brittle cookies. Old family recipe from her Irish nan.' He offered her one and Lilly happily accepted.

'Just what I need for fortitude, thank you,' she told him, grabbing her pen and pad, and rising. 'I am off to the funeral parlour to find a story that involves a marriage and a death.'

She noticed Fergus Griffith look at her suspiciously.

'Why that look? The editor has specifically asked for it. I assure you I am not about to kill a bride or groom in order to bring the story to life,' she said, taking a mouthful of biscuit.

He gave her a raised eyebrow and the smallest of smiles. 'It is funny all of your stories seem to come from one funeral parlour in particular.'

Lilly reddened and raised her chin in defiance, mumbling with her mouth half full, '*The Economic Undertaker* is the most forthcoming and my dear friend, Phoebe keeps interesting stories for me,' she said and heard him say on her departure.

'And her brothers are most handsome.'

That she couldn't deny, especially Mr Julius Astin – any excuse to be in his company was a good excuse.

Phoebe heard the sound of the horses and the hearse returning and knew her brothers were back from the funerals. They were often quick when there were few mourners or the ceremony was perfunctory; it was not yet midday. Hearing footsteps on her internal stairs, Phoebe turned to see her grandfather descending.

'Hello my dear, the boys are back. Come up for some lunch and sunlight,' he suggested, eyeing the surrounds of the cool, dark room in the basement of *The Economic Undertaker.* He did not see what Phoebe saw, namely Mr Walker as he sat in the corner in his morning dress, top hat included.

'A break would be good,' she said, smiling at her grandfather.

'Yes, we don't want the clients thinking you are the walking dead, and you scaring away business.'

Phoebe laughed, covered Mr Walker's body for now, and with a nod in his direction, she followed her grandfather up the stairs and into the sunny kitchen where her eldest brother Julius was sitting, and Ambrose was taking a sandwich from the plate Mrs Dobbs had prepared for their lunch.

'About time, Phoebe, dear,' Mrs Dobbs said with a shake of her head. 'I fear one day we will forget you are down there altogether.'

Phoebe kissed Mrs Dobbs's cheek as the men chuckled. 'I could use a cup of tea.'

'Solves the problems of the world,' Mrs Dobbs said filling the cups from the large pot.

The goodly woman in her sixties, with a large bun of grey hair tucked neatly upon her head, was a kind-hearted widow, her husband buried by *The Economic Undertaker*. After that, she was at a loss for what to do with herself and having not received a proper cup of tea during the process of meeting with *The Economic Undertaker*, she volunteered to come in daily and manage the kitchen, namely, their morning and afternoon teas, luncheons, and supply clients with the ample cups of tea they needed during their dark times. Julius insisted on paying her and they agreed on a small rate – that Julius topped up with a large Christmas bonus – which she heavily invested in ingredients for baking to her heart's content, knowing the three men enthusiastically enjoyed her offerings. It also meant she did not ever change out of her mourning black dresses, as the uniform was most appropriate to her surrounds.

'Did Rose have many mourners?' Phoebe asked sitting beside Julius as Ambrose was tasked with bringing milk and sugar to the table. Mrs Dobbs liked to keep him occupied so he was not underfoot.

'Just on a dozen not including us,' Julius said. 'It was a dignified ceremony, although I was inclined to punch her smug husband into the grave on top of her and shovel in the dirt myself.'

Phoebe hid a smile. 'I'm sure your scowling looks in his direction were threat enough, Julius.'

'Sadly no. It goes to prove that looks cannot kill,' he added.

'Regardless, I am relieved a good number were there to farewell Rose. There is nothing more forlorn than a funeral with no attendees.'

'Sometimes age dictates it, my dear,' Mrs Dobbs added.

'Indeed. My father, your grandfather,' Randolph paused to look at his three grandchildren, 'outlived all his friends, so it was family only at his wake. Had he not lived as long, the church would have been overflowing. He was a very social man.'

Julius accepted a sandwich from the plate Phoebe offered. 'She looked lovely in the little memorial chapel, well done, Phoebe,' he said and she nodded her head grateful for his praise.

'Several of the young lady mourners were making eyes at Julius. They have no shame,' Ambrose said with a quick grin.

'A missed opportunity, Julius,' Randolph said to his eldest grandson. 'You could have picked yourself up a wife at the same time,' he teased. 'Lord knows, it is not for lack of trying on my behalf to get you all partnered. Might I never attend a wedding or have young ones on my knees for storytelling hour?'

'Wouldn't that be lovely,' Mrs Dobbs said with a smile.

Phoebe could not hide her amusement as Julius rolled his eyes, refusing to engage in their trivial banter.

'It's that handsome, brooding demeanour, mark my words,' Mrs Dobbs said. 'That's why Julius catches the eye of the ladies, they want to save him. Not to mention the success of the business makes you both very eligible young men.'

Julius grimaced, attempting to ignore them as he focussed on the week ahead booking sheet his grandfather placed before him.

'Even if it is an odd business and death is not a subject many like to discuss,' Ambrose said, 'but it did not deter the ladies today.'

'Did they not see his handsome younger brother?' Phoebe asked Ambrose.

'No, and that mystifies me too, dear sister.' Ambrose sighed with a shake of his head. 'I am clearly the better-looking brother,' he said in jest. 'All I can think of is that they are fans of those terrible gothic romance novels and think Julius has stepped out of the pages of one.'

The family chuckled and Julius gave his brother a similar look of exasperation to the one he gave him earlier and set about ignoring him as he often did when Ambrose attempted to vex him. 'When will Mr Walker be ready?' he asked Phoebe.

'Ah yes, Mr Walker's sister hoped to have a small gathering for him here in a few days, and then bury him thereafter,' Randolph said. 'She would like the casket to be open if he is not too blue.'

24

Phoebe frowned. 'He will not be blue but, in truth, he is not in a hurry.' She paused. 'In fact, I think it might be best to ask the police if they would consider reviewing his case, and perhaps Julius, your private investigator friend might be interested in taking a look. You see, Mr Walker was himself a private investigator and his death might be as a result of his last investigation.' Phoebe saw the men exchange glances and added. 'Yes, he said he was murdered. A most odd story it is too.'

Mrs Dobbs made the sign of the cross over her chest and muttered, 'Lord, bless us.' She had become conditioned to the eccentricities of the Astin family and Phoebe's special skills, but still liked to protect herself with a good blessing on a regular basis.

'What makes it odd?' Ambrose asked, none of them questioning how Phoebe came about the information or the validity of it. Those concerns had long since been answered and proven.

'Mr Walker said while attempting to find a missing woman, he lost his own life in the most terrible way. He believes he was hit in the back of the head and deliberately pushed in the river. He also believes others might have met a similar fate at the hands of the same man.'

'I think we should seek out Detective Stone about this and ask if he will investigate Mr Walker's death appropriately,'

Julius said. 'The death has obviously been considered an accident or misadventure if Mr Walker is here with us for burial.'

'That is what Mr Walker believes as well,' Phoebe said.

Julius continued, 'Detective Stone might be new to town but was respectful after our first encounter and I have met him several times socially since. We can trust him, I feel.'

'I believe so too,' Randolph said. 'I shall send a note asking Detective Stone to meet us at his earliest convenience.'

Phoebe nodded. 'Thank you, Grandpa.'

Julius finished his tea and a sandwich, refusing the extra round Mrs Dobbs offered his way and thanking her, rose. 'I'll get word to Bennet now. It will give him a chance to secure some work if a case can be made from it,' he said referring to his friend cum private investigator, Mr Bennet Martin.

'The men will need to act with caution by the sounds of it,' Randolph said, 'a villain is on the loose.'

Mrs Dobbs blessed herself again.

Chapter 4

DETECTIVE HARLAND STONE KNEW that his colleagues were laughing behind his back at the situation he found himself in. At six foot three, with fighting skills honed from boxing in his spare time, and with the odd mix of rough edges but a sterling private school education, there were not many prepared to laugh in his face. Still, Harland had consented to the work agreement and had made his bed.

'Let them laugh,' he mumbled to himself as he watched the passing scenery from the hansom cab he rode in. 'I might do the same in their situation.' He glanced at Gilbert, relieved his young partner had not heard his words above the rattle of the wheels on the road.

Being one of eleven detectives on the payroll across the state, a death in the city office saw him offered, on merit, the chance to leave the north and work in a city. It was not his birth city, but Harland was keen for the change and agreed. It came with a proviso as Harland was only just beginning his third decade and younger than several applicants to the post – he had to take a fast-tracked young detective under his wing. Normally the thought would not fill him or his colleagues with trepidation as most young detectives were keen and eager to go the extra mile, and that was true of his new partner, Gilbert Payne. But Gilbert was the son of a friend of the commissioner whose father had saved the commissioner's life in battle or in business or whatever the tale was, Harland did not care, he was lumped with the young lad who had not spent enough time on the beat to warrant his fast-tracking nor shown enough skills to be considered for a detective. The young man was a fact-gatherer and fascinated by how things worked. Harland was convinced he would make a better engineer or inventor, than a detective.

Still, Gilbert was enthusiastic and bright, neat and polite. Harland glanced at the young man with his perfectly parted hair and pressed suit. He was someone's pride and joy. Harland was determined he would make a detective of the young man yet.

'Harness your strengths and play to them.' He heard the words of his mentor in his head, they had been instilled in him many a time, and he would find Gilbert's strengths and do just that. Thus, Harland and Gilbert were a team of some amusement and derision.

'How does one lose an entire family?' Gilbert asked as the hansom pulled up outside of the residence of Mr Zachariah Beaming and the men alighted. He tilted his head to the side while he thought. 'I would understand if there were a dozen or more family members that one of them might be misplaced, but surely a head count for four children is not too challenging.'

'I think you might be taking the word "lose" too literally. There are several ways I imagine,' Harland advised his young protégé as he paid the hansom cab driver. 'The wife may have deserted her husband, taken the children with her and does not want him to know where she is. Thus, they are lost to him.'

'Yes, that could work,' Gilbert agreed.

'The husband may have bumped off his wife, and the children to boot,' Harland continued, lowering his voice as they made their way up the small garden path to the home, 'or it might be a misunderstanding and the family is on holidays or simply not corresponding with their relatives as expected, hence causing alarm.'

Gilbert nodded taking in the options. 'Or he might have lost them... say if they took separate means of transport home after a holiday like by ship or rail. If the ship sunk or the train crashed, well they would be lost. The *Agnes* sank recently but no one was harmed, but the *Quetta* sank merely two months ago taking 134 souls with it! I am not aware of any recent train accidents, I am sorry,' he admitted as if it were a fault.

Harland looked at Gilbert – restraining a sigh – and gave a small nod. 'Perhaps, but I imagine there would have been a list of the names of those missing at sea or deceased, and the operators would answer for it.'

'Ah, true,' Gilbert said, rubbing his chin in contemplation.

Harland had not expected to find Zachariah Beaming home when most men would be at their industry, but the door swung open and a man of medium height, with a full head of neatly combed salt and pepper hair, dressed and holding his hat and a cane answered the door.

'Ah, you caught me just departing – a lunch engagement,' he said, smiling. 'Zachariah Beaming at your service, how can I help?'

Harland took a moment to study the man before him; well groomed, with a British polished accent, clothing neat and refined, neither expensive nor tailored.

'Detectives Harland Stone and Gilbert Payne, Mr Beaming.' Harland did the introductions.

'Goodness, I hope everything is alright, Detectives?'

'May we come inside?' Harland asked, and on consent, followed the man inside his neat cottage home. He glanced around studying the area and noted his young protégé was doing the same... good, one lesson that had sunk in.

'I am on my way to meet a lady friend so forgive me if I don't offer you refreshments,' Zachariah said and indicated a sitting area.

'We won't delay you any longer than necessary,' Harland assured Mr Beaming and declined the invitation to sit. 'I am enquiring after the whereabouts of your wife and children.'

'Ah, that's a relief,' Zachariah said his hand going to his heart. 'I thought you were here to tell me bad news.'

'So you know where they are then?' Gilbert asked, confused.

'That I don't, Detective. The wife left me.' He adopted a sober look. Clearing his throat, he added, 'We were married when we were very young and in the first throes of love. The children came along quickly and... her nerves, you understand.'

'No Sir, what do you mean?' Gilbert asked blundering along.

Harland turned to the young detective. 'Mrs Beaming was not able to cope.'

Zachariah nodded. 'I am keen to find her, Detective,' he said to Harland, 'and I thought she might have returned to her parents, but it is not so. Unless they are not telling me the truth and want to keep me from her.'

'They are telling you the truth,' Gilbert said. 'They are the ones who have alerted us to them being missing.'

Harland gave Gilbert a look that he interpreted quickly and stopped talking. Harland did not want a potential suspect to know who was investigating him, or that he was the subject of investigation less he should change his behaviour. And the man in question did just that. He stood straighter, his brow furrowed and his jaw tightened.

'So, they believe my wife and children have come to some harm and I am responsible?' he asked of Harland.

'I cannot say where they lay blame, Mr Beaming, but why have you not been to the police to report your family missing?'

'Detective Stone, while they are missing from my life, I do not believe they are in any danger. If my wife chooses to depart with the children, surely putting the police on her and dragging her home would not solve any of our problems,' he said, tapping his cane on the ground as if that were a foregone conclusion.

'How do you know they are not in danger?' Harland asked picking up on his words.

'The lady is travelling with four children,' Zachariah said as if it were obvious. 'There would be much easier subjects to harass or harm I imagine.'

Harland nodded, unconvinced by the logic.

'That is a good point, Mr Beaming,' Gilbert agreed, 'but only if the children were of age to protest or assist their mother.'

'My eldest is ten years, her sister seven years and her brother is five. Old enough to protest and protect. The youngest is a child in arms,' Mr Beaming informed Gilbert.

While Gilbert discussed semantics with Zachariah Beaming, Harland took the opportunity to study the room while the subject was distracted. He noticed there were no family portraits or items that spoke of a family in attendance. The house was quite masculine in its appearance.

'Have you spoken with a private investigator by the name of William Walker?' Harland asked returning his attention to Zachariah Beaming.

'I have not. Should I be expecting him on my doorstep next?' Zachariah asked his voice displaying his displeasure.

'I cannot say but I am prepared to tell you that your wife's family has hired him to find your family.'

'Preposterous! The private investigator will get no audience here,' Zachariah Beaming said puffing out his cheeks.

'Do you have a cordial relationship with your wife's family?' Harland continued.

'I didn't have a great deal to do with them. As I mentioned, we married young, and have lived abroad for many years.'

Harland studied the man and then gave a quick nod of his head to signal they were done for now. 'We will leave you to your business, Mr Beaming, but please do notify us as soon as possible should your wife and children contact you. Just send a message to me at the Roma Street station.'

'I shall, I assure you, Detective Stone,' Zachariah said seeing the detectives out.

On their return to the station, Harland pointed out some observations to Gilbert, including what the young man did well and not so well. He was taking seriously his job to bring the young man up to scratch, and if he did not succeed, it would not be from lack of trying. In the meantime, a family was missing and Harland was not convinced that Zachariah Beaming knew nothing of their disappearance.

'Where to next?' Gilbert asked.

'You tell me, Gilbert, where would you go next with the investigation?' Harland knew exactly where he intended to go.

The young man thought a moment. 'I'd go to some of the women's homeless shelters and see if she had been there.'

Harland smiled. 'Bravo, Gilbert, we'll make a detective of you yet.'

Gilbert beamed with pleasure.

'So, you shall do that. Go to as many as you can,' Harland suggested. 'First though, when we return to the station, see if that detailed description of the family has arrived by telegram.

If not, you'll just have to describe the lady and children as best you can – the two daughters, ten and seven, a lad of five, and a baby girl. If Mrs Beaming sought help, hopefully, someone will remember them.'

'What shall I do if I find them, Sir?'

'Do not remove them from their safe premises, nor advise Mr Beaming. Just inform me and we shall act from there. Make sure they know they are not in any danger from us and we can afford them some protection if needed. Also, as you are not in uniform, take a constable with you so your enquiries look official, less you should alarm the ladies.'

Gilbert gave a nod. 'What will you be doing, Sir?'

'I need to finish the report and paperwork on our current case and then we can fully commit to finding out if Mr Beaming's family has met with foul play. Visit the shelters first, if no success, we shall start our investigation in earnest in the morning by seeking out the private investigator, Mr William Walker. I wish to find out if we should be more worried about Mrs Beaming and the children than Zachariah Beaming appears to be.'

Chapter 5

I F BENNET MARTIN – private investigator and artist – had known he would have a legitimate reason to visit Miss Phoebe Astin this afternoon at *The Economic Undertaker*, he would have felt lighter of heart all morning as he worked. Unlike many of his fellow artists, he was usually up early. He loved the light streaming in his windows first thing in the morning and putting aside his private investigator work – toil that did not involve a paintbrush or easel – he made time to indulge his art which he hoped would one day sustain himself and a future wife.

As he had recently finished a case and had nothing pressing, Bennet remained in his loose bedclothes and painted until late morning. His blond locks fell across his forehead, his hazel eyes studied the scene before him, and a strong square jaw added to his most desirable looks. A polished British accent, and a dash of talent and mystery, made him a formidable catch for the single ladies of the city and he had set many a heart aflutter, but he had eyes for one woman only. Fortunately, or unfortunately, her brother was his closest friend since arriving in this country.

He could not help but think of Miss Phoebe Astin as he worked on the river scene inspired by the view from his window. He would bide his time; it was all he could do while she was seeing that gallery owner, Gideon Hayward. He hoped that connection would amount to nothing and that he had not missed his opportunity to court her.

Satisfied with his morning's efforts, Bennet cleaned his brushes before undertaking his own grooming and rinsing the paint out of his hair – a bad habit he had developed from running his hands through his wavy strands as he stood back to study his paintings, thus streaking his hair with blue or red tints. He dressed and took the stairs to the lower level of his South Brisbane abode, where his office bearing the sign *Bennet Martin Esq. Private Investigator* was opened to the passing foot traffic.

It was just after midday when he presented himself with aplomb as if the day could now begin. His clerk, Daniel Dutton, glanced at his timepiece as Bennet entered.

'Do not say it,' Bennet said, warning the young man whom he believed overstepped his mark all too often, and seemed to enjoy doing so. 'I got caught up.'

'In the bed linen with company?' Daniel asked.

'So impudent!' Bennet exclaimed and sat at his desk. 'If you were not so invaluable to me, I would let you go.' Bennet jested, having delivered that threat many a time before.

'Then who would make your sales, collect debts, greet your customers and write your reports?'

'Who indeed,' Bennet agreed. 'Good morning or rather, good afternoon, Mrs Clarke.' He greeted his housekeeper, as she appeared with a cup of tea for him.

'Mr Martin, did you find inspiration?'

'Indeed I did, thank you, Mrs Clarke,' he said and sighed, thinking of the painting on the easel that was calling to him. 'But now, a man must make a respectable living if he chooses to remove himself to the colonies and cut himself off from his inheritance by doing so.'

'How nice to have the option,' Daniel said drily.

'Will you take an early lunch now before I tidy your rooms?' Mrs Clarke enquired.

Bennet looked to Daniel. 'Will I?'

'If you please, but you might have a new case. Julius Astin has requested you call at your convenience.' Daniel waved a note at his boss. 'I'm sure Miss Phoebe will be present,' he teased.

Bennet sat up straighter. His best friend often summoned him if there was the whiff of a case, and any mention of Miss Phoebe Astin required his immediate attention. 'When did you receive the message?'

'Just five minutes ago. I heard you moving around so I suspected you were on your way downstairs, hence I did not interrupt you.'

'I shall go immediately. Thank you, Mrs Clarke, but I shall forgo lunch.' He finished the cup of tea in three large sips.

'But you have not had breakfast either, Sir,' she said alarmed. She was a portly woman who believed a man must be fed, and fed well. Her husband was proof. 'I will prepare you a sandwich to eat on the way.'

'He's fading away to a shadow,' Daniel agreed with a shake of his head and a small smile at Bennet.

'Fear not, both of you, I shall encourage Julius to come to lunch.'

Mrs Clarke made a clucking sound. 'Such a serious young man, that Julius Astin. Unlike you, Daniel Dutton!' She clipped him with her towel as she departed.

'Ow, Aunt, I am most serious and studious!' Daniel protested.

Bennet chuckled. 'You only have yourself to blame, recommending your aunt for the position of housekeeper.'

Daniel smirked and rubbed his ear. 'You will be pleased to know the hospital board settled your account today.'

'I am pleased to know that indeed, thank you, Daniel. Guaranteed employment then for all three of us for the next few months,' he said with a wink.

'Such a relief,' Daniel exclaimed drily. As Bennet's bookkeeper, he was well familiar with Bennet's financial situation and the business was in top shape, but he played along. 'What a blessing it is for me to have secure employment.' The young clerk's employment was never under threat while Bennet's mother continued to send him large 'charity' cheques for his upkeep. Whether Bennet's father knew of the household funds or his mother's spending money going to his disinherited son was another matter.

Bennet chuckled. 'A few more of those types of cases would be most welcome.'

Daniel grimaced. 'I for one do not enjoy hospital mix-ups and bodies being stolen, but you are correct, the investigation was spirited.' He could not help but grin at his own pun, as Bennet rolled his eyes, grabbed his hat and was gone as quickly as he came, hailing a cab not far from his office.

The hansom cab driver – an older man who looked worn from work – glanced down from his high seat at his passenger and frowned.

'You look very much alive, Sir, are you sure you want to go there?' he asked.

'I do, thank you my good man, and I will tip you handsomely to take me there,' Bennet assured him. 'Fear not, death is not catching.'

Bennet settled himself in the hansom and fidgeted with his neck tie, ensuring he looked his best for the Astin family, one member in particular. Granted, the death industry was an unconventional business but his friend, Julius, was an unconventional man. Bennet recalled their first meeting. He had stormed the premises of *The Economic Undertaker* of Tribune Street, South Brisbane, seeking information for a case he was working on. Bennet had a talent for the private investigation business – it was his pedigree. His father was a senior detective at Scotland Yard in England and hoped his son would follow suit and forget his art inclinations. It wasn't to be and to escape the constant demands of his father to man up and take proper employment, he sailed to Australia to carve his future.

Bennet had expected to find some resistance that day at *The Economic Undertaker* but instead, he found the business's founder, a young man of his own age, most helpful. From that moment on, he enjoyed the company of Julius Astin, who included him in his social circle and club activities, thus ensuring his arrival in Brisbane was not only fortuitous but most enjoyable. And Bennet admired Julius greatly for his business acumen.

The hansom pulled up, Bennet paid the man generously as promised and slowed his pace so as not to enter the solemn business too gleefully. After all, clients may be inside and in mourning. He opened the door, entered, and allowed his eyes to adjust to the darker surrounds. Bennet hurriedly removed his hat, as Randolph – Mr Astin senior – saw an elderly woman to the door. Customers preferred the distinguished and mature face of silver-haired Randolph Astin when it came to matters of death than that of the younger staff.

'My condolences, Madam,' Bennet said as he caught the eye of the lady in mourning.

She gave a nod and a small smile. 'Thank you, it's a bit of a relief actually.'

'Is that so?' Bennet said and restrained from laughing.

Randolph bid her farewell and as the door closed behind her, Bennet looked to Randolph for an explanation.

'Goodness, don't tell me her husband has dropped off this mortal coil and she's happy about it?' Bennet asked.

'Quite a few are, trust me,' Randolph said with a chuckle. 'Good to see you again, Bennet. The boys are in the kitchen, you know the way.'

'Thank you, Sir,' he said and grimaced as the front door beside him opened and a woman he recognised entered. Lilly Lewis. Sigh. The most aggravating woman in the world, and he knew without a doubt the feeling of dislike was mutual.

'Mr Astin,' she said her face lit up in her greeting of the gracious family patriarch. She looked to Bennet and her smile diminished. 'Mr Martin.'

Bennet Martin bowed as he offered her a greeting. She was attractive, he'd grudgingly admit, but she had a mouth that left a lot to be desired – always ready with a barb to fire his way and often.

'How delightful to see you again, Miss Lewis,' Bennet said with very little sincerity.

'Oh, the pleasure is all mine, I assure you,' she reciprocate with a pained smile that made Randolph laugh.

'I imagine you wish to speak with Phoebe, Miss Lewis? I shall gather the family, come into the kitchen and we'll keep the waiting area clear in case of clients,' Randolph said as he ushered the pair into another room.

In moments, the large kitchen at *The Economic Undertaker* was crowded with the Astin family, Mrs Dobbs, and the two visitors – Bennet Martin and Lilly Lewis.

'Goodness, it's a full house and everyone is alive,' Ambrose exclaimed as Mrs Dobbs rushed around putting out more biscuits and cakes, while the kettle boiled. The ladies sat while the men remained standing.

'I have been tasked with finding a feature story involving both a marriage and a death,' Lilly proclaimed explaining her visit.

'How terribly morbid,' Mrs Dobbs said and missed the surprised looks on the rest of the family. They had become so accustomed to death in all its life guises, the idea that it was morbid did not naturally occur to any of them.

'I might have just the thing,' Phoebe said.

'But it is just speculation at this stage,' Julius hurriedly added giving Phoebe a warning look not to reveal too much.

'Oh yes, I'm referring to the recent death of young Mrs Rose Beatty, married but a few years and her husband buried her today,' Phoebe assured her brother.

'And Julius almost buried her husband with Rose,' Ambrose added in good humour.

'Oh this sounds interesting,' Lilly said. 'Although, am I to assume there was another story too? A speculative story not involving Mrs Rose Beatty?'

'That is what I am here for I imagine,' Bennet said with a raised eyebrow in Julius's direction, who agreed with a nod. Bennet turned his attention to Lilly. 'You cannot wish to report on a story where there is no evidence or proof? A quick way to get yourself dismissed.'

'Thank goodness for you, Mr Martin, I might have fallen headfirst into that trap and not had the facts to back up my work,' she said giving him her best withering look that had the table guests hiding their smiles. Lilly turned to Phoebe. 'We are so lucky to have men to guide us, aren't we?'

Phoebe gave a small laugh. 'Oh, they always know best, I'm sure of it.' Lilly, Phoebe and Mrs Dobbs all exchanged a smile and Julius frowned more so than usual. Bennet looked less than pleased to be shown as wanting in front of Phoebe.

'I suspect we are being made fun of mercilessly,' Ambrose said looking from one lady to the next.

'Heaven forbid!' Phoebe exclaimed and returned her attention to Lilly. 'I shall give you this story first and inform you should the other story come to light.' She hurriedly gave Lilly the story of Rose and her early demise. 'If you succeed in finding any way to shine a light on the injustice of Rose's death that would be a great kindness to her. I suspect that she was not clumsy as her husband insisted.'

Julius shook his head in disbelief. 'It is a great shame it is not being investigated. I believe Detective Stone would have gotten to the bottom of it. He's rather dogged.'

'He is,' Bennet agreed.

'That's the new detective that has arrived from north Queensland, is it not?' Lilly asked but continued before anyone could answer. 'I hear he is a very interesting man and strikingly handsome,' she said with a glance to Phoebe which Bennet did not appreciate nor Phoebe's reactionary slight blush in response. Surely, she harboured no feelings towards the detective when she had already drawn the attention of gallery owner, Gideon Hayward.

The party waited for Lilly's departure, and armed with the information on Rose and a few next of kin addresses, she left promptly, along with Mrs Dobbs who had taken herself to the post office.

The remaining small party moved to Phoebe's work area, Bennet following the Astin brothers in front of him. He could not help but think what a very odd family the Astins were and how fitting that they worked in the death industry. They were all quite light of heart – except for Julius – and comfortable around death, he thought, as they entered the cool room. Nearby, a covered corpse lay on the table and Phoebe was about to tell them of a crime she believed had been committed as told her by a spirit. Yes, it didn't get much stranger than this. He could imagine his father's consternation if he knew this was what his son was doing.

As Phoebe adjusted the curtains to allow in more light, Bennet reached into his suit coat for his notebook and pencil.

To say he was uncomfortable was an understatement. Bennet's life of privilege was so different from the Astin family's humble beginnings they might have been living in different worlds. While Bennet struck out for independence, he was assured of a decent inheritance despite his father's threats. Julius, Ambrose and Phoebe had a business born from misfortune – the loss of their parents when they were younger. It was most likely why Julius was more serious than a man his age need be, but he was a man committed to family and hard work.

He had told Bennet the story after some persuasion and a few drinks. Julius was old enough to witness firsthand his parents' death. He recalled Julius's words: 'I will never forget seeing the pain my grandparents were in at the loss of their son and daughter-in-law, my parents, and then struggling to pay for their funeral and give them a deserving farewell when they now had three grieving grandchildren to raise, it was a terrible time.' He would not speak of the brutal manner of his parents' death but added, 'There was a fear and a stigma of not sending them off appropriately, the shame, was appalling on a poor family.'

And so, when Julius was old enough to lease a premise, he stepped up for the poorer families of the town providing an alternative funeral option – *The Economic Undertaker*. The Astin family offered modest and caring funeral packages with a very affordable 'middle option' so no one felt like they were choosing the cheapest send-off. A stroke of genius by Julius, he was astute.

As Phoebe moved to the corpse, Bennet studied her delicate face, large blue eyes and the wild and wavy blonde hair restrained by a white ribbon. He found himself quite distracted until a slap on the back brought him around.

'Are you alright, Bennet?' Ambrose asked. 'We're used to the dead; we can talk upstairs if you prefer.'

'No, not at all,' he assured them. 'Bring on your tales from the dead.' He did not feel as brave as he sounded but was grateful to benefit from the inside information and he swore to keep the family's secret.

'Mr William Walker is present; he too is a private investigator,' Phoebe said and delivered her briefing. Bennet could not see, nor did he wish to see Mr Walker. He found the whole thing a little disconcerting and would hate to run up the stairs to the sunlight and have Phoebe think he was fearful of what she faced every day. His exposure to death had been minimal at best.

'Mr Walker suggests you take up the case, Mr Martin,' Phoebe concluded. 'If you are interested in doing so, you should contact Mrs Beaming's family with haste, tell them of Mr Walker's demise and that you have been working with him, and offer to continue to investigate on their behalf to find their daughter.'

'That is very considerate,' Bennet said with a nod.

'Mr Walker suggests you make haste to his rooms and collect his files before the landlady clears them away,' Phoebe said.

'Yes, indeed, thank you,' Bennet said with a glance at the corner. 'I will go to Mr Walker's room now, hopefully be on hand when you meet with Detective Stone, and then speak with the family, in that order.'

'I have not had a response from him yet. Perhaps he is out of the office today,' Phoebe said.

Delighted to have a potential new meaty case and thrilled to see Miss Phoebe Astin he excused himself and left the room, doing his best not to make his exit too hasty for fear of giving himself away but he was never happier than he was that day to see the sunlight and walk the street. It was not far to Mr Walker's former residence and he decided to make the trip by foot, finding the neat but humble abode and a most unwelcoming landlady who size him up.

'You're the second man to appear on my doorstep within the hour but at least you are well dressed. And who might you be? Have you also come about the room?' she asked before Bennet had the chance to introduce himself and continued without drawing a breath, 'A handsome fellow like you will attract the ladies, and that is not encouraged. This is a respectable boarding house.'

'Good morning, Madam. I am William Walker's business partner and I've come to collect his papers if that is suitable for you?'

'Ah, right then. So you aren't looking for board?'

'No, Madam.'

'Come this way then. Will you take his personal belongings as well?' she asked, grabbing for a set of keys from a pocket in the front of her apron and unlocking the door to a room near the entrance.

'I shall leave that for his next of kin. He would only want me to collect his business papers so I can continue his work.' Bennet entered behind her to find a most orderly and sparse room. William Walker was a man light on possessions. Maybe his private investigator work meant he travelled frequently, unlike Bennet who had an artist studio and staff to maintain. 'Did anyone visit Mr Walker here recently?'

'No, he wasn't one for guests, but he came and went a great deal. I rarely saw him except for meals and he missed a lot of those.' She stood in the doorway and watched Bennet. Assuming she was not intending to depart, and somewhat relieved for fear Mr Walker might appear to him as he appeared to Miss Phoebe Astin, Bennet found a briefcase in William's possessions and packed the paperwork contents of his desk and drawers. Finding half a dozen files on a small timber table in the corner, Bennet thumbed through until he found one labelled 'Mrs Mary Beaming' and pulled it free.

Excellent! He had found what he came for but nevertheless, finding three more files that were not stamped 'Complete' as the others were, he took them should there be the opportunity to work those cases as well.

'Would you know to whom Mr Walker might have been meeting down by the river on the last evening of his life?' Bennet tried again, not expecting to be enlightened.

'No, but...'

Bennet looked at the landlady with hope.

'He did receive a message late in the afternoon. It was brought here by a young lad and I took it to his office. He read it, pocketed it and thanked me.' She shook her head. 'I heard he was found in the river, so I am guessing if he drowned, that message will be in his pocket and pulp now.'

Bennet slumped. 'I suspect you are right, Madam, but thank you for that information.' He had a glance in the bin beside Mr Walker's desk in case there were papers there to be retrieved but as expected, the room was spotless and the bin emptied.

With his bundle of papers, notably the file he wanted, Bennet thanked the landlady, departing as another young man appeared and received the same reception Bennet did. Only this party was interested in a room to rent and was hurried inside as Bennet was pushed out. By now the afternoon light was fading and the beautiful hues of dusk softened the end of the day. Bennet decided he could manage the weight of the briefcase and would walk home to enjoy the twilight. He had secured the papers not a moment too soon for fear they might have been destroyed by the new tenant.

Chapter 6

ZACHARIAH BEAMING WAS ROMANTIC, Anne Norris could not deny it, but her instincts made her wary of him, and not just because of his haste to partner. Something was not right about that man and Anne had very good instincts when it came to people. Her mother had always said she could sort the wheat from the chaff. Besides, she was no debutant. Marriage had long since passed her by and now in her fortieth year, she was a sensible and practical woman who didn't mind a bit of wooing but was not desperate for love. Zachariah Beaming on the other hand appeared to be very keen to form a union.

'You can't afford to be too fussy, Annie,' her neighbour, a policeman who had never risen the ranks but claimed to like the foot patrol of his street beat, reminded her over a cup of tea as they enjoyed the last of the dusk from her verandah.

Anne scoffed. 'You can talk, Edward Smyth. Any one of the lovely church ladies could have stepped into the role of Mrs Smyth if you'd put your mind to it. Lord knows you've enjoyed their gift of baking long enough.'

He chuckled. 'Ah, neither of us is inclined to marry. I've got my job, good company,' he said with a nod in her direction, 'and I'm set in my ways.'

'That we agree on,' she jested. 'My mother always said at my age, all men want is a purse or a nurse. I have some savings that might appeal to a man, but I have little patience for nursing. But, Zachariah is charming, however...' She shook her head in the negative rather than finish her thought.

'So, you have considered accepting his hand?' Edward turned side on to study the friend and neighbour he was not keen to lose to another man. He had no romantic interest in Anne but he did not want to lose their friendship and social engagements. He was comfortable in her company and she was pleasing to the eye – of medium height, well-endowed and sprightly, with brown hair that looked auburn in the dusk light and hazel eyes that sparkled with mirth when the occasion was right.

'He's a married man but claims his wife abandoned him taking the children.' Anne sighed. 'A sad tale if you choose to believe him. They had long since fallen out of love and are not companionable to carry on, he says.'

'He'd be missing the children I imagine.'

Anne gave a small shrug. 'Some men are more fatherly than others. I rarely saw my father – he spent his days at work and his evenings at the pub.' She shook her head. 'There's something not right about Zachariah though. We had lunch today and now he has hurried away on urgent business elsewhere, so I have time for a little bit of investigating of my own. Then I might confide in you, in your capacity as a policeman, not a friend.'

'I am open to that. I admit I'd be happy to impress Detective Stone. He's an interesting young man, new to our branch. He doesn't say much but is fair and gets the job done. Not that I'm seeking a promotion at my age, but a little respect wouldn't go astray.'

'Detective Stone, you say?' Anne said distracted as she thought about Zachariah Beaming.

'You think Mr Beaming is up to something nefarious?' Edward asked, studying her.

'I cannot say. Yet.'

Edward narrowed his eyes at Anne. 'You'll not be getting into any trouble now, will you, Annie? I'd hate to have to bail you out of my cells.'

Anne chuckled. 'I'll do my best to stay on the right side of the law.' She said no more as they finished their tea and watched the last light leave the sky. And then she added softly, 'It is odd though... I have seen him sit by me, talking gently of the things that women like to hear from lovers, and suddenly he would change completely... his eyes seemed capable of looking on and gloating over infamy or cruelty.' She gave an involuntary shudder.

'I think it best you steer well clear of him then,' Edward said his voice taking a serious edge. 'If you think something is amiss, do you want an audience with Detective Stone? I could organise it for you, and you could tell him of your concerns... it won't hurt for him to take a look. If he hasn't the time, at least speak to the officer in charge.'

'Thank you, Edward, maybe when I have my suspicions confirmed. There's something not right about that man,' she said again, 'and until I find out, there'll be no advance on our romance.'

Chapter 7

I T WAS A RESPECTABLE hour the next morning when the landlady at Mr William Walker's residence looked startled at the tall man – who identified himself as a detective – standing before her asking to speak with Mr Walker.

'But he's dead, your people told me that some days ago,' she said, her hand going to her heart. 'His sister arrived from the south to identify him. How can be dead and missing now?'

Harland took a step back to appear less imposing and to calm the lady as best he could.

'My mistake, Madam,' he said. 'I am new to the precinct and I have been ensconced on another case, I've been remiss in catching up with the news.'

'Goodness me,' she said. 'It was quite a shock the first time, I would hate to hear the man had suffered further by being lost.'

'Do not alarm yourself, Madam,' Harland said with a small smile. 'If your tenant has passed, then we shall leave him rest.'

Harland noted she was now studying him with some intensity. He expected she either wanted a tenant or was sizing him up for a young lady she had in mind for him. That seemed to be the common path mature women took in his company, except for several who were widowed and very confident, and best not to go there.

The landlady glanced behind her at a closed door and turned back to Harland. 'Someone's got to collect his things, but he's paid up until the end of the month so there's no hurry for his sister or the next of kin to get here,' she said generously. Many a landlord would have boxed the possessions and got another tenant in to secure additional funds.

'I will ensure the uniformed men inform the next of kin. Thank you for your time, Madam.' Harland placed his hat back on his head and gave the landlady a small bow.

'You wouldn't be looking for a room would you, since you are new to our city?' she called after him. 'Unless you have a wife, the room is for a single man only.'

'Thank you, but I have accommodation. Good day.'

Harland made his way back to the waiting hansom, pleased he had asked the driver to wait.

'To the morgue, if you will,' he instructed the driver and seated himself in the back mulling over this turn of events.

A missing wife, four missing children and now the man investigating their disappearance has turned up dead. A very unfortunate turn of events.

His mind strayed to other matters brought to the fore by the landlady. A wife... it was high time he thought about settling down, after all, he had recently turned thirty and Lord knows he had indulged in the company of ladies over the years, as well as enjoyed all the pleasures that came with the prestige of winning boxing bouts, the money splashed around from his prize winnings, and the drinking that had accompanied it.

There had been a lady up north that had caught his eye but she was too insistent with her attachment and impatient with his working hours. That would never do. But he would like to return at night to a warm home, a lady in residence, and maybe even his own brood – several boys and girls. As an only child, he wanted his children to have the love and support of siblings. The picture in his mind was not unpleasant.

The hansom came to a stop and jolted him forward out of his reverie. Harland opened the door at the sight of the large building in William Street that temporarily housed the morgue while the former premises was being repaired after a landslip. He paid the driver with thanks, dismissing him now that his police station was within walking distance, and made his way inside, through the corridors and downstairs to see the coroner.

Harland was pleased to find Dr Tavish McGregor alone. Like himself, the coroner was a younger man, new to the office but not to the role. They had met a few times of recent at a boxing tournament, sharing an ale and an appreciation for the sport. Harland was surprised to come upon him in the coroner's office several days later. This morning, Tavish looked worse for wear – his red hair ruffled, a stubble that suggested the razor had eluded him and blue eyes shot with red and somewhat blurry in their glaze. Harland remembered the look and grinned.

'Don't tell me the stress of the job is driving you to imbibe and keep all hours?' he joked as Tavish welcomed him. 'Thank goodness your clients aren't here for operations, or not the sort that require their surgeon to be sharp.'

Tavish chuckled. 'Good morning to you, Harland. And where were you last evening? Julius and Maxwell were in attendance. Or did you choose to box instead?'

'I went to watch the boxing but did not participate. Then I had an early night... I've got to be some sort of example now that I have a protégé.'

Tavish raised an eyebrow and with a look that said he knew of the protégé asked, 'And how is that going?'

'Boxing is easier,' Harland answered and earned a laugh. 'I'm looking for a dead man.'

'Well, you've come to the right place. Who can I offer you?' Tavish waved a hand in the direction of the storage area.

'I'm looking for a private investigator by the name of William Walker,' Harland said as he wandered around Tavish's workroom.

'Yes, he's very dead,' Tavish confirmed and grinned at Harland's smirk. 'The poor fellow was found in the river but not drowned, death was from a blow to the back of the head. If my memory serves me correctly, it was an odd pattern from the instrument... almost like a square waffle shape, but it must have been heavy or the killer had some force behind him; hell of a blow.'

'Murdered, you say?'

'Unless of course he fell, struck his head on something with that pattern and it cracked his skull, and then he plunged into the river. He still had his possessions on him so he was not slain for the purposes of theft.'

'But what did you recommend to the detective in charge?' Harland pushed.

'That it most likely was murder but an accident was not out of the question. It was Burton and Lou... I don't think they were too keen to investigate, especially as I believe Mr Walker is a single man and there will be no pressure to bear.'

Harland gave a shake of his head in frustration. 'Disgraceful. The sooner we find ourselves wives, Tavish, the better for fear we are bumped off and someone gets away with it,' Harland said.

'Fair point. I shall go seek a bride this very evening.'

Harland exhaled and smiled, remembering not to take his work to heart. 'May I see Mr Walker for myself?'

'He has gone to the funeral parlour for burial. I believe he has a sister who wanted to have him presented properly for a brief mourning window... Mr Walker was a little grey from the water.'

Harland grimaced. 'I imagine so. I shall seek him there and hopefully, he has not been buried yet. Which funeral business?'

'*The Economic Undertaker*. Julius's family business. You know of it?'

'Indeed, we had some dealings in my very first case here.'

Both men turned at the sound of a sharp knock at the door and without waiting for an invitation, the door swung open.

'Good morning, gentlemen,' Lilly Lewis said, walking into the sombre work area with a beaming smile and a pale blue dress that did wonders for the atmosphere.

'Well, if it isn't Miss Lewis,' Tavish said with an exaggerated bow before straightening and wincing slightly. The motion had not been good for him with his terrible hangover. 'Back for more stories for your death column.'

'Dr McGregor, how good to see you again and yes, you are going to be one of my main sources for tales of the dead, I imagine.' She clapped her hands together as though declaring it an exciting thought. Lilly turned to the detective and gave him a polite smile. 'Detective Stone.'

'Miss Lewis,' Harland said with frostiness and formality.

She grimaced. 'Why do I always get that reception from men of the law?'

'I can't imagine,' Harland retorted remembering only too well his introduction to Miss Lewis while working his last case and her goading him for information. 'Is it perhaps because you push and prod us and then write things not in our favour?'

'Who me?' she exclaimed all innocence and Tavish laughed.

'Butter wouldn't melt in your mouth, Miss Lewis,' Tavish said clearly enamoured by the sassy young writer. 'You will never get that frosty reception from me, I assure you.'

Lilly shot him a little grin. 'Thank you, Dr McGregor. But do not try and charm me with that Scottish accent of yours. I am sure that works on all the ladies, but not me.'

'Shame then,' he said with a wide grin.

'I shall depart,' Harland said interrupting their banter. 'Thank you, Doctor.' He addressed Tavish more formally in the company of others.

'May I ask whom you were enquiring after?' Lilly asked giving him her most enchanting look which Harland appreciated but did not feel moved by to share.

'No. Good day, Miss Lewis.'

'Would it be Mrs Rose Beatty?' Lilly pushed on.

'No. And what pray tell, is Mrs Beatty's story?' Harland asked. 'I don't believe that case has come across my desk.'

Lilly shrugged and glanced at Tavish. 'That is what I am here to find out. My friend, Miss Phoebe Astin from *The Economic Undertaker,* said Mrs Beatty was just laid to rest and was recently married. I write about births, deaths and marriages, so I am killing two birds with one stone, so to speak. Speaking of which, were you not catching up with Phoebe yesterday?'

'Unfortunately, I did not receive her letter of request until late, so I have messaged to advise I will be there this morning,' Harland said. 'But regarding Mrs Rose Beatty, was it a natural death?'

'Very unlikely but it is hard to prove a fall was not a fall,' Tavish said easily recalling the lady recently on his table. 'Having said that, she was covered in marks that would indicate someone in her life – possibly her new husband – considered her property to be manhandled.'

Harland sighed and rubbed a hand over his forehead.

'You cannot save all the world, my friend, and if her case was handed to one of the other detectives, I imagine – since

Rose has been buried – they determined there was not enough evidence to go on to make a case,' Tavish said and hit him on the back. 'Go find your Mr Walker.'

'Mr Walker?' Lilly's ears pricked up.

'Never you mind, Miss Lewis, I have this in hand.' With a farewell to them both, he departed to visit *The Economic Undertaker* in the hope that Mr William Walker was still above ground.

Chapter 8

O N HIS RETURN FROM inspecting the vacant shop next door with an agent, Julius Astin entered *The Economic Undertaker* with a speed usually observed by his brother, Ambrose, startling his grandfather who stood behind the counter studying the diary of pending appointments. Julius hurriedly shut the door behind him, stole a glance through the curtains to the street outside and then as an afterthought, looked at the foyer, sighing with relief that it was empty.

'Yes, and a good thing we have no customers at the moment,' Randolph said reading his grandson's mind. 'It is not good for business to startle the bereaved or appear to be in a rush. After all, we know only too well that—'

His sentence was cut off by Ambrose who joined in and finished his grandfather's well-known saying.

'—death is inconvenient in order to remind us to slow down and take stock,' Ambrose said in a sing-song voice and laughed as his grandfather narrowed his eyes at the cheek of him.

'Sorry, Grandpa, you are right of course,' Julius said hurriedly as if hunted.

'What has happened, lad?' Randolph asked using the term of endearment that the boys had never grown out of, but given the size of the men today, they were quite capable of fending off any disgruntled parties should Julius be under threat. 'Are you alright?'

Ambrose moved away from the counter and to his brother's side. Moving aside the curtains he glanced out and laughed.

'It is not amusing, Ambrose.' Julius headed to the stairwell in haste. 'I am detained on business should anyone ask,' he called and hurried down the stairs to Phoebe's workroom.

'What on earth is going on?' Randolph asked, frowning at his youngest grandson.

'Mrs Reed and her daughter, Hannah, are on their way, they are just paying the driver now,' Ambrose said. 'She will have her daughter wed to Julius if it is the last thing she achieves on this earth.'

Randolph rolled his eyes and relaxed. 'Well, that might work in our favour should we get to perform her service. Do you wish to be detained elsewhere too, Ambrose?'

'No, I wouldn't miss it for the world,' he said, enjoying the sport of a good flirt.

The door swung open and Ambrose greeted both ladies with a small bow.

'Mrs Reed, Miss Reed, how delightful you both look on this glummest of days,' he said, his charm at the ready.

Miss Reed dutifully battered her dark eyelashes and moved a strand of light brown curl from her cheek. She did her best to look demure; her mother took charge.

'Mr Astin, and Mr Astin,' she said seeing Randolph behind the counter. 'A glum day indeed. If now is convenient, we have come to a decision on my husband's headstone at last.'

'Ah good,' Randolph said. Mr Reed had been buried a year now and the time was right to put a monument on his grave. 'Perhaps we could move into the small meeting room and Mrs Dobbs can bring us some tea.'

Both ladies nodded their consent, and while Randolph went to alert Mrs Dobbs, Ambrose escorted the ladies.

'Is not Mr Astin, your brother, in today?' Mrs Reed looked around as if Ambrose might have hidden Julius under the counter. Miss Reed blushed prettily at the thought of Julius attending her and Ambrose restrained a grin.

'Unfortunately, my brother has been detained on a matter of business. You will have to make do with me, I am afraid,' he said humbly.

'Oh, that is delightful,' Miss Reed finally spoke up and realising her enthusiasm was both awkward and inappropriate, especially in their surrounds, looked down again at her clasped hands. The ladies followed Ambrose into the small room tastefully decorated with a mahogany meeting table and chairs, and a fresh bouquet in front of the window, masking the passing traffic.

On his grandfather's return, Ambrose stayed long enough to enjoy the glances Miss Reed made in his direction, and a stolen smile or two before excusing himself at the sound of the bell above the door tinkling, leaving Randolph to conduct business which both gentlemen knew would take several more visits to conclude if Mrs Reed had her way.

Phoebe gave Julius an affectionate smile as he moved to the stairwell, listened and returned to her side.

'Poor Miss Reed,' she said and pouted.

'Poor me, you mean,' he said in good humour. 'One would assume working in a funeral parlour that I'd be safe from scheming mothers, and that their daughters would have no business to visit here.'

'Well, I assure you, Mr Reed did not meet his death so that Mrs Reed could put her daughter in your path regardless of how handsome you might be.'

Julius made a scoffing sound and Phoebe continued, 'He died of natural causes; believe it or not.'

Julius grunted. 'I would not put it past her. Why can't Miss Reed move her attention to Ambrose? At least he'd enjoy it.'

'Because you are the head of the family and the primary business owner. You own two properties and have a share in our cousin's carpentry business. Quite a catch,' she said and laughed again at his uncomfortable reaction.

'And how is that public knowledge?' he said and shook his head in frustration. 'Speaking of business, I am keen to pursue another interest. The store next door will soon be available for lease—'

'The dressmaker, your idea for a mourning tailor!' Phoebe said cutting in enthusiastically.

'Precisely. There is a big market for mourning clothes and it is ideally situated next to our business.'

'And there are different levels of mourning wear, so the dressmaker can provide dresses for the early days of mourning and that which is required in the last six months. Customers will have a reason to return,' she said with a view to future business.'

'Very true. They could also make and sell shrouds too if families are in need for their deceased. We have so many borrowed and not returned, I have lost count.'

Phoebe cocked her head to the side and admired him. 'It is a very good idea, Julius. Perhaps you should act without delay while the shop is available and find some staff. I am happy to assist.'

He nodded his thanks. 'I welcome your input, Sister.'

'Uncle Reggie is here,' Phoebe announced, 'and Mr Walker said I am to call him when we are ready to discuss his unfortunate departure.' She smiled at her great uncle who was her only regular visitor, not that she had ever discovered why he continued to return. He would not – or could not – say what kept drawing him back to the world.

When Phoebe first told her grandfather of Reggie's appearance, he was most upset, unable to enter her workroom for several months and Phoebe was distraught for distressing him. Randolph and Reginald had been as close as any two brothers could be and Reggie's accidental death at age forty had shattered his older brother and the family. But eventually, in time, Randolph came to accept his brother's visits and Phoebe passed on messages that showed Reggie was as rambunctious as ever. Very much like his grand-nephew, Ambrose.

'He knows I am here,' Reggie said and smiled. In his ghost state, he was still a man of forty, only two-and-ten years older than Julius. He understood the young man only too well.

'Uncle Reggie sends his regards,' Phoebe said ignoring her uncle.

Julius did not comment and she gave Uncle Reggie an apologetic look.

'He has the gift like you and your mother, Julius chooses not to use it,' Reggie added and gave a small shrug.

Phoebe studied her brother as he returned to the staircase to listen for voices from above. She wasn't sure that Julius did see or hear the dead, or why her brother would choose not to if he could, but she was not going to push him to do so. It took her some time to feel comfortable with the spirits and their secrets.

'I would understand if he didn't want to see me should I be hideous,' Reggie joked, 'but it is well known I am the most handsome of the Astin family men, a great loss to future generations that I did not reproduce.'

Phoebe chuckled at his brazenness.

'It must be time to get a priest in for the clearing of spirits in here,' Julius said not looking in Reggie's direction but with a small twitch of his lips into what might have been a smile. Reggie laughed and Phoebe wonder if indeed Julius could see and hear Reggie.

'That only applies if the spirit is evil or annoying, and so far, I am managing them well,' Phoebe told him.

'Hmm.' Julius made a disbelieving sound.

'I am worried about you, Julius,' Uncle Reggie said, not using Phoebe to transmit the message. 'You are of marriageable age and here you hide from a woman seeking your attention. I worry you are like me and will end up with no wife and no children, just a collection of friends who have priorities to their own families. You have a lot to offer and you need not carry the worries of the world on your shoulder, not by yourself. You have done admirably and the family is well established.'

'Should I repeat your message, Uncle?' She turned to see her brother folding several of the shrouds in the corner as if taking stock.

'He can hear me.' Uncle Reggie sighed. 'It is as if Julius got all the serious traits and Ambrose received the ingredients to keep life amusing. They need to share some with each other, they would both benefit.'

Phoebe was impressed by her uncle's sincerity; he was normally more like Ambrose in personality and did not lend himself to serious thoughts, preferring to make her laugh and keep the mood light. She looked to Julius for a reaction and saw his jaw was firm and he did not look pleased with the discussion of his nature, but he did not let on he had heard Uncle Reggie's words.

'You have always made Ambrose and I feel so safe, but do you still feel you are responsible for us, Julius?' Phoebe asked.

'Of course not, but Grandpa and Grandma are not getting any younger and the business—'

'—the business is a success,' she cut him off, 'and it is time for you to start thinking of yourself now. Planning for the future... sons and daughters to take our place in the business, a lady to bring a smile to your face.'

'Phoebe, enough. I did not come down here to escape one pursuit only to be lectured on the topic.'

'Would you like to meet several of my lady friends?'

'No!'

Phoebe sighed.

'Forgive me.' He came to her working table. 'I don't mean to snap but I don't know why everyone insists on telling me what I need and trying to make me who I am not. I am very happy in my work, and my circle of friends, and I am open to a relationship with the right lady. But at this time of my life, I don't need to have your friends settled upon me.'

'Why not?' Uncle Reggie asked continuing to stir Julius into action. 'What delightful friends do you have for Julius to meet, dear Phoebe?'

She looked at her brother. 'Uncle Reggie asks after my friends,' she explained in case he could not hear Uncle Reggie and wondered why she persisted in talking of friends he did not want to meet. 'Well, there is Kate who is a photographer and a most interesting lady. She has been commissioned for many family portraits and has her own studio. She is quite lovely, if not a little flighty.'

Julius listened. 'She sounds perfect.'

'Really?' Phoebe brightened and seeing his small smile she gave her brother a smirk. 'And here I was thinking you were serious. I think I shall book us in for a family portrait for the business... it would be good to promote our services.'

'Very smart,' he agreed drily understanding her motive for doing so.

'There is also my friend Emily. She runs a grooming school for young ladies. You are both as formal as each other, so perhaps she is not for you. I believe a free spirit like Kate might suit you more and lighten you a little.'

'I don't need lightening.'

Uncle Reggie scoffed in the corner.

Phoebe continued, 'Of course, there is the lovely Lilly, my journalist friend whom you have met.'

'Ambrose cares for her.'

Phoebe wheeled around to look at her brother. 'Does he? I had no idea.'

'Nor does she apparently.'

'Did he tell you that?'

'No, but it is evident, is it not?'

'Well, I did not see it. But perhaps you are right, I may have been more focussed on watching your reactions to my friend than Ambrose's expressions in her company. That is most interesting.' Phoebe stored the information with a trace of a smile.

A sound on the stairs made them both start and Julius look around for cover.

'It is likely the detective, Ambrose would not out you to Miss Reed, surely,' Phoebe whispered and then they saw the suit-clad legs of the incoming guest on the stairs and moments later Detective Harland Stone appeared in full, and Reggie disappeared from Phoebe's sight.

'Detective Stone,' Phoebe said, 'Thank you for coming.'

'Miss Astin, my pleasure,' he said and smiled on seeing her brother. 'Julius, good to see you again, and my apologies to you both that I did not see your request yesterday until after hours. Is all well?'

'Murder and mayhem, Harland,' Julius said keeping his voice low as the men shook hands.

'Why are you whispering?' Harland asked with a glance at the covered deceased body in the corner as if that might explain something.

'I am avoiding a lady upstairs who is looking for a suitor.'

Harland laughed, a welcome sound that Phoebe enjoyed hearing. There was seldom any laughing in her life, and the detective was most handsome when he did so.

'So you are hiding with Miss Astin and the dead in preference? Goodness, she must be a dragon,' he said.

'On the contrary, Detective, she is quite lovely,' Phoebe said in Miss Reed's defence. 'Julius on the other hand is most averse to being trapped.'

'We are of the age,' Harland said to him with a small shrug. 'I saw Tavish this morning looking considerably worse for wear. I am sorry I missed you at the club last night, I went to see a bit of sport.'

'Ah, I left Tavish before he and Maxwell were well on their way to a big evening.'

Phoebe returned to his former comment. 'If you are of the age and open to a courtship, Detective, perhaps Julius, or rather Ambrose, can introduce you to Miss Reed while she is in attendance,' she suggested with another motive in mind. She was uncommonly attracted to the detective for reasons she could not yet explain and wanted to understand his situation in matters of the heart.

His expression shifted and for just a moment she thought he looked bemused as if she had rejected him out of hand. She hoped her comment did not give offence or infer that she would not welcome his attention.

He cleared his throat. 'Thank you, Miss Astin, but I believe I need to get settled here and establish myself in my work before I think to inflict myself on some poor unsuspecting lady.'

Julius chuckled and Phoebe smiled and gave him a nod.

'Your work would be most demanding I imagine, and no doubt you are on call as we are, often at all hours.'

'Exactly so, and Julius, Tavish and I must find wives that would tolerate that lifestyle,' the detective said, and added, 'and I imagine Miss Astin, you will need to find a husband who is open to the same unless you intend to give up your profession?'

'No, I do not intend to give up my work or supporting my family business,' she said most confidently.

'But you would still welcome someone to care and provide for you?' the detective asked, and before Phoebe could respond, another visitor could be heard making their way down the stairs, the sound of the footfalls indicating it was a man, and Bennet Martin appeared before them.

'Ah, this is timing,' he said on seeing the small party.

Phoebe introduced the two men – the detective and Mr Martin – who were such opposites of each other physically. One dark and rugged, the other fair and polished.

'We have met socially and I believe on my last case. You are a private investigator, are you not, Mr Martin?' Harland asked.

'Yes. My office is in South Brisbane. I only take on a few clients as I have a studio above that,' Bennet explained.

'Ah,' Harland said and nodded. 'An artist.' The word was said with neither condescension nor fascination.

Phoebe observed the two men who studied each other warily. Bennet interrupted her thoughts. 'Have you told the detective of the crime you believe is in motion, Miss Astin?'

'Not as yet,' Phoebe said.

'I just arrived but moments before you on a business matter, but do you wish to proceed with your reason for summoning me, Miss Astin?' Harland asked.

'No, please go ahead in case your business is pressing,' Phoebe said inviting him to speak.

Harland focussed on Phoebe and Julius. 'I have been contacted by a couple in the United Kingdom who are looking for their daughter, Mrs Mary Beaming, and her children. I have not been able to give it my full attention until now, but I believe they hired a private investigator from this city, Mr William Walker to find them. I visited his place of abode and was told he had departed this world and was waiting for burial.'

Hearing his name as if it were a summons, Mr Walker appeared and took his usual seat in the corner of Phoebe's room. She acknowledged him with a small nod.

'I can confirm that,' Phoebe said with a glance to Mr Walker. She looked back to see Harland frowning and looking from her to the corner and back.

He continued, 'The coroner tells me he is in your care. May I see him?' Harland asked.

'Of course. It seems our business is one and the same, Detective Stone. That is why I requested an audience with you.' Phoebe moved to Mr Walker's body and Harland followed.

Julius asked, 'Did Tavish believe Mr Walker's death was suspicious?'

'He did,' Harland admitted candidly, happy to share with the small party, but not before a cautionary glance in Bennet's direction. 'However, I don't believe the two detectives who looked over Mr Walker's file were as concerned about the manner of Mr Walker's demise. Are you intending to pick up Mr Walker's current cases, Mr Martin?' he asked Bennet.

'Just the very case you mentioned at this stage – that of the missing Mrs Beaming and the children – if the family wishes me to do so,' Bennet answered. 'I would be happy to share learnings, Detective.'

Harland nodded. 'That could be useful,' he agreed uncommittedly. He stood over Mr Walker and nodded as Miss Astin pulled back the sheet. Harland studied the body carefully, notably the wound to the head, and motioned to Miss Astin when his inspection was complete.

'I imagine he looks a good sight better now than he did when he came in since your work is done?' Harland asked.

'That's the truth,' Julius answered.

'You have some information, Miss Astin?' Harland asked as Phoebe covered Mr Walker.

Phoebe glanced at Julius and hesitated.

'An assumption made from studying the body perhaps?' Harland persisted and Phoebe's breath hitched.

'Detective, my information is not gleaned from fact.' She shifted, uneasy about how to introduce her source. 'I assure you I am not a soothsayer, I cannot see the future...'

Julius cut to the chase. 'We trust we have your utmost discretion so that this information is not traced to us?'

The detective nodded and Julius continued. 'The spirits sometimes linger to ask Phoebe for assistance if their business is unfinished.'

Harland could not hide his surprise but added, 'I see, most unconventional. You have my guarantee of discretion, Miss Astin, Julius.'

Phoebe breathed a little easier.

'And you are familiar with this, Mr Martin?' Harland asked the private investigator.

'Only of recent and it has been to my benefit,' Bennet said.

'Are you a believer, Detective?' Phoebe asked.

'I don't disbelieve,' he said. 'There are many things I have seen and many I don't understand, and that's just in human nature.'

Julius smiled and Bennet chuckled.

'So true,' Bennet agreed.

'Please, speak freely if you will.' Harland encouraged Phoebe to share her insights and with another look at her brother and the spirit of Mr Walker, present in the corner, she told Detective Stone what she had learned.

'As you know, Mr Walker is a private investigator. He was hired by Mr and Mrs Hames of Pembrokeshire in the United Kingdom to look for their missing daughter, Mrs Mary Beaming. She sailed to Australia three years ago with her husband, Zachariah and three children. She has had a fourth child since.'

Phoebe glanced over Bennet's shoulder to where Mr William Walker sat in the corner and listened for a moment before saying, 'Mr Walker was several weeks into his investigation and had made a major discovery. He determined that Mrs Mary Beaming had in fact returned to the UK with Zachariah and the children late last year. They were to have Christmas with her family. But they did not.'

'Did her family even know they were nearby, in England?' Harland asked.

Phoebe looked to Mr Walker and responded to the detective, 'Mr Walker said he is unsure as he was yet to tell the family of his discovery that they were in the country.'

'Were they in the same area?' Julius asked.

'No. For some reason, Mr Beaming took premises in Rainhill while Mrs Beaming's family lived in Wales,' Phoebe said.

'How far is that?' Harland asked Bennet as the best source for British information in the room.

'It's a good two days by carriage if you rested overnight, or if the family took a steam train, it would take them over 20 hours or so... Wales is not as well served by trains as some English towns I believe,' he said.

'So, they were but a few days away compared to across the ocean and her family was not informed, it appears,' Julius said, his eyes narrowed as he thought. 'I wonder if Mr Beaming said he would send them word or if he had no intention of seeing Mrs Beaming's family.'

'Knowing this information, it does not bode well for the family,' Phoebe agreed. She looked to the corner again and then added, 'Mr Walker found no record of Mrs Beaming or the children leaving Rainhill, nor Mr Beaming doing so either.'

'Is that so?' Bennett said. 'So, Mrs Beaming's family cannot reach her in Australia and believe her to be missing but she may still be in England and might be alive in Rainhill?'

He waited as Phoebe consulted Mr Walker and then shook her head.

'There is something else significant. Mr Walker found out that Mr Beaming is back here, in the country without his family. He must have travelled on a false passport but he is using his name here as normal,' Phoebe said.

'I can confirm that,' Harland said. 'Before my last case was finished, I was given this case and the request from England to enquire after the missing Mrs Beaming and her children. I met with Mr Beaming and as he claimed his wife had deserted him and taken the children, I did not prioritise it but finished up the other case first. It now appears very unlikely that he was deserted as Mrs Beaming surely would be with her parents if she were alive and living in the U.K. He also now has a lead on me and has likely slipped my grasp.'

Julius came to Mr Walker's side as the deceased lay on the bench covered before them. He asked his sister, 'Phoebe, did Mr Walker approach Mr Beaming with his concerns?'

'Yes. They agreed to meet and then the last thing he remembers was being struck in the back of the head, which must have rendered him unconscious and he dropped into the river where he was found. Mr Walker has no other explanation as to why he ended up in the water. I believe his body was snagged under a deck for a short while, delaying his discovery,' Phoebe said lowering her voice. She added, 'Mr

Walker fears that other ladies in Mr Beaming's company might find themselves in peril.'

'I too have some information as I have just visited Mr Walker's premises, at his invitation,' Bennet added, 'and obtained the file on Mrs Beaming.'

'I would be keen to see that,' Harland said, not claiming it as police property given the two detectives had ample time to collect Mr Walker's business papers but dismissed the case. 'Perhaps the sharing of information is a good idea,' he said warming to the concept.

Bennet then told of what he had learned – that Mr Walker had received a note delivered by a courier that afternoon before his death and he headed out, possibly to meet the murderer.

'The landlady told me the same,' Harland agreed. 'As the coroner did not mention it, I suspect the note was not legible when Mr Walker was pulled from the water.'

Phoebe looked to Mr Walker and said: 'It was a note from Mr Zachariah Beaming asking Mr Walker to meet with him.'

Harland nodded. 'Thank you. I shall visit Zachariah Beaming's residence again but I imagine my last visit most likely startled him into action and he is gone for good. I will also conduct research to determine if his family travelled to England and if Mr Beaming returned to Australia without them.'

'You are not prepared to take my word, Detective?' Phoebe challenged him and as they did not have any knowledge of each other, he was not aware that she was teasing him. He shifted uncomfortably until he saw all the men were smiling. 'Do not fear, I won't hold it against you,' she grinned.

He looked relieved and gave a small smile. 'Miss Astin, you are a unique lady.'

'She is indeed,' Julius said proudly looking at his sister who blushed at their praise and looked away.

Harland prepared to depart and turned back. 'The murder weapon... Dr McGregor, the coroner, said it left a square waffle pattern. Perchance did Mr Walker see it?'

Phoebe looked at the deceased gentleman, listened and nodded. She turned to the detective. 'Mr Walker said it all happened very quickly. Mr Beaming pulled an instrument from his coat and stepped behind to strike Mr Walker. He could not be certain but it looked like a cast iron meat tenderiser.'

The detective's eyes widened. 'Thank you. I will collect my young partner and head to Mr Beaming's residence.' He turned to Bennet Martin. 'If you could read through that file and pass it on to me or supply the relevant information, that would be appreciated.'

'Immediately,' Bennet agreed.

'I shall ask Mr Beaming of his business in Rainhill in the United Kingdom, and whom he resided with while there,' Harland said. 'We may find a party who is aware of the family's whereabouts.'

'If needed, Detective, my father is a detective with Scotland Yard. I am sure he would put a resource into service for us to call upon anyone we may need to question in England,' Bennet said.

'Excellent,' Harland said pleased, 'although I may need to go through the appropriate protocols via my office for that contact.' He gave a small sigh.

'I understand,' Bennet said.

Harland showed he could match Miss Astin if teasing was required. 'Is your client happy with that outcome on his behalf?' he asked cocking an eyebrow in her direction.

Phoebe smiled, looked to Mr Walker in the corner, and back to the detective. 'He is, Detective, but suggests you hasten to it.'

Harland smiled and needed no encouragement. With a quick farewell to all parties, he departed. Phoebe watched him with a smile until she realised her brother and Bennet were watching her.

'Have you two not got business to attend to?' she asked.

'If the coast is clear, yes,' Julius said. 'Come, Bennet, let's leave my sister to the company of her clients.'

'Three very likeable young men,' Mr Walker said from the corner of the room after Julius, Harland and Bennet departed.

'That is true,' Phoebe agreed. 'It is amazing whom you meet at a funeral home.'

Mr Walker laughed and then sobered. 'Thank you, Miss Astin. I believe I have done all I can now to set the wheels in motion. I shall bid you goodbye with my sincere appreciation and wish you a happy and healthy life. However, should you need to call on me again, do not hesitate to do so.'

Mr Walker stood and Phoebe returned his small bow, as he disappeared from her sight and workroom.

Chapter 9

BENNET WAS OUT OF sorts. His eyes had regularly found their way to Miss Phoebe Astin, but not once did she catch his eye any more than necessary in the course of the conversation. However, he was sure she looked at the detective as if he were the most fascinating man in the world. The man was polite and interesting, Bennet would grant him that, but his appearance was rough, and his face had seen a fist or two in its time. Surely a lady like Miss Phoebe Astin would not be attracted to him. Would Julius approve of that match? Come to think of it, would Julius have a say in his sister's choice of husband? After all, Miss Astin was quite modern.

'You are most out of sorts, what is wrong?' his young clerk asked.

'I have this bothersome clerk,' Bennet fired back but looked up to smile at Daniel Dutton. 'Forgive me, I have a lot on my mind and I must read through this file – a new case,' he explained. 'I will call on you to read it as well so you can assist me.'

'Willingly. Aunt has left to collect the post, I shall make us tea,' Daniel said, able to be serious when the situation demanded.

'And lock the door, for safety,' Bennet called after him but did not elaborate. If Mr Zachariah Beaming had already killed one private investigator, he might not hesitate to harm another. He waded through Mr Walker's notes and looked at the copies of tickets in the file – ah ha! Here was the first bit of proof required – passage to England for two adults and three children. The baby must not have required a ticket, he mused.

I wonder how many children Phoebe might desire if she were to become Mrs Phoebe Martin. He smiled at the thought of introducing her as his wife and having a brood of children that took after her.

Another piece of paper dated months later was a passage to Australia for one adult. What of the wife and children's passage?

Phoebe was three-and-twenty, she should be married. But was she ready to take a husband?

There were no other receipts in the file. So, had Beaming's family returned at another time or were they still in England? Perhaps Mrs Beaming refused to leave, but then one would think she would seek out her family in Wales which to date she had not.

Is Phoebe still seeing the gallery owner, Gideon Hayward? Or does she no longer seek his company?

He rifled through papers indicating Beaming had been in trouble with the police both in Australia and overseas. Petty crimes of theft and fighting. A man not averse to being cunning or using his fists.

Daniel reappeared with tea for them both and Bennet exchanged paperwork for the cup of tea.

'Please put this in order and I will deliver the file to Detective Stone at the Roma Street Police headquarters this afternoon.'

'I can do that delivery for you,' Daniel offered.

'Thank you, but I want to see if he has gleaned any information that could be of value to the case. For now, will you send a telegram for me? I wish to introduce myself to Mr Walker's clients and offer to take over the search for their missing daughter and grandchildren.'

'Right away,' Daniel said excitedly. 'That sounds like a case to get our teeth stuck into.'

'Yes,' Bennet agreed, 'but I fear the outcome will not be good for anyone.'

Anne Norris recalled her recent lunch with Zachariah Beaming before his hurried departure. She did not flinch when he took her hand across the table in the restaurant; he was a tactile man and even though she harboured suspicions about his nature, she was not immune to accepting the attention and flattery of a gentleman. Besides, she had told her policeman neighbour of her suspicions of Zachariah's character and felt a little safer for doing so, lest any harm should come to her. Still, it was an uncomfortable conversation as she recalled his parting sentiments.

'I am afraid I have to go away for work, head west,' he explained. 'I would be a very happy man if you might consider accompanying me.'

Anne was surprised. 'Thank you, Zachariah. Well, that is most thoughtful, but my commitments don't allow me to just depart on a whim, sadly. I have several people whom I care for and who rely on me. Duty, you understand.'

It was not a complete lie, but not necessarily true either. Anne wanted more time to understand the man; she did, after all, harbour grave suspicions about his character. She continued, 'Perhaps on your return, we might get to know each other more intimately.' Offering him a bare amount of hope.

'I would like that greatly, my dear, and that thought will brighten many a day in your absence. However, I am not sure how long I will be away. It may be days or it might be months.' He straightened and released her hand. 'I am sorry to say that I have never believed absence makes the heart grow fonder. I much prefer to have you by my side.'

'Nor have I,' she said in agreement. 'Not that I am a woman who strays, but one learns to fill one's day. Allow me to think on it if you will?'

'I'm afraid I leave immediately, this very afternoon,' he said and apologised. 'It is a situation I must deal with urgently, and most unfortunate.' He gave her a charming smile and a boyish shrug as if his life was in such disarray and his presence of great importance.

Anne sensed he was determined to have her consent, and while the idea of having an adventure appealed – she was by nature impulsive and he was handsome – but she did not feel it would bode well for her.

'Goodness, that is immediate. Why don't I follow in say a week or two if I can manage that?' Anne had no intention of doing so but it would allow them to part agreeably and delay the inevitable.

'That could work well for both of us,' he agreed, brightening. 'I shall write you with my address once I arrive.'

'What of your home? Would you like me to water your garden for you, collect your post and messages, and ensure it remains respectable?' she asked.

'That would be most kind. At least until you see to join me, then I will make other arrangements or advise the landlord if I am not returning.' He reached for her hand again. 'Are you sure I cannot convince you to come with me this very day?'

'Disappear just like that?' she said and clicked her fingers. 'A rather exciting thought. Speaking of which, did you read of that terrible story of the family in that small town out west, just disappearing?'

'No doubt they have been murdered,' Zachariah said releasing her hand again and topping up both of their glasses of wine before the waiter reappeared.

'How could that be so?' Anne asked. 'How could a family be murdered and hidden completely from the police? I would think it were impossible.' She grimaced at the thought.

'I disagree, your mind is too innocent,' he said with a warm smile.

'Perhaps. How would you suggest it was done then?' she prodded him, fascinated and keen to see more of his true nature. Would he take pleasure in the telling of the family's demise or would he show empathy and regret?

He webbed his fingers in front of him on the table and leaned forward. In a low voice, Zachariah Beaming said: 'It would be the easiest thing in the world to dispose of unwanted persons and bury them in quick lime. What better place, for example, than under the hearthstone at home? It is inside work and no one would bear witness.'

'Quick lime?'

He nodded, keen to elaborate and show his knowledge. 'The family might have met their end at the hand of the killer, who in the privacy of his own surroundings, dug up the floor in a room where space permitted – near the fireplace would be ideal as there is rarely furniture placed nearby that requires moving – and then buried the family, covering them in quick lime which cements them in. The murderer could work at his own pace unseen by anyone, and then repair the hearthstone near the fireplace. It is so very convenient as the bodies do not need to be smuggled out into the night.' He sat back self-assuredly and smiled. 'Perhaps I should write radio plays.'

'Oh yes, how very underhanded and ingenious,' she said trying not to show her shock and the heightened alarm washing over her at his glee.

Now, a day later and having had time to mull over the conversation, she could not deny she was pleased that Zachariah Beaming had departed on urgent business although she questioned the validity of his claim and wondered if he was evading debt collectors.

Putting their last date behind her, Anne Norris stood on the footpath out the front of his residence and studied the small, attractive house. The curtains were drawn on every window and the place had the air of desertion. He was a man who put great stock in haste. He had asked for her hand within a week of meeting her but Anne's father always said "Marry in haste, repent at leisure" and she was a practical woman of nature not prone to swooning.

Despite her belief Zachariah was gone, Anne made a show of checking his mailbox, and finding it empty, moved up the pathway, through the small garden and knocked on his door. There was no answer. She wandered around the back of the house and taking the few steps to the verandah, bent to glance through a gap in a curtain allowing her to see the kitchen and down the hallway. There were no hats or coats on the rack and no movement inside.

Anne straightened and looked around, her skin prickling with fear... caution... trepidation... she could not put a finger on it. But she was no wilting flower and took a moment to straighten her dress and pat her hair to ensure she was still presentable – a ruse for catching her breath and calming herself.

Taking the steps down from the verandah, Anne ventured to a small shed that opened on the first go. She felt herself physically brace as if expecting to find something untoward, and once her eyes adjusted to the light and she saw all the normal things one would see in a shed – a gardening fork, a spade, a watering can – Anne gave a small chuckle at her dramatics. That was until she saw the sack of quick lime in the corner of the shed. Hurriedly, Anne stepped away, closing the shed doors, for fear someone might close the doors behind her, entrapping her inside. But the yard and surrounds were still. She was alone, there was nothing to fear.

'I am convinced there is something not right about this man,' she whispered to break the silence and to give herself fortitude. His words came back to her as clear as day: "It would be the easiest thing in the world to dispose of unwanted persons and bury them in quick lime. What better place, for example, than under the hearthstone at home? It is inside work and no one would bear witness."

Anne took a deep breath and felt it was her duty to investigate. She knew where Zachariah Beaming kept a spare house key from a previous visit and if it was not there, she would attempt to break in regardless. She prepared several stories in her head in case she was interrupted by a nosy neighbour or worse still, by Zachariah himself lying dormant.

'I told Mr Beaming I would water his plants and I thought I heard a cat's mewl inside. For fear the poor creature was locked in, I thought it was my duty to investigate.' She nodded. That would work. Or perhaps if it were the man himself, 'Zachariah, you took me by surprise. I came by to say I would travel with you only to find the house closed up. I knew you would not leave without saying goodbye and I feared you were inside, injured. What a relief to see you.' That would take some work to say convincingly, she thought, but under duress, she could sound convincing.

With a deep breath for fortitude, Anne returned to the back verandah, lifted a copper figurine of a native bird and the key was there! She hurriedly grabbed it and moved to the door. The longer the exercise took, the more she feared she would not undertake it. Anne turned the key in the lock and opened the door, she waited, listened and observed. It was deathly silent inside. She wedged the door open with a nearby door stop placed for that purpose.

'Zachariah, where are you my dear?' she called and waited. 'Are you alright?'

Silence. Anne nodded as if permitting herself to go forward and with abundant trepidation, she moved through the kitchen, down the hallway and into the master bedroom, the only sound that of her footsteps on the timber floor. A glance in the bedroom wardrobe told her that Zachariah Beaming had indeed departed, the wardrobe was empty of clothes and shoes. She pulled open a drawer and found a few stray items – a comb and a pair of grey socks. In the corner, she saw a card and pulled it from the edge where it was wedged. It was an invitation for Major Williams. She threw it back in the drawer, a former tenant no doubt. Anne closed the drawer and opened the one below it. She gasped.

A photograph.

It was a portrait photograph of a family – a formal one with the family posed and the head of the family was Zachariah Beaming himself. Next to him stood an attractive woman with a babe in arms, and three small children sat in the front, one looking the wrong way impatiently.

"It would be the easiest thing in the world to dispose of unwanted persons and bury them in quick lime."

She dropped the photo, closed the drawer and made her way to the drawing room, to the hearthstone. Standing at the back of the room, she looked at the floor hoping to not see what she guessed to be true; it was uneven. The strangest feeling overcame her as if she wasn't alone anymore and she hastily turned and fled out the back door, locking it hurriedly and returning the key. She moved as fast as her skirt would allow her. It was time to visit the police and tell them of her suspicions. She would write down her observations tonight and visit first thing in the morning. It appears Zachariah Beaming has a family or at least once did.

Chapter 10

NOT AWARE OF THE visit made by Miss Anne Norris one hour prior, Detective Harland Stone returned to Mr Zachariah Beaming's residence with his protégé, Gilbert Payne, hoping the man might be in residence.

'Are we intending to arrest Mr Beaming?' Gilbert asked following Harland up the path.

'No, we are just inviting him in for questioning, whether he returns home after that will depend on his answers to our questions. I suspect he has slipped through my fingers now.'

'There appeared very little untoward about the case at that stage, Sir, and we were juggling another.'

'Yes, very true, Gilbert. I want to have a subtle look around for a square waffle-shaped heavy instrument that might have blood on it.'

Gilbert's expression relayed his trepidation. 'Should we have backup? He's not a big man but if he is wielding a heavy instrument... I have read that often when people are angry, they develop more strength than they characteristically display. Although, I cannot vouch for that personally.'

'Is that so? Most interesting, I have experienced similar. But I am not worried, Gilbert, and I don't believe we need backup yet. That's what you are here for, I am sure you will rise to the occasion,' Harland said and hid his smile when he caught the look of alarm on the young detective's face.

The two men arrived at the front door noting the closed curtains. Gilbert knocked dutifully and after a brief wait, he tried the door to find it locked. Harland moved around the back of the house; all of the curtains were pulled closed across the windows and on testing the back door, he found that locked as well.

'I think he might not be coming back for some time,' Gilbert said.

'I agree, Gilbert. I believe we might have alarmed Mr Beaming on our last visit, especially if he has something to hide, and he has departed in haste.' Harland sighed, and seeing the shed, went to look inside.

'Do you want me to break into the house, Sir?' Gilbert asked. 'It's a lock that won't withstand a good push to the door. My father has one similar and once when he lost his keys after a late night at the pub, he let himself in with a hardy shove.'

Harland waited for Gilbert's story to end and advised him, 'No need to break in. It is him I wish to see and I doubt he is hiding inside. Will you try the neighbours on either side and ask when they last saw Mr Beaming and if he mentioned his travels or when he would return?'

Harland opened the shed door and entered. He suspected Mr Beaming threw the weapon away. It had not been found in the river and there was a slim chance he might have thrown it in the shed. After conducting a brief search, Harland discounted that idea. He may have washed the tenderiser and returned it to the kitchen drawer – a ghastly thought but one to follow up. But Mr Beaming must have always intended to harm Mr Walker if we went armed for attack.

Tomorrow, he would return in case Mr Beaming was home, and if not, he would force entry to the premises. For now, to the train station and then to the river to see if anyone witnessed the meeting of the men.

Chapter 11

THE *VEXED VIXENS* WERE due to meet at any moment and Lilly Lewis had been looking forward to it all day. She rushed home from work after submitting her copy by the required deadline, her story on the marriage and death of Mrs Rose Beatty, and while it brought a tear to the eye, it was not the mystery she sought. On face value, she had to agree with whoever handled the initial case, there was nothing to say Rose didn't fall, except everyone who knew her husband knew he was handy with his fists. But Rose had loved her husband, and in his own way, he had loved her, like a possession.

Now, Lilly wanted to sink her teeth into something dramatic, to break a story even, imagine that. The thought filled her with frustration – that was never going to happen while she wrote the births, marriages and deaths column.

Never mind for now, she told herself and brightened at the thought of her evening ahead with her dearest friends.

The ladies attempted to meet on a regular basis but work and life inevitably derailed their plans, so now, the hostess of the gathering selected the date, and whoever was free, attended. Tonight, Lilly was hosting; her parents were abroad and the house was her own. The housekeeper had promised to prepare a supper worthy of four hungry young ladies and Lilly looked forward to relaxing in their company and sharing their news, and gossip. Changing into more relaxing attire from her corseted work dress, Lilly checked her appearance and ran down the stairs ready to welcome the ladies.

They had named their small party of four the *Vexed Vixens*, but did not seek to grow the circle unless another young lady of the same disposition to fit their group made herself known; they were all unique in their outlooks and occupations. Tonight, everyone was punctual.

After greetings and settling themselves around the table, Kate closed her eyes and savoured a bite of pie. 'Your cook's pie is so much better than my mother's,' she pronounced and then opened her eyes wide in alarm. 'Do not repeat that when you come to my place for goodness' sake. I'll be chased down the street with a rolling pin.'

The ladies laughed at the thought.

'Your secret is safe with us,' Lilly said placing a cup of tea down beside Kate and pouring her own last, she joined the ladies. 'I shall voice my vexation first as the hostess if no objections?'

'Proceed, please,' Emily said also enjoying the bite of pie on her fork and savouring the taste.

'I am so frustrated with my lot at work. I want to write serious stories, and I am stuck with babies, lovers and the dead. No offence, Phoebe,' Lilly said.

Phoebe leant over and squeezed her hand. 'No offence taken. I am happily stuck with the dead. I find them good company and they do not overstay their welcome.' She returned her attention to serving herself some vegetables and offered the ladle around.

'I wish I could say the same, my clients always overstay their welcome,' Kate said with a roll of her eyes. 'I set them up to take their photographic portrait and then they fidget and ruin the shot. Why is it that no one can stand still for five minutes?' Kate noticed Lilly's constant movement and rolled her eyes. 'Clients like Lilly for example,' she teased her friend. 'So, we must do the photograph again. Of course, once they see themselves on the plates, they are fascinated and I cannot move them out quickly enough. Although one man ran from the building believing I had now stolen his soul and captured it,' she said and chuckled.

'I am sure none of you face the daily vexations I do,' Emily the eldest of the group at eight and twenty said. The manageress of Miss Emily's Deportment School for Young Ladies sighed. 'I am seriously considering changing the name of my business to – Miss Emily's School for Baby Elephants.'

The ladies laughed freely.

'I have several such ladies at the moment and I am expected to create miracles with them.' Emily gave a small shake of her head in despair. 'I never mind if they are trying their best, but one young miss stomps through the house like a herd of cattle. I have tried all the usual training methods, from placing a weight on her head to slow her down and fix her posture, to dancing lessons for gracefulness, all to no avail. Another young lady slurps her cup of tea as if it were soup.'

All three ladies self-consciously adapted the manner in which they were sipping and Emily waved a hand in the air. 'Do not fear, you could not match these young clods if you acted that way intentionally.'

'That is a relief. Slurp on then ladies,' Lilly joked. 'I am sure you have them well in hand, Emily. Pray tell, what happened at *The Economic Undertaker* today?' she asked Phoebe. 'How are your most handsome brothers, not vexing surely?'

'Always vexing as brothers are by nature, but generally unchanged,' she said with a smile. 'Ambrose is not serious enough about the business for Grandpa's liking, and Julius spends half his day hiding from the misses who find a reason to call, which one would think given we are a funeral business would be challenging in itself.'

Lilly sighed. 'He is quite the catch, I'm sure I can think of half a dozen reasons to call in to set eyes on him.'

Kate smiled and glanced at Phoebe and away again.

'I saw that look, Kate, what did that mean?' Lilly asked, narrowing her eyes suspiciously.

Kate laughed. 'I heard that you had a gentleman who was rather smitten with you.'

Lilly's heartbeat hastened hoping it was Phoebe's brother but was that why Phoebe stiffened beside her? Was she concerned Lilly was going to try for one of her brothers, or another thought occurred to her, maybe both Kate and Lilly shared affection for the same suitor? Lilly coughed lightly, clearing the tightness in her throat and tried to approach the subject in a relaxed manner adding in jest, 'I have a number of men who run when they see me coming. But do tell? Whose eye have I caught?'

'A certain coroner has lost his heart to you,' Kate said with a wide smile. 'He is handsome and Scottish, a doctor mind you, and quite eligible.'

The ladies all cooed and Lilly shook her head, grinning at their antics. 'Dr Tavish McGregor is not for me, but yes, I agree he is charming. How do you know of his interest in me?'

'The police photographer is an acquaintance of mine and saw you and me taking tea on one occasion. Knowing we were friends, he told me Dr McGregor was quite smitten with you and could not take his eyes off you when you came upon a crime scene where the good doctor was in attendance recently.'

'I saw him but yesterday,' Lilly said, 'but I shan't pursue that suit.'

'Ah, poor Dr McGregor,' Phoebe said and sighed.

'What of your beau, the very handsome gallery owner, Mr Hayward?' Kate asked.

'Gideon and I have decided to remain firm friends but not pursue romance,' Phoebe said.

'Oh no, are you heartbroken?' Emily asked. 'I will go around and box his ears if you like.'

Phoebe laughed. 'Thank you for your loyalty, dear Emily, but I assure you it is mutual. I like him a great deal but we are not well-matched in nature. He is more social in art networks than I desire to be and while I enjoyed the outings initially, I am, I fear, a homebody at heart and content with little company and the solitude of my family and dear pets.'

'There is nothing wrong with that,' Lilly said.

'You would die if you could not be out all the time,' Emily said looking at Lilly incredulously.

'I know, but my sister is a quieter soul and enjoys select company rather than crowds. She leads a very happy life and we have both learnt to respect that.'

'Exactly,' Phoebe said. 'Neither Gideon nor I am pained, it has been a lovely friendship and we shall see each again socially, I am sure. But I am convinced he and his gallery assistant, Miss Warren, may be suited.'

'Ooh, is she lovely too?' Kate asked.

'She is and they share a passion for art and making the gallery the best it can be. She is quite witty when one gets to know her and I think she keeps Gideon on his feet. I have mentioned it to his sister, Matilda, who will take matters in hand. I am convinced once they encourage their attraction, they will be most suited and happy.'

'Well, that is that then. So, is there anyone who had caught your eye?' Emily asked leaning into the conversation a little as if Phoebe was going to whisper a great secret. 'Someone less outwardly convivial perhaps?'

Phoebe smiled. 'There is a certain gentleman in my acquaintance whose attentions I would welcome.'

Lilly nodded her understanding. 'Someone calm, handsome and in control like your brother, Julius.'

'But perhaps not quite as sober,' Phoebe said. 'My mission is to make Julius smile at least twice a day.'

'I am sure that must be lovely when he supplies it,' Lilly said and sighed as if she might never be so fortunate to have Julius's smile bestowed upon her.

'It is hard-earned some days. His responsibilities started so young in life, that sometimes I fear Julius has forgotten he no longer is responsible for us,' she mused. 'I am grateful that he has a group of friends with which he can forget himself for a little while in their company, but it would be lovely to see him cared for by a lady.'

Lilly hoped Phoebe might see her as this lady but she did not offer any insights or a special smile or glance her way. She did however add, 'I might have a story that will help your career—'

'—goodness, do you? How wonderful,' Lilly cut her off, then seeing her friend's sombre look, reined in her enthusiasm. 'I can work behind the scenes, if need be, I can be subtle with my research and writing.'

'I am sure you can.' Phoebe said with full trust in her friend. 'However, it is a current investigation and I suspect your interference won't be welcome unless you promise not to print anything that will hinder the investigation, or until Detective Stone authorises it.'

'I can do that,' Lilly assured her, 'unless I sourced the information myself.'

'Of course,' Phoebe agreed, 'and then you can be a step ahead of the detective!'

'Is Detective Stone single?' Kate asked.

'Focus dear Kate,' Emily scolded her. 'You should be good at that given you focus through that camera of yours all day.'

Kate smiled. 'Forgive me. Carry on. I shall ask after the detective later then,' she said with a wink in Emily's direction. 'I am asking for both of us, Emily... he might be interested in a lady with good deportment.'

Emily would have snorted but the manageress of a deportment school did not do that.

Phoebe started her story. 'It begins with a private investigator who was murdered and left to die in the river and a man that he was investigating whose family is missing.'

The ladies gasped.

'Oh dear, this does not bode well for the family,' Emily said her hand going to her heart.

'I just did a death portrait for a family. Such awful things,' Kate said and shook her head. Then noticing everyone looking at her, held up her hand. 'My apologies, no more comments unrelated to the topic at hand.'

Phoebe grinned at her friend. 'Given that is how we met, I cannot regret that you do the occasional death portrait, but I am glad the desire for them is diminishing.'

Kate placed her cutlery down and reached for Phoebe's hand. 'Our friendship is indeed a wonderful thing born from that sad portrait.'

'I am calling order,' Lilly said and tapped her teaspoon against her teacup. 'No more interruptions until we hear the full story. Phoebe, please continue,' Lilly insisted and Phoebe took the floor and told the ladies what had unfolded.

'Can you tell me what the man's name is? The accused man?' Kate asked.

'I suppose there is no harm in doing so if we keep it to ourselves,' Phoebe said with a glance around the room as if checking for eavesdroppers. 'But please do not say a word, his family may be alive and well, and he has not yet been charged or imprisoned.'

'But you do not believe he is innocent?' Emily asked, observant at reading people from years of working with young ladies at the deportment school.

'No, and as Mr Walker spoke with me of how he died, I believe this man to be Mr Walker's murderer and violent enough to harm his family,' Phoebe said. Her friends were well familiar with Phoebe's visions and peculiar relationship with the inhabitants of the other side.

'Who is this villain?' Lilly asked. 'We, the *Vexed Vixens*, promise none of us will tell.' She held up her hand in a salute; the other ladies followed suit.

'His name is Mr Zachariah Beaming,' Phoebe said.

'Beaming.... Beaming...' Kate muttered. 'Why I did his family portrait! He has a wife and four young children; the

113

littlest was but a babe in arms. Mrs Beaming is so lovely and a wonderful mother.' Kate's eyes widened. 'Do not tell me they are dead?'

Phoebe bit her lower lip in concern and then answered, 'We do not know yet, but they are missing. Would you have that portrait? A copy perhaps?'

'Of course. Shall I bring it to you tomorrow?' Kate asked. 'I shall print it tonight.'

'Yes, please, Kate, that would be so appreciated. I shall ask the detective to collect the photo. He will be pleased to be able to identify them for his enquiries. Perhaps that might be an opportune time for you to drop in, Lilly?' Phoebe asked.

'That would be wonderful. It will give me an excuse to be there... I will say I heard about it and wish to report the story or assist where possible,' Lilly said.

Phoebe suggested a time in the afternoon and advised she would send notice if it did not suit the detective.

'And to think while you are all wrapped up in mystery, I shall be training cattle.' Emily sighed, breaking the tension.

'I am rather fond of cows,' Kate contributed, and the subject matter became lighter. But Lilly could think of nothing else but her potential story break and the family that may now be no more.

Chapter 12

THE POLICE SERGEANT GAVE an exasperated sigh as if his time was being wasted. He was a competent officer with considerable experience, but time and duty had wearied him. Nowadays with his retirement approaching, he aimed for a day with little interruption and even less taking of notes. It was also nearing his morning tea break and he was keen to be rid of the mature woman before him. Sergeant Henderson looked at the statement he had taken from her, dated it, and passed it over the table for the lady's signature.

Anne Norris signed her name and turned her attention to the sergeant.

'I fear you are dismissing my concerns somewhat, Sergeant,' she said, pulling her shawl tighter around her in the chilly police interview room.

'I assure you, Madam, we will take your observations onboard and review them most seriously.' The elderly police sergeant gathered the papers and rising to convey the interview was over, added, 'I must say, so as not to give you false hopes, that there is little to go on here but the finding of a family photo, a discussion of the death of a family and a means of disposal suggested by the man you name as Mr Zachariah Beaming.' He held up his hand as Anne went to speak. 'Granted, it is a discussion that should not have been conducted with a lady, but I don't think that is a crime.'

Anne's lips narrowed in frustration and she rose to leave as he opened the door indicating the interview time had come to an end.

'It will take only a little manpower to investigate if he has a family, if they are missing and if the hearthstone has been recently laid, surely Sergeant? Mr Beaming told me he was an unmarried man, and the photograph alone proves that to be a fabrication.'

'Unfortunately, Madam, I could not arrest every man who has lied about his marital status in order to win the hand of another lady, our cells would be overflowing.' He cleared his throat as if such indiscretion should not be spoken of out loud, as common as it might be. 'And, sadly, we are very short on manpower, Mrs Norris.'

'Miss Norris,' she corrected him and he gave her a curt nod.

'But I assure you, I will give this my attention.'

Anne thanked him and departed down the hallway, the sergeant watching her until she left through the station's front doors. He returned to the desk.

'Anything of note?' the desk clerk asked, as the sergeant threw the statement in a tray upon his desk.

'No,' he said and gave a small chuckle. 'Just the unfounded fears of a nervous woman.'

Detective Harland Stone was barely in the office for fifteen minutes when his planning was interrupted by the desk sergeant slipping him a piece of paper with an address scribbled upon it. He recognised it immediately.

'That is the address you asked me to search for recently is it not, for that Beaming fellow?' the desk sergeant asked.

'Indeed, and thank you for remembering,' Harland said to the efficient, senior officer.

'Did you find him in residence?'

'The first time, yes. But not on our return visit when we had more questions. I intended to go back today and see if he has returned.' Harland ran a hand through his hair – an action he often did when contemplating.

The desk sergeant nodded. 'You have an additional reason to now. A gentleman dropped in but moments ago and asked could a policeman meet him there within the hour... he is the home owner. He was showing a prospective tenant through but he thinks something might be amiss. He did not elaborate but I thought it best it comes to you.'

'Exactly so, thank you, Sergeant, we shall head there now.' Harland looked at the address again and suppressed a groan. He reached for his coat, slipping it on as he thought – Mr Zachariah Beaming was not coming back if the house owner was showing a tenant through... so where exactly was Mr Beaming? And what was amiss? Had he stolen something to add to his list of amassing crimes?

He looked at his young partner writing furious notes at his desk in the corner of the room.

'We are returning to Mr Beaming's residence, Gilbert. Ready?' Harland grabbed his hat.

The young detective jumped up, slipped on his jacket and grabbed his hat, hurrying to catch up with Harland as he strode down the hall.

'I bet he had no intention of returning,' Gilbert said. 'Who closes up like that if they are just going away for a day or two?'

'My Aunt Ethel because she believes the sun fades her rugs,' Harland said dryly as they exited the building and motioned to a hansom cab.

'I've got an Aunt Ethel too,' Gilbert said brightening. 'Do you think they know each other?'

Harland looked at the young man trying to understand how Gilbert's mind worked. 'No, I doubt that very much.'

'You're probably right,' Gilbert agreed. 'They would have to move in the same circle or be the same age. Or be in a club of ladies named Ethel. Such clubs do exist, believe it or not.'

Harland smiled at the thought. 'I have never come upon another with my name. It would be a lonely club indeed.'

'You may need to adopt your middle name then, Sir.'

'Grayson.'

'Oh,' Gilbert said flatly. 'You will have to make friends some other way, Sir. Maybe a hobby.'

Harland laughed, and they entered the hansom, advising the driver of the address.

'Tell me, Gilbert, why do you want to be a detective or have you been coerced into the occupation? The discussion is private between ourselves and there is no right or wrong answer,' He assured him.

Gilbert's jaw dropped open and he was silenced, deciding what to answer.

'That is fine, perhaps tell me another time if you feel comfortable doing so,' Harland said.

'Are you firing me?' Gilbert blurted out.

'Of course not. I am getting to know you as we begin our partnership together. Perhaps your other interests may tell me about your strengths. You certainly are very good at facts.' He kept to himself that it might help him move Gilbert onto an area of police work that was more suited to his skills.

Gilbert breathed out a sigh of relief. 'I am not sure why facts remain with me, but I have always gathered and stored them.'

'Like a walking encyclopedia, no less.'

Gilbert reddened slightly. 'If only I were that useful, Sir.'

The discussion was forgotten for now as they pulled up outside Mr Beaming's house. A man in trade clothing paced outside the house. On seeing the hansom pull up he hurried to meet them. Harland asked the driver to wait.

'You're the detectives?' he asked.

Harland nodded. 'Detectives Stone and Payne. You are?'

'James Blake. I own this house, or rather my parents did, now it is mine, inherited. I am leasing it out. I've got a butcher shop too, my trade. The shop's in the main street and I live above it,' he said hurriedly spilling out information as Harland found nervous people often do, to his advantage.

'Mr Zachariah Beaming was your tenant?' Harland asked. 'We called recently and found him in residence. He departed hastily.'

'Yes, he was paid up for a few weeks more but I received a telegram from him that he was discontinuing the lease. Urgent business has called him away.' James Blake frowned, fidgeting with his hands.

'May I have that telegram so I can attempt to trace his whereabouts?' Harland asked.

'It is at my residence.'

'I will send Gilbert around to collect it,' Harland said with a nod to his partner. 'You have some concerns then?'

'There is a most peculiar smell. In the drawing-room, near the hearth.'

Again, Harland restrained a groan. The worst-case scenario made its way to the top of his mind. He informed Mr Blake, 'It was not there two days ago when we were admitted, but the house has been locked up and it is quite warm.'

'He seemed quite a fastidious man,' Gilbert said surprised. 'I'm surprised he didn't have a cleaning lady, but that was probably his wife.'

'I don't think it is a domestic smell, Gilbert,' Harland suggested.

'Oh no,' Gilbert uttered appearing to have caught up with his superior's thinking, and Harland gave him a nod pleased he had reached the same conclusion until he said, 'I hope he did not have a pet and left it to fend for itself. I cannot abide animal cruelty of any kind.'

'Nor I,' Harland agreed with a small sigh and moved on, not waiting for his partner to get the full picture. Gilbert's naivety was surprising. Harland returned his attention to the butcher. 'I understand your concern and inference, Mr Blake.'

'Something's not right.' Mr Blake nodded. 'The floor's different too, like it has been freshly laid. I can assure you my parents did no maintenance of that sort on this house nor did I for my tenants.'

Harland grimaced 'Show me through to the area in question then if you please.' He turned to the hansom cab driver. 'Five more minutes if you will?'

'I've got all day if you are paying,' the driver called back and relaxed in his seat.

Harland and Gilbert followed James Blake up the front stairs and waited as he unlocked the door. They entered the premises and the smell hit them immediately.

'Good Lord, that is foul,' Gilbert exclaimed. 'That's a dead smell if ever there was one. Not that I've had much experience in that, although when I was on the beat, we found a man who'd been dead in his shed for a week. Put me off my dinner for days.'

Harland braced himself and walked in the direction of the unpleasant odour. James Blake was correct; it was coming from the drawing room and more specifically from near the hearthstone. Harland ran his foot over the area and noticed the new quick lime in place. He moved to the far end of the room

122

and then walked to the other, Gilbert observing him the whole time.

'Do you see anything untoward about this floor, Gilbert?' he asked and held up his hand to stop James Blake from answering as he started to speak.

Gilbert followed the movements of Harland from one end of the room to the next.

'It's uneven, Sir. Looks new too, I'd say.'

'As would I,' Harland agreed. 'What about the substance?' He decided to use Gilbert's knowledge to his best advantage and watched as the young man studied the floor.

'Quick lime!' Gilbert said. 'It can be flammable if water is around, Sir, it is quite amazing stuff. My uncle used lime water to save several of his cows who ate too much grass. Just mixed the quick lime with about three or four pints of water and when settled, the cows were given it as a drench. Worked a treat.'

Harland waited patiently and saw the surprised look on Mr Blake's face.

'And it's purpose here... what do you think?' Harland pushed Gilbert to wade through his mind to the most relevant fact.

'Oh, yes,' Gilbert said, looking at the ground and up at Harland. 'It's used for burials, of course, to cover corpses.'

'That it is, and with the smell, we can draw a likely assumption.' Harland saw Gilbert's shocked realisation as he turned to Mr Blake. 'Did your tenant, Mr Beaming, have a family?'

'If he did, I never met them. He was the only one I dealt with,' James said. 'So, what now? I am not going to be able to lease my house until—'

Harland cut him off and motioned for the men to remove themselves from the room.

'One moment, Mr Blake, please. Gilbert, will you return to the station and bring back officers with the appropriate tools for digging and breaking a hearthstone?'

'Really?' Gilbert asked wide-eyed.

'Really, Detective.' Harland returned his attention to the butcher.

'Who's going to pay for that damage?' James Blake's face reddened with anger.

'Mr Blake considering what we might find, that will be the least of your problems.' Harland saw the sad acceptance dawn on James Blake's face as he came to fully understand the question related to Mr Beaming's family.

Harland continued, 'Mr Blake, I will take the keys please and I suggest you return to work and mention this to no one until we investigate. I will let you know the outcome. Share the cab with my detective if you like.'

'Gladly,' James Blake said and handing over the keys made his way to the waiting vehicle.

'Make haste, Gilbert, and tell no one except the officer in charge.'

'Sir,' Gilbert agreed and raced to the hansom, swinging up into the seat next to James Blake and directing the driver to return him to Roma Street station.

Harland watched as it pulled away and then he re-entered the house, levering up the windows in the drawing room in an effort to release the smell. And then he waited.

Chapter 13

Bennet Martin looked worse for wear this morning. His sleep had been disrupted by thoughts that Phoebe fancied that detective. All the months he had been finding reasons to see her, savouring every moment his closest friend, Julius, had mentioned his sister's name, and biding his time waiting and hoping affections would cool between Phoebe and Gideon Hayward – he had not counted on another suitor undercutting him.

He moved to his painting of her, almost finished but never finished. Every time he declared his work done, he saw some imperfection on the canvas that the subject herself did not display. Bennet glanced at his other portraits of Phoebe leaning against the wall in the corner. Some were painted in moments of passion when he felt free with his colours and strokes, the result being a charming picture of exuberance and affection. But the one in front of him on the easel was his best. Should he gift it to her?

Maybe it was time to speak with Julius and ask permission to court her or to broach the subject. He imagined Julius would tell him the decision was Phoebe's but speaking with the head of the Astin family first was the right thing to do, and Julius accepted this role, even though his grandfather was by rights the senior Astin. He will not deny me, surely, Bennet mused. After all, she has no fortune to speak of, even though Julius is a wealthy man, and not many suitors will care for her eccentricities.

He moved away from the portrait and cleaned his brushes. There would be no painting this morning, he was not in the mood. Bennet frowned hearing footsteps hastening up his stairs and he panicked, unable to move the painting before there was a quick rap at the door, it opened and his clerk stuck his head in.

'Sorry to interrupt your work,' Daniel Dutton said with a glance at the painting.

'Then don't,' Bennet snapped and rolled his eyes as Daniel retreated, closing the door. 'You are here now, tell me what is the matter,' he called with a raised voice.

Daniel opened the door and grinned. 'You look most dishevelled this morning and you are grumpy again. What is going on? Perhaps you need to have some female company that is not on a canvas, even if it is just for relief purposes,' he said with a nod to the bed.

Bennet was about to explode when Daniel continued, 'Oh, that is the problem, you are in love. Why didn't you say so?'

'What is it you want?' Bennet ground out the words attempting to ignore Daniel.

'There is a letter from Miss Astin requesting your attendance at two o'clock as she has some information to share on a case. Her man awaits a response?'

Bennet brightened. 'Absolutely. Tell her I shall be there.'

He ignored the satisfied look from the departing clerk and hurried to do his grooming. Now that his day had a clear direction, he would get to work on the Beaming case and go to the post office to see if there had been a reply to his telegram. Hopefully, Mrs Beaming's family will engage him in Mr Walker's stead and he can begin work on the case of the missing wife and children in earnest.

Detective Gilbert Payne returned to Mr Beaming's former lodgings with a couple of constables in tow and behind them a few more men armed with tools for starting work. 'There's a note for you, Sir.' He handed Harland a folded piece of paper.

Harland stuffed it in his pocket for a moment as he showed the men into the house and the room in question but not before assuring a neighbour there was no cause for alarm as he saw the small lady in the floral dress looking over the hedge.

'Agh, this can't be good,' one of the older men declared as the smell assaulted their senses on entering the drawing room.

'I fear you are right,' Harland said. 'It was much worse on arrival with the house closed. Perhaps start digging here.' Harland indicated an area where the lime did not seem as set and might break more easily.

'Right you are then.' A younger man with a spade said and struck the first blow into the ground.

Harland moved away and read the note in his pocket.

Good morning, Detective Stone. Should you be free at 2pm today, we have something that might assist with Mr Beaming's case. If that time is unsuitable, please advise a suitable time at your convenience. Yours sincerely, Phoebe Astin, The Economic Undertaker.

He pocketed the note. Two o'clock will be fine given it was just on 11 o'clock and he envisioned they would find what they needed in a very short time. In fact, he might not need what Miss Astin had to offer, but it would be pleasant to see her again. The thought annoyed him as much as it did surprise him. He had enough on his plate settling into a new role and new city, without the internal tension of a new romance.

'What do you want me to do, Sir?' Gilbert asked interrupting his thoughts with a frustrating question that a thinking detective should not have to ask his superior. Other partners did not have this dilemma. Before he could respond, one of the diggers let out a loud curse.

'Detective, you'll want to see this,' he said, and two men lifted a piece of hearthstone to reveal the source of the smell. A young lady lay partly clad and decomposing, her body covered in broken stone and dust. The sight was both mortifying and devastating.

Gilbert raced outside, nauseous, the smell was overwhelming and another constable followed in his wake, he too was overtaken by retching.

'Thank you, gentleman,' Harland said. 'Can you remove all the new stonework laid? I need to be sure there is no one else buried beneath.'

'Strike, how many more are you expecting?' the older digger asked and Harland grimaced as he answered, 'Four children.'

The young man made a sign of the cross and continued raising the floor. Harland went to the window and called Gilbert. 'Will you fetch the coroner please?' He saw the look of relief on Gilbert's face at the opportunity to leave the grounds.

Back inside, the men laboured, making quick work of the job, and stood back when finished.

'Just the one then, Detective,' the younger man said, wiping his brow. The relief of everyone in the room was palpable.

Harland breathed out, the vice on his chest releasing for the first time that morning. He thanked them as they packed up to depart. Harland studied the woman again. She was not long decomposed and if it was Mrs Beaming, where were her children?

Chapter 14

CATHERINE TOUNSELLE WAS A practical young lady but nevertheless quite easily distracted by flattery. The voyage on the steamer, *Adelaide*, was coming to an end and it had been the most romantic of trips. Only last year her sister had wed and now Catherine felt the pressure to do so as well. She had known romance but nothing that would lead to a walk down the aisle, and she did want to do so sooner rather than later. Fortuitously, on the voyage, she had met a dashing man – even if he was quite a bit older than herself – who claimed to have completely fallen for her charms. She wasn't sure what those particular charms were that attracted him, and even if she was not in love, she was in love with the idea of being in love. A retired military man, he cut a dashing figure and had won the respect of all on board.

After dinner that evening, the gentleman in question slipped her hand through the crook of his arm as they took the customary walk around the deck, enjoying the scent of the ocean and the blackest of skies out on the seas, littered by stars.

'I am saddened for it to end,' Catherine said, with a sigh.

'The journey will soon end, but we need not end our connection, dear Catherine.' With that, Major Zachariah Williams dropped to one knee and Catherine gasped. Random guests around the deck stopped to watch, their faces alive with delight.

'Miss Catherine Tounselle, will you do me the great honour of being my wife? Of allowing me to care for you for all your days? Dear Catherine, will you marry me?'

'Yes!' The word sprung from her lips with no hesitation whatsoever and later she would realise she did not love him at all, but the moment was ever so romantic and the ring he presented was ever so big. He was a handsome man, well-groomed and was, according to him, in possession of a sizeable fortune. What more could a young lady of marriageable age want?

'I am overwhelmed by the honour you bestow upon me,' he said to her rising from his kneeling position. They embraced and in the joy of the moment began to recall their most romantic times on board, and plan for all that was to come.

Catherine flushed with delight. 'You are a terrible flatterer and have pursued me from the moment you laid eyes on me, I am sure. We do barely know each other – it has been the shortest of journeys.'

'Yet I know all I need to know. I had no chance from the start, smitten I was, and I know I cannot continue without you,' he said making her feel beautiful and desirable when no one else had done so in the past. 'One must not delay when happiness is within reach.'

So, this was what it was like to be truly loved and desired, she thought, content. Catherine could not wait and tomorrow before they docked, she would ask the crew to wire her mother and sister of her good news.

'You will never regret it... we shall get a lovely home in Albany—'

'Albany?' she said alarmed. 'Western Australia is a great distance away.'

'We need not live there forever, but I have work lined up commencing next month, and a steamer ticket for my departure.'

Catherine gave a small nod. 'We shall see how we fare there then.'

'Of course,' he agreed. 'But I want you to come to me as soon as you can. Go home, make plans to travel and I shall book your passage. While I wait for you, I shall find us a home.'

'I am returning to Brisbane to see my parents first. But I shall prepare my trousseau there and come by train, I prefer it,' she said.

'Then it is all planned,' Zachariah Beaming or rather Major Zachariah Williams said and kissed her hand, relieved now that Miss Anne Norris had not agreed to accompany him as Miss Tounselle was younger and no doubt an innocent in the bedroom. 'We shall be wed as soon as you arrive and begin a new life together in a new place. You will want for nothing, my darling. Nothing.'

Chapter 15

Detective Harland Stone had a day like no other. A dead body under the hearthstone, an appointment late in the day with the coroner, Dr Tavish McGregor, to know more about the deceased lady, a report that had just come to hand indicating a lady by the name of Miss Anne Norris had advised the police of her suspicions of Mr Zachariah Beaming, and a 2pm appointment at *The Economic Undertaker* of which he was on his way to now. He had sent Gilbert off to find Miss Anne Norris and ask if she would come to the station this afternoon or if more convenient, he would call on her this very day. He expected the young detective to meet him at the offices of *The Economic Undertaker*. He was quite looking forward to Gilbert's reaction to being told of a ghostly vision. What facts would he dig up concerning that, Harland wondered.

He stopped short of entering the building as the door to the funeral parlour swung open and a couple with two older children – all dressed in black – departed the premises. When they were further along the street, he entered slowly, casing the reception area and seeing it clear.

'Ah, Detective Stone, good timing,' Randolph said, rising from a stool behind the front counter.

'I just saw a mourning party leaving and thought I'd give everyone a moment.' Harland removed his hat.

'Most kind. Diphtheria took the littlest one. We don't see it as much these days, thank goodness.'

'Thank goodness you have a funeral plan they can most likely afford,' Harland said with all sincerity. 'Miss Astin requested I call in, my partner, Gilbert Payne, will soon be joining me.'

'I will keep an eye out for Detective Payne and make sure we don't accidentally bury him,' Randolph said, earning a spontaneous laugh from Harland.

'That would be appreciated.' No sooner had he said the words when the door opened and Gilbert stuck his head in, glancing around warily and looking relieved on seeing Harland.

'You have the right place, Detective,' Randolph said and the men introduced each other. 'Come this way, Detectives, Phoebe is expecting you in our meeting room.' Randolph

137

led the way. 'Gives you a break from seeing bodies in her workroom.'

'Much appreciated. I see my share without seeing more in Miss Astin's workroom,' he agreed.

Harland was struck once again by the sight of Phoebe – she was so ethereal, so different to all he normally laid eyes upon in the course of his workday. Earlier he had seen the rotting remains of some poor lady – a daughter, a wife maybe – and here was Miss Phoebe Astin, in a close-fitted pale lavender gown cinched around her small waist, with cream lace around her sleeves and neck, her long wavy blonde hair let down and tied loosely at the back with a piece of matching lace. She looked so delicate although he knew she was quite strong of nature; he could look at her all day. Then he noted the journalist, Miss Lilly Lewis, in attendance and his demeanour changed to wary. The two ladies were most formidable despite the delicacy of their beauty.

'Miss Astin, Miss Lewis,' he said with a curt nod and introduced Gilbert to the ladies in attendance.

'Detectives, thank you so much for dropping in when I imagine you are very busy,' Phoebe said. 'Miss Lewis and I have something which we thought might be of use to your case. It is a portrait photograph my friend, Miss Kate Kirby, took at her studio. She could not be here to explain due to a last-minute booking but—' Phoebe stopped mid-sentence as Bennet Martin rushed in behind Harland and greeted the party.

'Forgive my tardiness, my clerk lost a... never mind, what did I miss?' he asked looking at the group and greeting Miss Astin and Miss Lewis, and undertaking an introduction with Detective Gilbert Payne, then shaking both detectives' hands.

Before Phoebe could respond Julius rushed in wearing his dark morning coat having just come from a funeral. He smiled at his friend, Bennet, and greeted Harland with an affectionate slap to the detective's shoulder.

'Harland! Good to see you again and this must be your partner. What have I missed? Do I need to be here?' he asked in one breath, then seeing Lilly acknowledged her attendance. 'Miss Lewis.'

Phoebe refrained from laughing but held up her hand. 'No one has missed anything, you all arrived at the same time and no Julius, you are not required and may depart.'

'Excellent, good day all,' he said and was gone as quickly as he came.

'May I ask why the media is involved?' Harland said addressing Lilly.

'What exactly are we involved in?' Bennet asked and Phoebe rolled her eyes.

'If everyone would indulge me and perhaps cease asking questions, I will inform you.'

Harland looked sheepish and gave a small smile and nod. He accepted the offer of a chair and the party sat around a timber meeting table. Mrs Dobbs bustled in with a tray carrying a teapot, cups, a sugar pot, a milk jug and a plate of cake. She deposited it and left the party to serve themselves so they could speak in private.

Harland did not realise how hungry he was until he saw the slabs of cake and happily accepted a slice and a cup of tea from Phoebe who played hostess. He noted Gilbert took a small slice and surmised the young man scored tea and cake at Anne Norris's residence. He was pleased to see Gilbert studying the party and would welcome his observations later. As to himself, Harland was oblivious to the looks he received from the private investigator beside him or of Bennet Martin's feelings towards Miss Astin.

'We are here to briefly discuss Mrs Beaming and the four children and I shall be quick as I know everyone is busy,' Phoebe said.

'I have news on the case as well, should I begin while you pour?' Bennet asked and Harland tried to restrain his frustration that everyone seemed to be involved in a case of which they had no business owning, except perhaps for the private investigator.'

'Please do, Mr Martin,' Phoebe said most formally.

'I collected a telegram this morning and Mrs Beaming's parents wish me to continue the investigation for their missing daughter and grandchildren.' He accepted the cup with thanks. 'It is fair to say that they were shocked by Mr Walker's demise and are quite fearful for their daughter's safety, even more so now.'

'Understandable,' Harland said and gave Gilbert a subtle shake of his head to say nothing as yet. He was pleased to be able to eat while Bennet spoke of the case Harland appeared to be sharing with the party in attendance. Mrs Dobbs's moist fruit cake was quite exceptional and he meant to tell her so afterwards. He asked, 'Have you any insights that might assist us?'

'Yes. I have been in touch via telegram with a friend of mine in Rainhill as that is where travel tickets indicate the Beaming family were visiting. My friend is a retired policeman, a friend of my father's,' Bennet explained to Harland. 'I described Mr Zachariah Beaming as best I could from Mr Walker's description in the file, and he discussed it with several people in industry in the town – shop owners, the local priest, and even at boarding houses. This is where it gets interesting.' Bennet paused, making sure he had their attention.

'One moment, please,' Harland said interrupting. 'Forgive my directness, but Miss Lewis, I need to understand your involvement and what you intend to report out of this meeting?'

'I understand, Detective,' she said brightly. Lilly's energy could fill the room. 'My editor has requested I find a story with a bride, groom and death and I intend to take it further and provide a significant editorial piece.'

'To further your career?' Harland asked.

'I am hoping so, as you hope to solve cases to better your career, Detective.'

'She has a fair point, Sir,' Gilbert added and Harland saw the group hide smiles and looks at the senior detective being put in his place. Yes, Miss Lewis was right, he conceded, but it was his job to help others before furthering his career became a consideration. He was about to speak again when she elaborated.

'I assure you, Detective, as I assured Phoebe, I will be the soul of discretion, I will not publish anything without your prior knowledge and I will report the facts only.'

Harland felt a little more reassured by her sincerity. 'When might you be intending to run this piece then?'

'As news unfolds and hopefully before other news outlets have wind of it.'

'And what if one of your rival papers gets word of it first? Will you start embellishing the story and placing yourself in danger to have more to report?' Harland knew the game only too well.

'Absolutely not, well, hopefully I won't be in danger,' she said, deciding not to promise that which might be beyond her control.

Phoebe bit her lip concerned and added, 'We are pursuing a very shady character, capable of murder as we know from Mr Walker's death.'

'The crime rate and attacks against women are considerably high at the moment,' Gilbert spoke up.

Harland held up his hand. '*We* are not pursuing it, *I* am pursuing it, with the assistance of Mr Martin.' He conceded with a glance to Bennet. 'While I appreciate and welcome your insights Miss Astin and Miss Lewis, you are not to involve yourself with this man or anyone in his shadow.'

Phoebe nodded her understanding but Lilly's eyes brightened again, her blue eyes twinkling with mischief. 'This is where I hope we will strike a bargain, Detective Stone. I will promise to stay out of trouble and report only that which is factual or happened, and not print anything that you are still investigating for fear of derailing your progress...'

'And?' he asked sensing a negotiation. Lilly delivered her payoff.

'If you will guarantee me exclusive inside information, allow me to be on this case behind the scenes, and give me several quotes to include. I can take that deal to my editor.' She sat straighter, looking ready to fight and strike another deal if need be.

Harland could feel all eyes upon him as he thought, and then he gave her a curt nod. Lilly's eyebrows went upward at once.

'Really?' she exclaimed almost forgetting herself and he did his best not to smile at her enthusiasm.

'If and only if you stick to the terms of the agreement. Should you not, then it will be the first and last time we share information.'

'Agreed,' she said offering her hand across the table to shake on it to his surprise. With a frown, he took her hand and was even more surprised by the firmness of the young lady's grip. 'I have five brothers,' she said as if reading his mind.

'Heaven help us,' he muttered and looked to Phoebe with an air of amusement since she had teased him last visit and caught him unaware. 'Was this your idea then?'

Phoebe gave a small shrug. 'A joint decision I would say as a result of my ladies' meeting last night. We discovered something that might be of value to you and then I could not keep Lilly from the story.'

'I imagine so,' Harland said drily and turned to Bennet. 'Forgive me, Mr Martin, you were saying.'

'Bennet, please. We have met several times in Julius's social circle even if it was briefly. I am sure we can dispense with the formalities.'

Harland nodded his agreement.

'As I was saying, my contact, the retired policeman, thought the description matched a tenant of a landlady in his acquaintance. She remembered Mr Beaming, but not as Mr Beaming,' he said delivering the words with great effect.

Harland did his best not to roll his eyes at the theatrics and he sensed Phoebe was not one for dramatisation either as she hurried Bennet along asking, 'Had he taken an alias?'

'Indeed. He rented a house in Rainhill – that's about thirteen miles from Liverpool,' he added for Gilbert's benefit, 'under the name of Major Zachariah Williams, and pretended he was a military man.'

'Major Williams, that is very helpful,' Harland said, running a hand over his jaw. 'What of his family, were they seen?' He did not want to declare yet that he may have found Mrs Beaming's body but not that of her young ones, and had told Gilbert earlier not to mention it either.

'No and brace yourself,' Bennet said to the ladies.

'I imagine both ladies have been exposed to quite a number of fearful sights in their roles,' Harland said and noticed both ladies looked at him with appreciation.

'Then I shall brace myself,' Gilbert said breaking the tension as the group smiled at his honesty. 'I suspect this will be a fearful tale!'

'I suspect you are right, Detective,' Bennet said enjoying his moment in the spotlight. 'Major Williams, that is Zachariah Beaming, said he was a widower and began courting his landlady's daughter, Eliza. He wore a uniform, went to church, and was seen in all the right circles. But you will not believe this, a woman with four children was staying with him for a while and he told his landlady that it was his sister, nieces and nephew.'

'Good grief, the man has no shame,' Lilly said.

'Unless they were his sister, nieces and nephew,' Gilbert mused. 'But it would be a remarkable coincidence.'

'Time will tell,' Bennet agreed.

'That has been most helpful, thank you, Bennet,' Harland said giving praise where praise was due. 'And you, Miss Astin, Miss Lewis?'

'As mentioned, my ladies' group met last night and I was discreetly discussing Mr Walker's death – we often speak of our work in our small group,' Phoebe explained.

Harland noticed she did not mention Mr Walker was in spirit form. He may be spared from discussing her proclivities of speaking with the dead with Gilbert after all. For now, at least.

Phoebe continued, 'We were concerned that a wife and children could be missing. I mentioned the name of Mr Zachariah Beaming and our dear friend, Miss Kate Kirby, recognised the name.'

'She is a photographer and does family portraits,' Lilly continued the story when encouraged by Phoebe.

'That is an amazing art,' Gilbert said and turned to Harland. 'The technology is getting better and better. My aunt, uncle, and their daughters had a photographic portrait taken and she was quite shocked by how they all looked in it.' He leaned forward. 'She is convinced the photograph has drained some of her spirit.'

Harland tapped the desk impatiently not wanting to reprimand his young charge in front of the group but he saw Phoebe had read his signs of frustration and hurried the conversation along kindly adding for Gilbert's sake, 'Kate tells me that is not an uncommon thought, Detective Payne.'

She slid an enveloped photograph to the detective. 'Kate took a photograph portrait of the Beaming family only six months ago after the birth of their fourth child. We sourced a copy for you.'

Harland grabbed for the envelope and opened it hurriedly. He looked at Mrs Beaming and dropped the photograph to the table, his eyes staring straight ahead.

'What is it, Detective?' Phoebe asked, concerned, placing a hand on his arm. He was startled as if he had forgotten he was in company, and then seeing her hand on his arm, stiffened as if he did not require emotional support. She quickly withdrew her hand.

'Miss Astin, we made a discovery this morning, which is to remain within the confines of this group just for now until I see the coroner this afternoon.'

'Dr McGregor? Yes, agreed,' Lilly assured him again. 'What is it?'

'We discovered a body of a young lady recently murdered and buried under the hearthstone of Mr Beaming's house.'

The group expressed horror and Harland raised the photo to look at it again, adding, 'The children were not there and I fear for their whereabouts.' He looked to Phoebe. 'But thanks to this portrait, I can confirm the deceased lady is not Mrs Beaming. I don't know who she is, but I will know more this afternoon hopefully.'

Bennet grimaced. 'I wonder if Mr Beaming, or rather the major, left England with a new wife – the landlady's daughter he was courting – and they were residing in that house as husband and wife.'

Harland gave a contemplative groan. 'Could you wire your source and find out from the landlady or the local priest if they wed or departed for Australia together?'

'At once.'

'Detective Payne and I shall go directly to the coroner,' Harland said rising.

'May I come?' Lilly asked.

'No. But come to my office later this afternoon and as agreed, I will tell you what I know for your story tomorrow.'

'Thank you,' Lilly gushed. 'I shall go speak with my editor now.'

Harland saw her squeeze Phoebe's hand and the return look of pleasure Phoebe gave her. What brings a man to harm a lady, he pondered for just a moment as he watched them, and felt nothing but protectiveness. He bid them farewell and departed with Gilbert and Bennet on his tail. Harland had a dead body to identify and a young partner who was bound to regale him with a thousand facts related to morgues on the way there.

Chapter 16

AMBROSE ASTIN HAD LOST a body. It wasn't something that happened every day, fortunately, still, it should not have happened at all. He could imagine his brother's wrath and his grandfather's disappointed look. The man was dead, how far could he have got? It is not like he could hitch a hansom and leave town or go back to his former residence. Ambrose ran through the realistic worse and best-case scenarios in his head – the deceased might be buried by mistake, or best case, he is in storage. Ambrose knew neither would please the family of the deceased if he did not find the body soon.

'Blast it,' he muttered under his breath. He stood in the hallway outside the morgue, hands on hip, trying to recall what his grandfather had told him since the note he had scribbled down was incorrect. Was he to collect the body from the morgue or the hospital? Both places had told him they did not have a Mr Eldon for collection but the other options – private addresses, a hotel, a scene of a crime – he would have remembered. There was nothing to be done about it, he would have to return to the shop and ask again.

'Ambrose!'

He heard a voice call out his name and turned to see Tavish McGregor heading up the hallway. The Scottish coroner was a welcomed sight and he was beaming as if the sight of Ambrose was a pleasant interruption to his day.

'Tavish, fancy finding you here at the morgue,' Ambrose joked and shook the extended offered hand.

Tavish slapped him on the shoulder. 'I am pleased to see you; I don't get much living company at my place of work. It might not have been the best choice of occupation for a popular man like me,' he joked and Ambrose laughed.

'Ah, the dead are pleasant enough,' Ambrose said with a shrug. 'I've found some to be better company than the living.'

Tavish laughed a hearty laugh. 'What are you doing here then?'

'I've lost a body.' Ambrose looked sheepish and gave a small shrug. 'Julius will kill me and Grandpa will disown me.'

Tavish chuckled. 'It happens to the best of us. I've lost several but I have always found them. Do not despair, what is the deceased's name?'

'Mr Eldon. Your office manager tells me he is not here, if he ever was.'

'Eldon? I know the name Eldon and he was here. Died of accidental poison ingestion.'

Ambrose's hand went to his heart. 'Good, so I have the right name and the right building. But apparently, Mr Eldon has departed without me. Dying to get out perhaps.'

Tavish chuckled again. 'Julius picked him up earlier.'

'What? No! I shall kill him on my return,' he muttered angrily and reached into his pocket pulling out a note of paper. Another fell from his pocket onto the floor. He retrieved it and groaned. 'I was looking at yesterday's list, here are today's pick-ups for me.'

'Anyone I can help you with?' Tavish said trying to hide his amusement.

'No, I am off to the hospital. But thank you, Tavish. Do me a favour and do not mention this to Julius.'

'It will cost you an ale.' Tavish gave him a wink.

'Done, a small price to pay.' Ambrose shook on it.

'Tavish, Ambrose!' A voice called from further along the hallway and the men turned to see Detective Harland Stone approach.

'Right on time,' Tavish said welcoming the detective and noting the large hallway clock marked the hour of two. 'Got any dead you want Ambrose to take away while he is here?'

Harland shook both men's hands and looked to Ambrose. 'Do you only take the dead, because I have a partner who I might happily part with?'

Ambrose grinned. 'Only the dead, but you have the right contacts if you want to take it further,' he joked.

Harland had left Gilbert to pay the driver and to sign in for them. They could see the young detective coming down the hallway towards them, putting on his jacket as he walked.

'Whose body are you two meeting about?' Ambrose asked.

'A woman I found this morning... related to what Mr Walker told us in your rooms.'

'Ah, Phoebe is rarely wrong,' Ambrose said with pride. 'I shall leave you to it and get on before Julius sends out a search party.'

The men bid each other farewell and Ambrose hurried on to collect his corpse. Behind him, Harland prepared to learn the truth about the women below the hearthstone.

Lilly Lewis knocked on her editor's door and entered the den of his smoke-filled room when summonsed. He stopped what he was doing, and peered over the rim of his wiry glasses.

'Lewis, looking resplendent in blue.'

'Thank you, Mr Cowan, and that is a most striking tie,' she retorted since she was fairly sure he would not praise the attire of his male reporters, so she gave as good as she got. He chuckled in response and ran his hand down it. 'The wife makes them. She's handy with her dressmaking, the cooking leaves a bit to be desired.'

'How fortunate you have the club lunches then,' Lilly said frustrated with the small talk.

'Indeed, a man would starve.'

Mr Cowan was at no risk of that, she noted. 'I have a very important news story to share with you and I have been promised exclusivity by Detective Harland Stone if you permit me to write it.'

'Is that so?' he said with mild amusement and studied Lilly, blowing puffs of cigar smoke in her direction. 'What did you do to get that?'

'Not what you think, Mr Cowan,' Lilly said drily and made him laugh. 'I had a photograph that I procured that was of use to him.'

Mr Cowan held up his hand. 'Take a seat and take it from the top, young lady; make it snappy.'

Lilly smiled, sat, and laid the story out before him. He sat back, hands steepled across his girth, as she told him of Mr Zachariah Beaming, the woman under the hearthstone, the missing family, and her invitation to get a statement on the body found this very afternoon. When she finished, she held her breath, praying he would not take the story from her.

Mr Cowan leant forward. 'Brilliant. It is yours; I'll hold space for you for tomorrow's issue, work with Lawrence.'

Lilly grimaced and pushed her luck. 'Sir, Detective Stone will only give the story to me.'

'Then Lawrence can do his own investigating and you can combine your findings.'

'Can I pick my own partner, please?' she asked with nothing to lose – in for a penny in for a pound as they say. Lilly braced waiting for Mr Cowan's patience to run out but instead, he chuckled.

'You've got more front than a box of shirts, young lady, but I admire that in a reporter. I wish some of my men had as much. Who do you want to partner with?'

'Fergus. We sit next to each other and I have observed he is hard-working, always comes in early and leaves late, and has made some of the shipping stories most entertaining, would you not agree? We could both use the challenge.'

'Fergus Griffiths! I've got him doing the shipping news for a reason. He bungled a horse racing story that made me a laughing stock at the track,' he spat out, angry still.

'Mr Cowan, Fergus told me that was several years ago and he deserves a break.' She thought of the ruffled young man, a few years her senior with a mop of brown hair, intelligent dark

155

eyes, and with a wife and child to support. 'Surely you made an error or two in your early days.'

'If I did, I paid for it.' Mr Cowan grumbled. 'Alright then. But this is on you, Lewis. Let me down and you will both be writing about marriages, deaths and the incoming fleet until the cows come home!'

Lilly jumped to her feet. 'You will not be disappointed, Mr Cowan. I will have an amazing story for the morning edition, and you'll see, we will end up being your number one crime writing team.'

He scoffed again but indulged in a smile at her enthusiasm. 'Ah, while I think of it...'

Lilly tried not to grimace, it was hard to second-guess the editor's thoughts and what was to come.

'The piece you wrote on the deceased Mrs Rose Beatty...' he lifted some papers, rifled through his in-tray and waved a letter at Lilly. 'Got this letter this morning from Mrs Beatty's brother. The family wanted to thank us for the compassionate article on their sister and daughter. He made mention that Mrs Beatty's husband had an unfortunate accident and will be waylaid for some time.' The editor scoffed.

'Well, that is unfortunate,' Lilly grinned, 'I'll be sure to tell the detective and the Astin family at the funeral home.'

With a wave of his hand dismissing her, Lilly hurried from the editor's office. There was much to do, words to write, a detective to meet and a fellow reporter to get briefed for the job.

Chapter 17

THE CORONER, DR TAVISH McGregor, pulled the coverings away from the face of the deceased woman on his table and then replaced them just as quickly. 'Nothing to see there that I can't tell you about,' he said and noted the look of relief on the face of the young detective.

'I hope she was long dead before the quick lime was poured on her,' Gilbert said.

'Rest assured, Gilbert, she was felled by a blow to the side of the head, a blow that would kill her quickly,' Tavish said and added, 'cracked the skull.'

'Is there any indication of who she might be? I've since determined she is not Mrs Beaming... well not the first Mrs Beaming,' Detective Harland Stone said.

'There is nothing on her person that gives the lady an identity, except a wedding band so she is a bride. The side of her face would need to be somewhat reconstructed should you wish to do a drawing for identification purposes... the corpse has decayed.'

'Let us wait and see what comes from another line of enquiry,' Harland said. 'This may be an English lady, the daughter of Beaming's landlord when he recently resided in Rainhill.'

'Goodness, what sort of man is this?' Tavish asked.

'A man who will hang if he is caught and charged with two murders,' Gilbert said stating the obvious.

'Very true, Gilbert,' Harland concurred. 'Would you say the manner of death – the blow to the head and the weapon used – was similar to that inflicted on the deceased private detective, William Walker's skull?'

'Hmm, let me recall,' Tavish said and ran a hand over his slight red beard. 'Was he the gentleman found in the river?'

'That is him,' Harland said.

Tavish found his notes and concurred. 'Similarly shaped instrument and injury... not a distinct waffle pattern but he may have used the side of the instrument or the back of it. Did you not find a murder weapon on site?'

'There was a meat tenderiser...' Harland was about to say as Miss Astin advised but recalled himself and remained discrete,

'I believe that is the instrument found under the woman's body. It should be with you for analysis.'

'Ah, it is me that is at fault,' Tavish said grabbing a small box on his table and opening it. He lifted out the heavy cast iron tenderiser ensuring he did not touch the areas where he might lift evidence.

Gilbert said with a look of distaste on his face, 'I am sure I'll never eat a bite of steak again without thinking of it.'

'Nor I,' Harland agreed.

'There are hairs on this, excellent,' Tavish examined it. 'Are you thinking it is the same culprit then?'

'I am,' Harland confirmed. 'I believe Zachariah Beaming killed this woman and buried her under his hearthstone, and also killed the man who was hired to investigate what happened to Beaming's wife and children. He is the strongest suspect for both crimes.' Harland refrained from mentioning that he did not have any evidence at this stage except for the word of Mr William Walker's ghost, to the latter murder.

'I can release her for burial but if she is not identified, I imagine there is no family to claim her as yet,' Tavish said.

'Correct. I will let you know as soon as we hear from England about the landlady's daughter,' Harland said. 'For now, we are off to speak with Miss Anne Norris, a friend of Mr Beaming.'

'A lucky-to-be-alive friend I would say if this is the pattern of people in his company,' Gilbert said with a nod to the corpse in the corner.

'Yes, I am glad I am not making the acquaintance of Miss Norris in my rooms at this stage,' Tavish said. 'Miss Astin and I have the misfortune of knowing people when they are on their way elsewhere.'

Harland smiled. 'I guess that's one way of describing being en route to a box lowered six feet under.'

They bid Tavish a good day and jumped on the omnibus to Anne Norris's home where she was expecting them. On arrival, Gilbert – who had set up the meeting – introduced Harland to the mature, medium-height, slim lady, with her hair tied neatly in a bun, and a look of vigour to her face. Harland could imagine she might attract a mature man's company. They accepted the offer of refreshments.

'I imagine visiting witnesses is often the only time you young men eat during a busy day,' she said kindly, bringing the teapot to the table.

'I had lunch but Detective Stone often forgets,' Gilbert said, and eyeing the slice on offer added, 'but I can always eat.'

Anne Norris smiled with delight. Other than her neighbour and the church ladies, there were few to spoil with cooking in her life.

'I believe we must offer you an apology, Miss Norris,' Harland started. 'Your early suspicions about Mr Beaming have been brought to our attention and it is the reason we are drawing the net tighter.'

She smiled, pleased, and after pouring three cups of tea, placed the pot in the middle of the table, and pushed the plate of freshly baked chocolate slices closer to the two men, who both happily accepted with thanks.

'Well, thank you, Detective, for saying so. I did think there was something quite odd about him. But when I spoke to the police sergeant, he dismissed my claim.'

'The Sergeant said your suspicions were the unfounded fears of a nervous woman,' Gilbert stated.

Harland gave him a pained look – there was no need to further insult the woman with the internal bungling and rudeness of the police department, one sergeant in particular. He apologised again and she smiled and patted his hand.

'Detective Stone, thank you but do not concern yourself. I am a mature woman and am quite aware that we ladies are regarded as nervous creatures to be protected or ignored as the situation presents.'

'I assure you, Miss Norris, that is not the case, nor should it be, and certainly is not how I regard the ladies in my acquaintance.'

'Nor I,' Gilbert piped up and Harland cringed anticipating his next frank statement would set them back again. 'My mother would kick my butt to town and back if I treated her as a nervous creature to be ignored and protected!'

Miss Norris laughed aloud and Harland exhaled with relief.

'I like your mother, young man,' Miss Norris said.

Finishing a bite of his slice, Harland said, 'This is most excellent, Miss Norris, thank you. Could you please tell us more about your suspicions and your relationship with Mr Beaming?'

Miss Norris agreed and started her tale, including what she had told the sergeant at the police station about Mr Beaming's bragging on how to get rid of a family, the quick lime she found in his shed, and the hidden photo in his room of a woman with children, himself in the very same photo as the head of the family. 'Yet he continued to ask for my hand in marriage and to ask me to travel with him.'

'Are you rich, Miss Norris?' Gilbert asked with his usual bluntness. Harland intended to ask the same question but more diplomatically.

Miss Norris laughed again. 'I am self-sufficient Detective Payne and could provide for myself and a husband comfortably. I guess that is appealing to a man of limited means.'

'Your cooking would also be most inviting,' Gilbert said and on seeing the look from his boss, took a large bite to prevent himself from saying anything further.

Harland offered Miss Norris an apologetic smile and her look of merriment told him she understood his dilemma only too well.

'Did you witness any violence or anger from Mr Beaming during your acquaintance with him?' Harland asked. 'Anything that might make you think he was capable of killing his wife and children?

'Yes,' she responded honestly and openly and gathered her thoughts while topping up their tea cups. 'He could change in an instant from gentle to cruel with his comments and thoughts, but I did not see any physical proof. Mind you, he seemed to take delight in discussing that which brought misery or hardship to people. It was this behaviour, that put me on alert and even though he exercised an amazing fascination over me, I refused to marry him. Call it instinct or intuition, I was certain there was something wrong somewhere,' she explained.

'I believe your intuition to be most sound,' Harland told her.

Anne Norris continued, 'Thank you, Detective. I believe, because I had witnessed it and experienced it first hand, that women found him quite irresistible – it was his charm and attention. For fear of being indiscreet, he was the gentlest of lovers.'

Gilbert choked on his tea and Harland tapped him on the back until the young man ceased coughing and gave him a nod of thanks.

'Was he angry when you would not accept his hand in marriage?' Harland asked.

'He was frustrated and dare I say, surprised. I don't think he had ever been refused anything before. I declined his offer kindly, several times, saying I preferred a long acquaintanceship.'

'That may have saved your life, Miss Norris,' Harland said.

'I suspect his wife was not so lucky,' she added.

'Did he ever speak of a wife or children in any context?'

'Only to say he was a man deserted by his family and to adopt a most wounded countenance.'

Harland then told her to brace herself and spoke of the lady found under the hearthstone. Anne's hand went to her heart.

'I sensed it when I entered his house.' She stared at the men shocked. 'That must sound silly to both of you. But I remember my first visit as I stood on the hearthstone, there was a deep sense of tragedy, I could not put words to it.'

'It doesn't sound silly at all, Miss Norris,' Harland said, especially as he was chasing a conviction based on the hearsay of a funeral mortician and a ghost. Thanking her for the tea and slice and rising to leave, he added, 'Please take great caution and let us know should Mr Beaming return.'

165

'I can assure you, Detective Stone, you will be the first to know.' She rose to lock the door behind them.

Chapter 18

I T WAS A STREET of some decline that Julius Astin steered the horses and hearse into and proceeded down its length, searching for the house in question to collect a body for burial. As they made their way down the street, residents emerged, many wearing black, most likely to follow the hearse to the nearby cemetery.

'Goodness, I hope our hearse does not get stripped while we are collecting the body,' Ambrose said subtly with a glance around.

'I don't think poverty necessarily means they are criminals, but it won't hurt to be wary,' Julius agreed in a low voice.

He spotted it – a small and pitiful house. The garden was bare as if no one had the time or inclination to tend it, the house was in some disrepair and the neighbouring homes were not much better. Julius was not present in the office when the family had made their arrangements with his grandfather, but they had chosen the cheapest package available which was most unusual. There was little difference between the packages to allow grieving families to easily afford the middle package and feel better for doing so. In essence, they were all very affordable, but the lowest price package was favoured by charity organisations who sought to bury one of the paupers in their community, or an agency appointed to do the job and wanted no frills. In some cases, it was selected for the occasional black sheep of the family who was despised and buried only as a matter of duty.

'They obviously have done their best,' Julius said with a nod to the small wreath on the door to indicate a death had occurred. 'And, they have managed the mourning themselves.'

Ambrose nodded at several of the neighbours as they approached. 'The neighbours must hold the family in high regard given the number gathering'

Julius saw a small sign on the fence offering sewing, dressmaking and mending services.

'A young woman and her brother, you say?' Ambrose asked.

'Yes. The deceased is their grandmother, according to Grandpa's notes.' Julius mused, 'I hope the granddaughter is of age to work, for if the grandmother was the principal dressmaker, they are now bereft of their breadwinner.'

'As we were once,' Ambrose said quietly and Julius turned to study him. He gave a brief smile in remembrance of how far they had come.

'We were very lucky that Grandpa was gainfully employed as a clerk or I can't imagine how our grandparents would have kept us all together.'

'How you would have missed me if we had been dispersed to the winds,' Ambrose teased, lightening the mood as he often did when it became too sombre.

'I can't conceive it,' Julius retorted with a small smile and saw Ambrose was not sure whether he was jesting or sincere. 'Come then, let us collect the body.' He saw two teenage boys approaching from a nearby house. They wore dark, ill-fitting suits that appeared to be hand-me-downs. Julius alighted and asked, 'Perhaps you will hold the reins for us lads, for a small payment?'

'Sure, Sir,' one of them said, keen to pat the horse and be of importance. The other followed eagerly. 'You don't need to pay us.'

Julius was moved by the young man's integrity and pride but knew the money would help. 'Thank you, but I'd like to... it's an important job and you are doing me a service.' He slipped them both a coin and saw them pocket it fast.

'Don't take the hearse for a ride, will you?' Ambrose winked and both boys laughed.

As they opened the small gate a young woman took the three steps down from the house to greet them. Julius was struck by her beauty. She wore the expected black mourning clothes, but that only served to enhance her loveliness. Her dress was simple, trimmed with crepe, she had black lace around her wrists and neck which was normally considered highly inappropriate – such decorative flounces were not welcome in mourning, and she wore a striking black pearl necklace that would no doubt keep her in tea for a year.

She was Phoebe's height, about five-foot-five, with brown tresses and startling blue eyes. He was quite captivated. Remembering his duty, he gave her a solemn nod.

'Madam, our sincere condolences. Julius and Ambrose Astin at your service.'

'Thank you. Mr Astin. I am Miss Violet Forrester and my brother...' She turned to find he had not followed her outside and gave a small roll of her eyes. Then realising that was probably not appropriate in the circumstances grimaced. 'Forgive me, my brother is inside.'

'I understand only too well, Miss Forrester,' Julius said. 'I too have a little brother.' He glanced to Ambrose who feigned surprise and made her smile the most beautiful of smiles.

'Please, will you enter?'

She gave a small wave and nod of thanks to the neighbours and with a glance to the hearse, which seemed to bring the reality of the moment back to her, reached for the stair rail and steadied herself. Julius immediately reached for her arm.

'Are you quite alright, Miss Forrester? You may wait here if you prefer; I assure you, we have this in hand.'

She took a halting breath. 'Thank you. But no, I can do this, I've had quite a bit of practice,' she said with a small smile as if it were an accomplishment to have lost nearly everyone in your life and to come through it.

Julius admired her immensely and the two men followed her inside, Julius noting the feminine shape of her body and the delicate step of her tread. They entered a dark room where the small, slight body of the deceased grandmother was laid out, surrounded by fresh flowers, most picked not purchased as wreaths.

'It is simple,' Violet apologised, with a glance at the flowers, the mirror covered with a dark cloth and the attempt to present her grandmother in her best light in death.

'It is tasteful and more than adequate,' Ambrose assured her kindly. 'Where is this brother of yours then, and we shall begin your grandmother's final journey?'

'Here,' a voice said behind them and they turned to find a young man, thin and awkward as befitting his age; Julius guessed him to be fifteen or thereabouts.

'This is Tom.' She turned to her brother and smiled with affection. 'Mr Julius Astin and Mr Ambrose Astin.'

The men greeted the boy who reciprocated with excellent manners, and again Julius was impressed that Violet, in her time of distress, would recall their names.

'Would you like to walk in front of us as we bring Mrs Forrester to the hearse?' Julius asked and Violet nodded, leading Tom away. They stood like solemn guards on the stairs to see their grandmother in her coffin leave her house for the last time. Once the coffin was loaded, the last of the Forrester family – Miss Violet and Master Tom Forrester – stood behind the hearse, in front of the neighbours who would accompany them to the cemetery. The hearse slowly moved forward and they began the walk.

There was little talk, just a solemn procession but now and then the younger members of the party would speak. Julius was sure he heard one ask young Tom if they would remain in the house now. He turned just enough to check they were all still well and to hear the reply when he saw Miss Forrester misstep or perhaps the overwhelming thought of the future had enveloped her. He threw the reins at Ambrose and leapt down as the horses continued to slowly walk on.

Reaching her side, he found her supported by several neighbours and he thanked them and took her arm. 'I think it best you sit up front and I shall walk with your brother.'

'No!' she said eyes wide. 'I am not the fainting type, I assure you.'

'Shock can affect us all in different ways,' he said. 'There is no shame in it.'

'I'll be right, Sis,' Tom assured her and with the hands of a neighbour guiding her and Julius strong by her side, she allowed him to lead her to the front. Ambrose pulled the horses to a halt.

'Please allow me,' Julius said and did not wait for permission before placing his hands around her waist and lifting her beside Ambrose who saw to her comfort. He stood waiting for the hearse to pass and then fell into line beside Tom.

'Are you alright then?' he asked in a low voice.

'I am. We will be,' Tom said as if convincing himself. 'You been affected by shock?'

Julius gave him a confused look.

'You said shock affects people in different ways. Have you ever been shocked?'

Julius studied the young man before responding. He was never one for revealing too much about himself or his past, but what did it matter to this stranger in need of some comfort?

'I had a very public breakdown once when I was about your age.'

Tom's eyes widened in surprise. 'Did you go berserk?'

Julius chuckled and then restrained himself, they were at a funeral after all and he could feel his grandfather's look of reprimand without seeing it. Randolph was a stickler for

173

solemnity when it was required, especially at Sunday mass where as a youngster, Julius found himself and Ambrose often in trouble for not paying attention.

'No, I did not go berserk, but I...' He hesitated.

'You don't have to tell me,' Tom said. 'I understand.'

Julius's jaw tightened. To tell the young man would mean talking about that which he did not recall to memory ever if he could help it. That time had passed and he suffered through it; he was focused on the now and the future. Before he could decide what to tell Violet's brother, Tom started speaking again.

'I think I am in shock too because I just want to hit someone. First Mum and Dad both get sick and die, then Grandpa goes not long after – he had a fall and never got up again – and now Grandma. All in the space of a few years.' It was as if Tom could not stop talking now Julius had opened the floodgates. 'Some of my friends still have all their family. It's not fair, I hate everyone right now, everyone,' he said and drew a sharp breath, his lips thinning as he regained some control.

'It's not fair, you are right about that,' Julius agreed. Behind them, a hand reached for Tom's shoulder and Julius saw the young man grimace, as he would have, not being one for public sympathy. He continued, 'But do not do something that will get you in trouble or separate you from your sister, that would be worse for both of you.'

'Is that what happened to you? Did you and your brother get sent away?'

'No.' Julius inhaled, accepting he must reveal some of himself. 'But I felt the same way as you do for a long time – I was very angry that everyone else got more than us, they got what we too deserved.'

He read Tom's expression and the boy's need to make sense of everything that was going on. Julius relented, drew another deep breath and continued in a low voice, for Tom's ears only.

'When I was 14, my parents went to dinner to celebrate their wedding anniversary. My brother – who you see driving now – was 11 and my little sister, Phoebe was nine. My parents were struck by a carriage while crossing the street. It was out of control – the driver was larking – and they could not avoid it. They both died in a moment, trampled by the horses and the wheels in a brutal fashion, their life spent like that,' he said and snapped his fingers. Julius stopped talking and took a deep breath, looking forward and regaining his composure before continuing. 'I was very close to my parents, and I did not take it well. We went to live with my grandparents and like you, I was angry.'

'What did you do?' Then Tom's eyes widened to fit his imagination. 'Did you try and kill the driver?'

Julius avoided looking at him.

'You did!' Tom hissed.

'I did not deliberately think – I am going to find and kill him – but I knew who it was and I wanted him to feel my pain. I was planning with the mind of a 14-year-old and not at all in a rational state.'

'I am one year older than you were then. I feel very rational.'

'Perhaps I was more so than I care to admit.'

Julius glanced around but none of the mourners seemed perturbed by their low voices; several had taken it as an invitation to share their own quiet conversations. He looked back to see Tom studying him.

'What did your public breakdown entail then? Did you fight the killer in front of everyone?'

'No. But I was very angry at the funeral and when they lowered my parents into the grave, I... well, it does not matter now, but my grandfather and uncles could not restrain me. I was out of control, loud and disrespectful. It was very painful for my grandparents.' He grimaced at the shameful memory for a man who was so composed today. 'Then I ran away from the cemetery and did not return for three days; I believe they were quite distraught with worry.'

'Where were you?'

'I knew where the driver resided and I was watching him. I was in his shed the night of the funeral, plotting what I would do. I had a lot of ideas.'

Tom's eyes were huge. 'What happened?'

'The next night he came home from somewhere in a terrible state of drunkenness, driving his cart. He might have killed someone, again. I was enraged. But before I even made it to his back door to confront him, I heard a gunshot.'

'He killed himself?'

Julius nodded. 'I didn't go inside but I saw him on a chair, the rifle in his lap.'

'He must have felt really bad.'

Julius gave a small chin-up movement that said little of what he was thinking; even a psychologist who had studied the characteristics of the mind might find several explanations. 'I released his dogs and cattle so they did not starve should he not be found quickly and then I got out of there.'

'Did you go home?' Tom asked.

'No, I believed my grandparents would not want me anymore, so I decided to sign-up and join the national army. It took me a day to walk to the city, and I slept on the street for another night.'

'You were fourteen and you tried to sign-up!' Tom said and looked down to hide his grin from the mourners behind, his shoulders shook silently with laughter which made Julius smile and hide his mirth as well.

'It seemed like a good plan at the time,' Julius defended himself. 'They made me fill in a form and told me to wait for an interview, and not long after Grandpa walked in and took me home.'

'I bet you were punished for a year.'

'No, not even once. But I had little rope; he watched me like a hawk for a long time.'

Tom shook his head. 'Yeah, I don't think I'll do any of the stupid stuff you did.'

Julius gave him a look that made Tom grin again and turn away. He left the young man for a moment and went to assist Ambrose with the horses and hearse across a grate before returning to Tom's side.

'What happened then, did you stay with your grandparents?' Tom asked in a low voice.

'Yes, but it got worse before it got better. I heard my grandparents trying to work out how they could afford to keep us and there had been offers from aunts and uncles to split us up and separate us.'

'That would be awful,' Tom said and looked up at the back of his sister sitting up in the hearse's front seat beside Ambrose.

'It would have been more pain for all of us, and Ambrose and Phoebe were already mourning. So, being the eldest, I had to step up. I got a job after-school delivering newspapers and gave my earnings to Grandpa. Grandma helped me apply for a scholarship for the three of us. I scraped in and got one for three years of academic study.'

'Smart Alec,' Tom said and grinned.

'I almost lost it a few times, the examinations each year were hard,' Julius said with a smile. 'Phoebe got a scholarship for music and our uncle sponsored Ambrose, so we made it, I guess.'

'Yeah. I could get a job. Violet sews, Grandma taught her everything. She has her own clients and will probably get Grandma's now too. We can make some money to live on. Besides, she's going to sell Grandma's necklace after the funeral, the pearls, they should fetch a bit.'

Julius stored this information and gave the boy an encouraging smile. 'You will be fine as the man of the family now; I do not doubt it.' He saw Tom straighten, his shoulders broadened as if Atlas had just placed the world upon them and he stepped up to accept the role.

They walked in silence for a short while before Tom uttered, 'Strange job you do.'

Julius hid a chuckle but smiled at him. 'It reminds me to live each day to the full and do what I love with the people I love.'

'Yeah?' Tom turned his head up and squinted in the sun as he studied Julius.

'You love doing this?'

'It's better to be me than the dead, don't you think?'

Tom grinned. 'You're alright.'

And the cemetery came into sight.

Chapter 19

BENNET MARTIN PACED. THE hour was getting later, the workday had only a few hours remaining and he hoped to have answers today. Occasionally he ran his hand through his blond hair which flopped straight back into its former position reminding him a visit to the barber was long overdue. Not even three cups of tea from Mrs Clarke, the housekeeper, could relax him – in fact, he had no memory of drinking them except for the fact he still held the cup and saucer. Finally, the door opened and his clerk appeared waving a piece of paper at him. Bennet hastily put down his cup and raced to Daniel's side.

'The telegram is here,' Daniel Dutton said with a wide grin.

Bennet snatched the paper from him with excitement and read what he feared and knew to be the case in his heart of hearts. He said the words out loud even though he was sure Daniel read the message en route. 'It is true... Eliza, the daughter of Beaming's landlady in England came back to Australia with him. He pretended to be Major Williams and wooed her. They married before sailing here together.' Bennet exhaled and shook his head. 'She is surely the deceased woman found under the hearthstone. Her mother last heard from her when they settled in Melbourne.'

'In the house in which she was found dead no less,' Daniel added.

'I must go at once to see Detective Stone. That poor woman in England is bound to be frantic; we have a duty to identify the cemented bride.'

Daniel grimaced at the term. 'But that doesn't solve how you will identify her,' Daniel pointed out the obvious.

'Ah, yes, good point, Daniel. I knew you were worth keeping around,' he joked. 'Will you return and telegram them again? Ask for an urgent and detailed description of Eliza or a contact in Australia – a relative or friend perhaps – who might identify the deceased but do not imply she is deceased. Advise I shall pay for their return message.'

'I will. We can share the cab, drop me on the way,' Daniel said and called out to his aunty, the housekeeper Mrs Clarke, that they were off, soon to return.

'The comings and goings in here,' she said, entering the room flustered. 'Mr Martin, your hat,' she called after him as he raced by her, and Bennet raced back in, taking it from her with thanks.

It felt like the longest journey in the world to Bennet who was bursting with important information. He almost pushed Daniel out of the hansom cab at the telegraph office and the cab hurried on to the police station in Roma Street. He would have something to report back to Mrs Beaming's parents who hired him to find their daughter and grandchildren... some progress, although not heartening news from their perspective but at least it was not their daughter under the hearthstone. Racing up the stairs to the reception desk, he told the desk sergeant he knew the way to Detective Stone's office.

'He is not in, however, but we are expecting his return shortly.'

'Oh, blast it all!' Bennet said.

'I am right here,' a voice said behind him and Bennet turned to see the welcomed sight of Detectives Stone and Payne arriving.

'I have news,' Bennet said forgoing greetings. Behind the detective, journalist Lilly Lewis arrived, a flush of excitement upon her face.

'Here we all are,' she said approaching them.

'Timely, Miss Lewis,' Harland said, 'Bennet has news. To my office then.'

The small party made their way hurriedly up the hallway. 'I am on a deadline, Detective,' Lilly said. 'The editor has permitted me to run the story and the first article is to run tomorrow. I have drafted copy if you will agree on what I am to release and update that of course.'

'That sounds exciting,' Gilbert piped up. 'On deadline!'

Lilly laughed. 'It does rather.'

'Congratulations, Miss Lewis,' Harland said and stood aside to allow them all to enter the office first. 'Will you be seated?'

Lilly sat, Gilbert beside her, Bennet paced and Harland took his place behind his desk. Bennet recognised the detective was not a man given to impulses but he expected a reaction when he gave his news and he was not disappointed. Harland shot to his feet and ran a hand over his lower jaw.

'This does not bode well for your clients, Bennet,' Harland said, 'but at least we have a lead on who the deceased lady might be.'

'Oh my,' Lilly said, 'that poor lady. Alone in this country, thinking she had her whole future ahead of her and trusting the love of her husband.'

'My mother always says marry in haste, repent at leisure,' Gilbert said.

Bennet turned to Harland and noted a flicker of exasperation before the senior detective's patient countenance won over and he said, 'Bennet, this is the news we have needed, thank you. So, we have a reasonable belief that this lady found below the hearthstone is the second Mrs Beaming.'

'Yes, it is a reasonable assumption,' Bennet agreed. 'Her name, that is, her maiden name, was Miss Eliza Stubbings.'

'Next, we need to formally identify her,' Harland continued to think through the process methodically and out loud. 'You cannot name her in the press yet, Miss Lewis.'

'Of course not,' Lilly said, 'there is no concrete evidence it is her, yet.' She winced at her choice of words.

'The cemented bride,' Bennet said and gave a small shrug of apology at Lilly's reaction. He continued, 'I am ahead of you there, Harland. As we speak my clerk is telegramming Miss Stubbings's mother – Beaming's former landlady – and the priest for a full description of the current Mrs Beaming, and to enquire if any friends or family might be here on hand in Australia. Rest assured my clerk will not mention that she is deceased until identified.'

'Excellent, thank you.' Harland turned to Lilly. 'Miss Lewis, you may report on the finding of the lady and the manner of uncovering her. Also, that an identification process is underway but not who we believe the lady to be.'

Lilly waved her article at him and grinned. 'That is just what I have covered, plus I have mentioned the police are seeking the whereabouts of Mrs Beaming and her four children to ensure their safety. I know this will imply that Mr Beaming is up to something nefarious.'

Harland thought about the consequences of that for a moment and all waited for him to speak. 'I have no issue with that,' he added and Bennet read Lilly's obvious relief. 'I would appreciate it if you also reported we are seeking Mr Zachariah Beaming to assist us with our enquiries.'

'Thank you, Detective Stone,' she said and leapt up. 'I shall be off then and in touch tomorrow.'

The three men remained; Harland turned to Gilbert and said, 'We still have a missing first wife and four children. I suggest we get our British counterparts to look at the residence and the hearthstone in Rainhill where Beaming or rather Major Williams, was staying. His family may have been there with him for a period of time.'

'Yes, or as he claimed, his sister, nieces and nephew, very crafty,' Gilbert said with a serious shake of his head.

'We may need to dig that floor up if it shows evidence of being tampered with,' Harland concluded.

'I agree,' Bennet said. 'Do you wish me to contact my father at Scotland Yard to orchestrate the dig?'

Harland shook his head in the negative. 'Let's begin with the local police and detectives in the area and give them the courtesy of investigating first. I shall telegram now. I fear the worse.'

'That is six people he might have killed,' Gilbert said shocked, 'including the first private investigator.'

'Let's hope there are not more,' Bennet said and advising he was at the detectives' disposal, left to wait for his clerk and word from the family of the deceased bride's description.

Catherine Tounselle stood back and looked at her trousseau packed neatly in her travelling trunk. She was ready to take the long train journey to Western Australia to meet her fiancé, Major Zachariah Williams, soon to be her husband. The very last item she placed on top was her wedding dress wrapped in paper. Her sister, Frances, stood beside her and reached for Catherine's hand.

'I so wish I could be there and mother is quite distraught, not that she is fit for travel at the moment. If only you could have married here before your betrothed left for his work.'

Catherine's hand went to her heart. 'It is not as I hoped or dreamed, Frannie, but nevertheless, it is lovely to have prospects for the future. Of that, Father is pleased.' Her voice

186

hitched with emotion. 'I barely know my fiancé and I am not sure I am doing the right thing now that there has been some time and separation between us since the voyage.'

Frances smiled. 'From what you say, your brief time spent on the ship was very romantic. It is to be expected that we would all be caught up in it.' She studied her sister. 'You could delay the trip, see how your heart felt in time, a month or two maybe? He will be more established then as well.'

'That is true,' she said and moved away from her sister to the dresser where she lifted several sheets of paper – Zachariah's telegrams. 'He is clearly concerned for me and in haste to have me join him. Listen to this, "*Come at once or the rains will set in and travelling will be impossible. I cannot be without you*".' She looked up at Frances. 'I brought my trip date forward and received this from Zachariah once I notified him of my actions, "*I was all joy when I got your wire to say you were leaving earlier... knowing how happy I could make you... life without you would not be worth living.*" He writes with so much passion.'

Frances agreed, 'There seems no doubt of his genuine affection for you, and he is a dignified and handsome man.' She collected the framed portrait of the Major that Catherine had left on her dresser and handed it to her for packing.

After doing so, Catherine turned to Frances and the two sisters hugged.

'It is your time,' Frances said and looked at her little sister with concern and love. 'Be happy, Cathy dearest, and I shall come over and visit once you have set up your home, and then you can tell me everything.'

Catherine returned her sister's embrace and pulled away to dab her tears. 'By the end of the month, I shall be Mrs Zachariah Williams and managing my own home.'

'We shall both be wed,' Frances said and sighed happily.

'And soon, hopefully, we will both have families.'

The thought made Catherine believe she was doing the right thing. She closed the lid of her trunk. 'I will do this, I will go be a bride and wife, support him and live my best life.'

Chapter 20

RANDOLPH LOOKED AT HIS eldest grandson with frustration – it was usually Ambrose who was the recipient of his exasperation but not today. Julius looked his normal self but as they sat around the table before the business opened and Randolph told them of today's events, the young man was distracted, his brow furrowed, his thoughts elsewhere. Julius had agreed to whatever was proposed when he normally had a comment or suggestion to add, and even Ambrose and Phoebe were casting the odd glance his way.

'Julius, where are you?' Ambrose asked.

He snapped to look at Ambrose. 'Sorry, what was that?'

'Exactly, you are miles away, what are you concerned about?' his younger brother pushed.

'Nothing of consequence.'

'Then share it,' Phoebe added.

Mrs Dobbs entered with a pot of tea and a loaf of her freshly baked bread with jam and butter. It was a small repast for the party before the sign on the door was turned to read "Open" and they would disperse for the day to undertake their duties.

'Perhaps you are hungry. Have you eaten, Julius?' she asked and Randolph suppressed a smile as he saw Julius brace. He was the most stoic of the three, no doubt from what he had seen and experienced – young eyes that had seen sights they should not have. He did not like being the centre of attention, receiving sympathy or being fussed over, and was quick to divert attention from himself.

'I will eat now, Mrs Dobbs, thank you,' he said and accepted a slice of her bread loaf, buttering it with more concentration than required. He paused before biting and put the loaf back down. 'I was speaking with Phoebe about leasing the store next door and starting another business.'

'The tailor?' Randolph asked happily accepting a slice from Mrs Dobbs. 'I've always thought that was an exceptionally good idea.'

'As do I,' Phoebe agreed, thanking Mrs Dobbs as she sat beside her with her own cup of tea.

'Yes. Ladies' mourning wear and we could sell sheaths as well for those who don't wish to make their own. With the store becoming available for lease, it is the ideal time and the size of the store will lend itself to several dressmakers, a fitting and cutting area, and a changing room.'

'You have done your research on this,' Randolph said, 'although I don't know why I would expect anything less.'

Julius gave him a grateful smile. 'I may have found a dressmaker who could manage the store and any staff she needed.'

'When did you do that?' Ambrose asked surprised. 'I am with you most days – oh, Miss Forrester,' he said and smiled. 'I think she caught your eye for more reasons than the dressmaking sign on the fence.' He waved a slice of bread and butter at Julius before taking a large bite.

'Who is Miss Forrester?' Phoebe asked, fascinated now. She daintily spread bread and jam on her slice, unlike her brothers who slapped it on as though it were their last meal.

'From yesterday's funeral,' Randolph said recognising the name. 'The granddaughter of the deceased.'

'That is her. She was very beautiful,' Ambrose said, talking with his mouth full and watching Julius for a reaction. He swallowed and added, 'Petite, startling blue eyes and what you ladies call chestnut hair.' He glanced at his sister. 'She is about your age or thereabouts, Phoebe. Quite a catch, would you not say, Julius? And there was no suitor present.'

'It reminded me a little of our situation,' Julius said ignoring his brother's teasing. 'Miss Forrester and her brother, Tom, have been left alone in the world. They have even lost their grandparents. She is a dressmaker and Tom said she was most capable.'

'Did you get a chance to speak with her brother then?' Phoebe asked knowing conversation with the family at a funeral was most unusual, as the mourners tended to fill that role.

'Yes.' Julius did not elaborate but Ambrose did.

'Miss Forrester was quite overcome at one stage and Julius offered her the seat beside me on the driver's bench.'

'I walked beside her brother,' Julius added.

'What a lovely touch,' Mrs Dobbs said and sighed.

'And so young Tom said she was a capable dressmaker. Did you see any proof?' Randolph asked.

'Her dress was lovely,' Ambrose answered. 'Not that I am a fashion expert, despite how good I look.' He got a laugh from his family and Mrs Dobbs. 'She had lace on her dress and sleeves, I haven't seen that before.'

'Did she?' Phoebe asked wide-eyed. 'I like her already.'

'Of course you do,' Ambrose said with a roll of his eyes. 'But I don't think she is as unconventional as you. Time will tell, especially if we see her more, what do you think, Julius? Will we be seeing more of the lovely Miss Forrester?'

'What will become of them, Julius?' Randolph asked, seeing Julius's grimace towards Ambrose and saving Julius from having to respond to his brother's teasing again. 'Did Tom say anything of their plans?'

'Not in as many words and I don't know well enough yet to say, Grandpa,' Julius answered. 'There is a small sign on the gate advising of the sewing services on offer. The boy is five-and-ten and of working age, but is still at school. He must be fed and kept. The house is modest, but I am not sure Miss Forrester can maintain it or pay rent if she is renting, without the assistance of her grandmother, whom Tom said also sewed.'

'She might have inherited the house,' Phoebe suggested. 'Then she need only make enough to keep them in supplies.'

'True, but unlikely,' Ambrose added. 'It was very much struggle street.'

Julius nodded his agreement. 'Miss Forrester wore a set of black pearls that I suspect had been handed down. Tom said she would sell them after the funeral.'

Randolph exhaled, his face masking his sadness for them. 'We all know that struggle only too well. So, what do you intend to do, my boy?' he asked with affection.

'I was going to see what Miss Forrester's sewing skills were like and offer her a position. If she sewed the dress she was wearing, she will be most capable.'

'As long as she stocks the traditional wear,' Ambrose added with a look to Phoebe. 'We don't want her scaring customers off with outlandish modern mourning designs... there's a reason we keep Phoebe in the basement.'

The party enjoyed Ambrose's antics and Phoebe hit him playfully on the arm.

'I warn you now, Ambrose, should I have to attend your funeral I am wearing pink,' she teased him, 'and I will say it was at your request.'

'Outrageous!' he exclaimed theatrically. 'Although Miss Forrester did say the lace was a nod to her grandmother.'

'Did she?' Julius asked with obvious interest. 'What did she say?'

'Well, I complimented her on her appearance and said the lace was beautiful but unusual. She said that her grandmother insisted on it, to provide some relief from the morbidity of the dress. Miss Forrester also said that given they had been wearing black for the last year to mark her parents' passing, her grandmother did not want them to continue in black for another year.'

'Well let's hope they abide by her request,' Randolph said. 'I hate to see young people in black. What of the boy then? Did he seem bright, Julius?'

'Bright enough and if he can remain at school, that is ideal. But if he is not scholarly – and we all know you can be bright without being a good student,' he said with a look to his brother and earned a smirk, 'I believe our cousin is ready to take on an apprentice carpenter.'

'Excellent idea,' Randolph said. 'What do you need from us?'

'I shall let you know, thank you, Grandpa. Do I have a few hours spare now to call upon her and broach the subject?'

'Yes, but be back by 11 o'clock if you can. If not, do not fear. Ambrose and I will manage the funeral and Mrs Dobbs and Phoebe can manage the shop, perhaps?' Randolph looked to the ladies.

'My workload is not demanding, I can do that,' Phoebe said and Mrs Dobbs agreed.

'I will be back by 11 o'clock. I shall take the small trap,' he said and rose with a vigour they had not seen from Julius for some time. He stopped at the door and looked back at Ambrose. 'And do not marry me off just yet.' After seeing Ambrose's grin, he shook his head and departed.

'Well, what do you make of that then?' Randolph asked, his voice lowered.

'I am excited,' Phoebe gushed. 'Was she truly lovely, Ambrose?'

'She was very beautiful and feminine, yet strong in her determination. A lot like you, Sister.'

Phoebe smiled her thanks.

'Wouldn't it be lovely to see our Julius happy?' Mrs Dobbs sighed as if she had earned the right to claim Julius too, since working with the family.

'Nothing would make me happier, except to see these two settled as well,' Randolph nodded toward his remaining grandchildren. 'But I always thought Julius would pose the greatest challenge.'

'Despair not, Grandpa,' Ambrose said. 'It appears he has found someone else to rescue.'

'Perhaps she will rescue him,' Phoebe said with a smile.

Violet Forrester was at work in the front room of her home; the curtains were wide open to let in the light for her sewing projects. It was a lovely April day, brighter and cheerier than she felt, and the warmth and light were appreciated after a week of dark despair. She was alone for the first time; Tom was at school and the house once full, felt very empty.

What now? she thought. The pearls that were to be passed down from her grandmother to her mother to Violet will bring in enough funds to pay the rent for several months and provide food on the table. Her dressmaking work will keep them afloat, but any untoward expenses will see them reeling. She needed her grandmother's customers to grace her with their work, which would help them immeasurably, even if she had to toil day and night to get the work done. Tom must have what he needs, he is growing and will soon outgrow his boots and clothes. The thought made her heart flutter with anxiety, but she reined her thoughts into focus on her stitchwork, her source of income. One day at a time, she told herself, remembering her father saying, "Do not foresee drama that may never eventuate."

Violet heard the horse and carriage before she saw it arrive. There were no residents on her street who could afford to travel by hansom. The driver was not visible to her, but she saw the horse harnessed under the shade of a tree nearby and she saw it nibbling on the fresh grass moments after it was settled. She liked a person who put their animals before their own comfort. The sight of a man at her gate startled her; she was home alone and not aware of any debts due today. Then she recognised the stance of the man coming up the couple of stairs to her door, his broad shoulders and tall form – it was the man from the funeral directors. It was Mr Julius Astin.

Violet's heart fluttered, and she leapt to her feet and straightened her skirt. There was no time to consult a mirror – nor could she as it was still covered in black crepe; she was yet to put away the remnants of her grandmother's mourning, the thought had overwhelmed her last night so she left it for another day. Julius's knock startled her which was silly given she knew who it was, but she now had to move, to attend to him at her front door, and she had not expected to see him again.

Violet hurried to the entrance, took a deep breath, and opened it. He stood holding a large box and he offered her a small smile and a bow.

'Miss Forrester, please forgive the intrusion of my unexpected visit. I was here yesterday—'

'Of course, I remember you, Mr Astin. I was distressed yesterday but not so distressed to forget you in one day and you were so very supportive.' She greeted him kindly. 'Please, will you come in?' Violet did not say that he was quite unforgettable and that he did have his hands around her waist for one moment as he lifted her into his seat beside his brother.

Julius nodded his thanks and took the remaining step to the front door, entering her home and looking large in the small hallway. Violet need not worry that he would be appalled by her small home or the state of the worn furnishings, he had seen it all yesterday. The house was clean, that was the best she could do at this time.

'May I put this down in your kitchen?' he asked.

'This way please.' She led him down the hall and watched as he placed the box on the kitchen table and then removed his hat. 'Pray tell, what is that?'

'Just some items that I hope may be of use to you.'

She looked from him to the box and opened it to find fresh bread, tins of biscuits, tea, sugar, and a range of grocery items including a few treats.

'Goodness, how generous. Mr Astin, do you deliver this to all of your clients the day after a funeral?' she asked surprised. She felt the room was too small for both of them, he was too close and she wished Tom was home from school.

'No,' he admitted.

'You are very thoughtful, but I assure you we don't need charity.' Violet stepped away from the box and tried to keep the ice from her tone when his gesture was well-intended. She could certainly do with this charity and Tom would love it and deserved it, but pride prevented her from accepting it from a man whom she did not want to look at her as a charity case.

'It is not charity, I assure you,' Julius answered hurriedly, momentarily worried he had caused offence. 'It is a gift if you will be so kind as to accept it.' He appeared uncomfortable, which did not suit the aura of confidence he first presented. 'I hoped to call on you and I thought flowers – which I know are normally presented in these situations – are not needed in a house full of flowers from your wake. Besides, I am often too practical for my own good, or so my brother tells me, and I hate to waste means on flowers when goods might be of more value.'

She knew only too well the goods were worth ten times more in value and use than the flowers.

'Thank you, Mr Astin, it is indeed a practical and appreciated gift.' She saw him relax slightly and did not realise he was so concerned about having caused her offence. 'May I offer you tea?' She looked in the box. 'We have some now.' Violet turned to him and smiled and his gaze did not leave hers.

'If you are having tea, I would be happy to partake. Unless I am taking you from your work.'

'I am happy for the break. Shall we stay here and take tea in the kitchen? It is a sunny room.' She indicated a seat and invited Julius to sit. 'I am sure no lady in your company has ever made you the offer to sit in such salubrious surrounds.' Violet gave a small laugh at the thought and Julius smiled, relaxing a little.

'None so welcome or appealing,' he said and she felt herself short of a reply and unsure if he were referring to the kitchen or herself. No doubt he was very good at charming the ladies, she imagined they would fall at his feet. Violet busied herself making tea and did not open the tin of biscuits from his gifted supply, but chose a tin that a neighbour had baked for the wake.

'Thanks to our neighbours we shall not run short of biscuits for a month or so. There is a bright side to everything, is there not?' she teased and enjoyed his surprised reaction.

'You think very much as I do, Miss Forrester. Working in the death industry, my family and I forget sometimes that people fear it or see it as terribly morbid, and we must school ourselves not to make the occasional joke.' He cleared his throat. 'I imagine if Tom is like myself and Ambrose at his age, his appetite is rather ferocious and you might not get a month's worth of supplies from your stock,' he joked. 'How is Tom today?'

'His usual self, which pleases me,' Violet said bringing the pot to the table as Julius rose to assist her and she invited him to remain seated. She sat opposite him and rotated the pot as her grandmother did, she then poured. 'Tom is restless and talking about getting work.'

'You would prefer him to stay at school? I might have put the idea of after-school work into his head... I told him I did a paper run when I was his age.'

'Ah, I see. I would prefer what is best for him. He is not a great scholar, but I don't wish him to miss out on opportunities.'

Julius thanked Violet for the tea and declined a biscuit. He took a sharp breath before continuing, 'If I may be so presumptuous, I know of an apprenticeship for a carpentering and joining position that will be available with my cousin, Lucian, in the near future.'

'Carpentering and joining! Tom loves to work with his hands,' Violet exclaimed and noted Julius's expression shifted to one of almost relief.

'I called on Lucian this morning and he has not filled the position nor promised it to anyone; I said I might know of someone. The wages are good and Lucian does a wide range of work including making our coffins, traps and wagons.' Julius gave a small shrug. 'There is no pressure to bear, it is just something to consider if that would interest Tom.'

'You would recommend him?'

'Of course. He is a bright lad and not afraid of hard work from what I gather.' Julius smiled and added, 'Like his sister, I imagine.'

'Thank you,' she said and could not mask her relief or delight. 'I shall speak with Tom if you are sincere. He would love to earn his keep with his hands and what a great start to life to be apprenticed in such an industry. Thank you, Mr Astin.' She tried not to gush but if her brother got a good start in life, Violet was then not as concerned as to what became of herself. The weight would fall off her shoulders and how proud her parents and grandparents would be. She was quite excited by the thought. 'Thank you,' she said again.

'It is nothing.'

'It is not.'

Julius looked down at his tea, avoiding her praise.

'You are as uncomfortable accepting compliments, as I am accepting charity,' she said and saw him snap to look at her. She hurriedly added, 'Please forgive my candour, Mr Astin. I have been at home too long in the company of my family and have not practised my social skills.'

He inclined his head politely. 'It is refreshing, and I am sorry I gave so little consideration to how my gift might be perceived. I am afraid I am used to taking charge.'

'As am I. Besides, I have no grounds for pride when I have a brother to support. Your gift is gratefully received.'

They smiled at each other like two kindred souls, but Violet was surprised by one thing, this man, this beautiful successful man looked at her as if he wanted her. Even with her inexperience in matters of the heart, she believed she had read this correctly. It was most surprising. Violet scolded herself, she could not be right, after all, what did she have to offer him other than poverty, her young ward Tom, and her sewing skills? He must have any number of women at his disposal with wealth, charm and sophistication.

Julius shuffled and then straightened as though hearing some unspoken command from a parent telling him to sit straighter.

'Miss Forrester, I have a business proposition for you,' he said bluntly.

'You do?' she asked surprised. 'You are the bearer of much good news today then.'

Julius chuckled and she was amazed at the difference the smile made to his countenance. What a challenge to see that again, what a reward.

She smiled at him in return. 'What business do you think I am in?'

'Dressmaking, are you not? I saw the sign on the fence and Tom told me you and your grandmother were most capable.'

'Did he now? He is selling me rather well.'

'Tom said your grandmother taught you all her skills. If your grandmother sewed as well as mine, then I suspect you are most talented.'

'That would be a competition neither of us would renege on – whose grandmother was the best seamstress,' she said and smiled. 'You need a suit made perhaps?'

'No.'

She studied the handsome man more brazenly now, readily making direct eye contact. Their dialogue was flowing without the initial awkwardness when all they knew to speak of was the funeral of yesterday. Violet's shock at seeing him was also abated. In truth, she welcomed the company on a day she anticipated would be lonely and difficult. She continued to probe.

'Your wife or sweetheart needs a dress made, perhaps for a special occasion? I would be most honoured to do so,' she said and sipped her tea, her heart thundering as she waited to know his marital status while maintaining her best calm exterior.

Julius shook his head. 'I have neither. I intend to lease the shop next door to our business and I have long planned to invest in a dressmaking business specialising in ladies' mourning wear and sheaths.'

Violet's eyes widened in surprise. 'What an excellent idea and the proximity is ideal.' She blushed, realising he knew that as a businessman and did not need her endorsement. She hurriedly added, 'When my parents and grandfather died, Grandma and I made our own mourning dresses as lots of women do... but I have some clients that rushed to us when caught unprepared by death, and had nothing appropriate to wear. I am surprised, given the demand, there is not someone doing so already.'

'As am I, especially as I have been speaking of it for long enough. I thought one of my business connections would have taken the idea and developed it.'

'Why now?' She frowned looking at him and feeling a little suspicious of his intentions. 'Is this another charitable endeavour on your behalf?'

'Another?' He looked confused.

Violet looked at the box of goodies on the kitchen bench.

'The goods, the apprenticeship and now you speak to me of a proposition in business. Will you employ me as well?'

Julius stilled and she noted he chose his words carefully.

'Yes, or if not you, I will employ someone as the business will go ahead.'

Violet understood his meaning. If she did not take the position, someone else would, so why not herself, especially now when she needed financial security.

'Miss Forrester, I know very few people I could approach to work as the shop's manageress. The person in the role would not only make the garments but oversee the other dressmakers. When I saw your sign on the fence and the timing with the lease beckoned, I thought it most opportune for both of us.'

'Meant to be, maybe?' she said with a slight tease.

'My sister is more inclined to believe in such, but I assure you, it would be advantageous to me as well.'

'A manageress,' Violet said as if that was the only word she heard.

'Yes. What do I know about dressmaking? I will own the business, pay wages to the manageress and dressmakers and earn my profits from sales. I am open to a commission on dress sales too if that is what you wish.'

Violet stared at him, closing her mouth which she realised had dropped open.

'Mr Astin, I must confess I have never managed a store nor other dressmakers or been offered a wage.'

'Nor had I when I started my business, but I've done reasonably well.'

Violet laughed at his modesty. It was well known that his business was the biggest in the local industry and the Astin family, particularly Julius, was one of the most respected, generous and wealthy sons of the city. Her grandmother had told her so before her death when she insisted on organising details of her own funeral, using the company that had buried Violet and Tom's grandfather several years earlier.

'You need time to consider my offer, of course. I am happy to show you the store if you would like to see it and you may wish to contribute ideas to its layout,' Julius offered.

The thought of sharing a ride with Julius Astin and accompanying him made her quite excited and nervous.

'So, I would be in your employ?' she asked, clarifying her role.

'Yes, but I will not interfere in the business, I assure you unless my assistance is required for practical matters. My bookkeeper will manage the lease and wages but leave the shop manageress to purchase fabric, determine design and keep the orders on schedule.'

She cocked her head to the side. 'It appears you know a little more about the business than you let on.'

'I do my research. I would not wish to employ people without ensuring the business might be profitable.'

She nodded, impressed. Then a thought occurred to her. 'May I ask, are you an investor in the carpentry business?'

'Yes.'

Violet's eyes narrowed slightly as she thought. *Was Julius Astin buying her family?*

'What concerns you, Miss Forrester? Please speak frankly. We are both capable of it,' he said referring to their earlier admission.

Violet saw the businessman come out and she gave him a brief nod. 'Mr Astin, when you arrived, you said the box of goods was a gift and that gift would normally be flowers.' She saw from the look in his eyes that he understood her implications.

'Miss Forrester, I assure you there will be no impropriety. You need not see me in any capacity other than professional if that is your concern. I would never take advantage of my position or put yours and Tom's employment at risk because of a friendship, or... a liaison,' he added looking most awkward at having to spell it out.

'Thank you, Mr Astin. I would hate to lose the clients I currently have to accept an offer only to have it rescinded if I did not, well...'

'I understand.' Julius rose suddenly and Violet scrambled to her feet.

'Thank you for the tea and hospitality. We both have work to do today, and I am due back within the hour. Will you favour me with your answer regarding the dressmaking business and Tom's apprenticeship at your earliest convenience?'

'I will, Mr Astin, and I thank you for your generosity and thoughtfulness.'

With a brief nod and the collection of his hat, he was gone, his long strides echoing down the hallway and leaving Violet with so many thoughts and emotions swirling through her that she had to make a second pot of tea to calm herself.

Chapter 21

Lilly Lewis opened the door of *The Economic Undertaker* with far too much gusto for a place of mourning and realising the errors of her way, stopped in dismay, and cautiously glanced around the door. She heard laughter and saw Ambrose Astin behind the counter.

'A living person, lovely,' he teased. 'Do come in while you are still breathing.'

Lily grinned and relaxed. 'Forgive my invasion, Mr Astin, I forgot myself in my enthusiasm.' She waved a newspaper in his direction. She admired how strikingly handsome he was, just like Julius, but he was not Julius.

'Do not fret. We have clients in-house but safely ensconced with my grandfather in the meeting room.' He turned with a nod to the closed door behind him. 'Come in and may I offer my congratulations?'

'You have seen it?' she asked, moving out of the doorway.

'Who could miss it with a heading that size? Well done, Miss Lewis,' he said warmly. 'I am very happy for you and very proud to be amongst the acquaintances of such an important writer.'

'Thank you, Mr Astin.' She looked at him for longer than propriety allowed, touched by his genuine support of her which was not always forthcoming when a woman enters a man's world and dares to have a career. Lilly swallowed and asked, 'Has the victim, Mr Walker, reappeared since with any new angles?'

Ambrose smiled. 'Asked like a professional journalist. I do not believe he has and not to me. I don't see them.'

'I would not want to.'

'Nor I. I would rather admire the living.'

Lilly gave a light laugh. She realised he held her gaze, and reddening, she looked away just in time to save herself from being clipped as the door swung open and Bennet Martin entered.

'Well, this is a most social place this morning,' Ambrose said pleased to see his brother's closest friend.

'Ambrose! Good morning,' Bennet answered and turned to Lilly. 'Ah, you are here. Congratulations, Miss Lewis, and well done. You stole my title!' His smile relayed he was not upset.

Lilly grinned again. 'I did, my apologies, but I mentioned it casually to my editor and he grabbed it thinking it was most appropriate even if it was somewhat affronting.' She looked at the large headline reading the less than sympathetic title *The Cemented Bride*. 'So, thank you, Mr Martin!'

'The pleasure is mine,' he said and gave a small bow. Lilly did not see the narrowing of Ambrose's eyes at Bennet Martin. Instead, she smiled at one man and then the other, saying to Ambrose. 'I hope Phoebe has not seen it; I must have someone to surprise.'

'I can't speak for my sister, but she is in her room and you are welcome to head down there. She is not pressed this morning with a deadline. Is your editor pleased?' Ambrose asked.

'He is delighted. May I?' She indicated the stairs.

'Please do,' Ambrose said. 'I must remain here until Grandpa reappears.' He turned to Bennet. 'Julius is out, but due back shortly.'

'Then I shall accompany you, Miss Lewis, to visit Miss Astin if she is receiving in her rooms,' he said, happy for the excuse and followed Lilly down to the cooler workrooms.

Lilly smiled at Ambrose, oblivious to his racing heart, and took to the stairs, glancing over the railing as she descended to see her mortician friend, Phoebe, sitting at a desk doing paperwork. Phoebe looked up and smiled.

'Lilly, Mr Martin! I was just ordering some more of my products. This is a pleasant surprise.'

'We did not come together,' Lilly said hurriedly as if word might get back to Julius and he assume that she was interested in Bennet Martin.

'No, but timing is everything,' Bennet said equally pleased for the clarification, not that Lilly was aware of his intentions towards Phoebe.

'Have you seen my story?' Lilly asked.

'Yes! Grandpa and I were astounded. What a coup, Lilly.'

'It is thanks to you, Phoebe. I don't know how I will repay you, but I will, be assured of that.' She placed the paper on Phoebe's work table with her story front and centre.

'Nonsense.' Phoebe grinned and rising, hugged her friend. 'I simply tipped you off. You and Mr Martin did all the hard work.'

'Have you had any more insights?' Lilly glanced at the corner and back to Phoebe. She felt Bennet Martin stiffen beside her.

'Is he here?' he asked.

'No,' Phoebe assured him. 'Mr Walker left once you and Detective Stone accepted the case. I believe he thought his work was done.'

'I guess that is all he could do from the other side unless he wanted to give Mr Beaming a good haunting,' Lilly said.

'I'd be tempted,' Phoebe said and laughed to put them at ease. 'Do not fear, I do not recommend that to my spirit friends.'

'Is anyone here?' Lilly asked intrigued.

'I am sure Miss Astin does not want to reveal her secrets to us,' Bennet said, shifting uncomfortably and putting his hands in his pockets. Lilly turned to look at him.

'Mr Martin, do not tell me you are fearful of ghosts.' She gave him a look that would challenge any gentleman's manhood.

'I shall not tell you then,' he said in good humour and Phoebe laughed.

'I think you might be in the minority if you are not fearful, Lilly.'

'So, is anyone here?' She persisted, wide-eyed with interest.

'Yes,' Phoebe answered and before she could utter another word, Bennet jumped in.

'I am about to go by the telegraphic office and if I have received word from England about the deceased lady, I shall go straight to see Harland. I shall let you know the outcome if you like, Miss Astin.'

'Oh yes, thank you. I would like to keep Mr Walker up to date, in the event he does return,' she said, flushing somewhat self-consciously at the strangeness of her request.

They heard footsteps above and Bennet jumped slightly. Lilly's eyes went straight to the stairs, missing his reaction. But she had not got a fright, instead, her face held an expression of hope.

'Your clients are leaving or your eldest brother is back,' she said thinking Julius might appear any moment and keen to get upstairs should he be in the reception area. She turned to Phoebe. 'I'd best let you return to your work then, and me to mine. I could not resist coming by to thank you and show you my headline.'

'It is only the start of a brilliant career, Lilly,' Phoebe said with more confidence than Lilly felt knowing her editor was fickle and each writer was only as good as their last story.

'I shall head off too. I just swung by to lock Julius in for tonight at the club,' Bennet said. 'Would you let him know I will be in attendance?'

'I shall.' Phoebe agreed. 'I am glad you get him out for some relaxation and entertainment.'

'I do my best, but it is not without its challenges,' Bennet said with a grin in Phoebe's direction.

'May I come with you to the telegraphic office, Mr Martin, and if there is word, we can travel to see the detective together?' Lilly asked.

'Absolutely. We will share a ride. Never let it be said that I stood in the way of a good story. But mind you, I have clients to satisfy, so if you should hear of anything...'

'It is a deal,' Lilly agreed. 'Is the deceased lady likely to return in due course, Phoebe?' Lilly took to the stairs.

'Most possibly.' Phoebe walked behind the pair to see them to the front door. 'Best of luck then both of you.'

Lilly looked around and her heart sank, Julius was nowhere to be seen. She gave Ambrose a small wave and with Bennet, silently slipped by the couple in the reception area being farewelled by Randolph. She had enough death on her hands at the moment and did not need to see more raw grief, nor feel guilty for enjoying the chase, or in this instance, case.

Phoebe watched them depart, looking for signs of affection between them and saw nothing. How odd that Bennet Martin should be nervous of the dead she thought, especially when it was only Uncle Reggie with her previously. Bennet will never truly understand or wish to hear much of her profession then. She imagined how different their upbringings had been.

216

Returning to her room, Phoebe stepped up on the arm of a wingback couch to glance out her window. Being in the basement, her source of light was two egress windows that were high enough to see the back of the yard and escape in the event of fire or flood, but well above head level to see out. Peering through the window afforded her a view of the small stables at the back of their office and she saw the horse and trap arriving in the yard. It was as good a time as any for a break, she determined. Besides, she wanted to hear how Julius went with Miss Forrester and his business proposition.

Phoebe grabbed her completed paperwork and took the stairs, finding her grandfather and Ambrose at the front desk.

'Is that Julius back?' she asked as the door opened in the back room and Julius strode through the room to them. His face was unreadable but it did not speak of the anticipation and happiness that masked it when he left.

'You are back.' Phoebe stated the obvious.

'Yes.' He did not meet their eyes and looked hurried. He glanced at the clock. 'We best get moving, Ambrose.'

'But how did it go?' Phoebe asked. 'Was Miss Forrester happy with your suggestions?'

'Did she accept?' Ambrose asked.

'She will let me know,' Julius said curtly. He took the piece of paper from his grandfather with the details of their collection and thanked him. Julius turned and headed towards the back exit.

'But was she excited to see you?' Ambrose asked.

'Not now, hurry up,' Julius called back, his stride lengthening in his haste to depart.

'Did she make love-sick eyes at you and call you her hero?' Ambrose persisted following his brother.

'Ambrose, do not pester your brother,' Randolph called after him with a well-worn saying used greatly in their younger years.

The door closed and Phoebe looked at her grandfather. 'Oh, dear.'

'We shall see. Julius does not wear his heart on his sleeve but I suspect his interest in Miss Forrester runs deeper than a business arrangement,' Randolph said and Phoebe agreed.

'I can't imagine what objections she may have to the offer, but I shan't pick out a new bonnet right away then,' she joked and hearing Mrs Dobbs calling the kettle was on, handed her supply order to her grandfather for dispatching and they moved to the kitchen for a cup of tea.

Chapter 22

DETECTIVE HARLAND STONE ALMOST snatched the paperwork from the desk sergeant in his hurry to read it, thanking him as he strode down the hallway, young Gilbert in pursuit. He avoided unnecessary eye contact and gave a nod or a smile to those in his path who greeted him. The front page of the newspaper created great interest in his case and he had both senior and junior officers waiting to see the outcome and how the new, young detective with the undesirable partner would handle it. The upside was that Zachariah Beaming was now a wanted man and there were eyes all over the state on the lookout for him. Harland was pleased he had played the game correctly and warned his inspector last night of what was to come.

'What is it? Has someone found Beaming?' Gilbert asked, catching him up.

'No. I believe It is the update I was expecting from the English police officers; they have commenced their enquiries in Rainhill and at the house Beaming leased.'

'Ah. Ghastly,' Gilbert said, his voice fading off as they entered their shared office.

Harland removed his hat and his suit jacket placing the latter over the back of his chair. He came around to the front of his desk and perched on the edge as Gilbert moved to his. Tearing open the envelope flap, Harland unfolded the numerous telegrams, some long, others one line only... a cost his budget would bear as it was a necessity.

'I will need to inform the inspector,' Harland said reading the first line that told him all he needed to read. He put his head back momentarily and closed his eyes. 'They have been found,' he said, opening his eyes and sighing.

'That poor family,' Gilbert said softly. 'Dead under the hearthstone? It would be his signature all over it if that were the case.'

'Yes, exactly so, Gilbert. The bodies of a woman, three girls and one boy were found in the house he tenanted.'

Harland flipped to the next slip of paper and read out loud the succinct lines of each telegram peppered with interruptions from Gilbert.

'The last resident at Rainhill house was Major Zachariah Williams.'

'He is clever to pick a surname that would be prolific in military circles,' Gilbert said.

Harland looked up at him, surprised. 'Yes, you are right. It would take some time to check his authenticity, but why would you if he was a respectable middle-aged gentleman with capital? Who might challenge him and for what purpose?' Harland turned the page where a few lines were nestled together. 'The rent was paid weekly to the landlady's daughter, Miss Eliza Stubbings.'

'That's how he came to know the latest bride, I suspect,' Gilbert said. 'She was his rent collector. So, if the woman buried here is that woman, her married name in the register will be Eliza Williams, nee Stubbings.'

'Yes, I suspect so,' Harland agreed. 'And the deceased family now unearthed will be Mrs Beaming and her children. I must alert Bennet so he can advise his clients. They will have to travel to Rainhill to identify their daughter if they have not already been informed.' He continued to read the telegrams, some useful, some not. He gave a small shake of his head. 'This one is interesting.' He waved a slip of paper. 'They wed after the major's visiting sister and her four children departed.'

Gilbert scoffed. 'He is the worst of men. Telling his mistress that his wife was his sister!'

'Indeed,' Harland agreed comforted by Gilbert's moral outrage. Many a man saw nothing wrong with harbouring a mistress, including many of his fellow detectives. 'According to the landlady, their stay was brief and their departure mysterious and sudden.'

'We know where they went now,' Gilbert said interrupting again. 'They never left the house in Rainhill. It is a tragedy.'

'Ah, and here it is,' Harland said reading the line first before reading it aloud. 'Workman had obtained and prepared cement but were not permitted to enter the house. Beaming undertook the work at night. A neighbour saw him through a window smoking and drinking wine for refreshment during the task.' He looked at the final telegram entry. 'It has caused quite a frenzy in the small town.'

'I can only imagine. Here is Mr Martin now,' Gilbert said as Bennet arrived with Lilly right behind him, hurried and excited by the unfolding of the case.

'From England,' Bennet said waving a telegram. 'I have a detailed description of the lady found here under the hearthstone, and a spinster aunt is living in Australia who can identify her.'

'Good morning, Bennet, Miss Lewis,' Harland said, ever calm. 'The description will be most useful, thank you. I have just received distressing news; your client is best to get to

Rainhill as soon as possible. I cannot give you these but read them quickly before I see the inspector.'

The men swapped notes and Lilly read over Bennet's shoulder while Harland moved to Gilbert's desk and shared Bennet's telegram correspondence, allowing Gilbert to jot down the description of Eliza Stubbings on his pad.

'Is there anything that might tell us of his whereabouts?' Gilbert asked.

'No, but plenty that tells us of his character,' Harland said and read some of the information the priest and the mother of Eliza had shared. 'Eliza was a dutiful girl, according to her mother. She sailed with her new husband from England on the *Kaiser Wilhelm II* – check the passenger list, Gilbert, and what names they travelled under. It should be Major Williams and Mrs Williams.'

'Will do, Sir,' Gilbert said jotting down the name of the ship.

'They arrived in Australia ten days before Christmas and rented the house in Windsor,' Harland read.

'But...' Gilbert rifled through his notes. 'The coroner said she was murdered on Christmas Eve so they did not even have ten days together as man and wife in her new country.'

'I imagine they got to know each other a little on the long voyage over,' Harland said.

Bennet cut in, 'Beaming paid the rent for a further four weeks and wrote to Eliza's mother pretending all was well and

Eliza was so very happy. It is in there,' he said with a nod to the notes in Harland's hand.

Harland scanned them and found the man's words. 'Beaming says, "We have spent a happy Christmas. Eliza is the happiest woman ever seen. She does enjoy herself." It was all a fabrication.'

'She was dead then,' Gilbert agreed, and ever practical added, 'He didn't even have to buy her a Christmas gift.'

Harland thanked Bennet and returned the telegrams, keeping one with his permission – the contact for the aunt in Australia who could identify her. He turned to Lilly.

'Miss Lewis, report on all you have just learned as you see fit. It is another scoop and will not harm our case to have it released,' Harland said. 'Please ensure you include his alias of Major Williams.'

Lilly's eyes widened with delight. 'Thank you, Detective Stone. I shall make notes quickly and my partner and I will do it justice. Will you give me a quote?'

'As you desire,' he said and allowed her time to prepare. When they departed, he turned to Gilbert. 'Zachariah Beaming is a wanted man now on two continents, Gilbert. Go speak with the front desk and have them record every report of his sighting and we shall follow up, and then check the ship passenger records.'

'Yes Sir,' Gilbert snapped and jumped to his feet as Harland donned his jacket, grabbed the telegrams and headed to update his superior.

With her trunk onboard the train bound for Melbourne and her fears in check, Catherine Tounselle settled in her seat by the window. The carriage was by no means crowded which was a relief. Zachariah had sent her twenty pounds for the fare which impressed her parents to no end and convinced them he was a man of good character who cared a great deal for their daughter.

The first leg of the journey cost eight pounds in first class and she would stay overnight in a hotel in Melbourne recommended by her sister from previous travels. It was a hotel considered proper and safe for young ladies travelling without companions. The next morning, Catherine would be free to recover at leisure and do a little bit of sightseeing before the express train departed for Adelaide at 4.50pm, arriving the next morning at 10.10am. Then, it was onto another train to Perth where Zachariah would meet her for the final leg to Albany. The thought of Zachariah waiting for her caused her heart to flutter with equal excitement and trepidation.

Am I making the right decision?

It is too late now.

No, it is not. I could get off this train immediately.

But then I shall be a burden on my parents or need to find myself employment or a husband, and I have a potential one.

It is just pre-wedding jitters. I believe everyone has that feeling and mine are more daunting than most with a trip across the country to a new life as well.

Catherine was stirred from her reverie as the carriage filled and she greeted an elderly man who introduced himself.

'Mr Walter Kilsby, at your service.'

'Miss Catherine Tounselle, a pleasure to make your acquaintance, sir.'

The well-groomed and tidy gentleman sat in the middle seat opposite. Both undertook the silent agreement to refrain from too much conversation too early – it would be a long journey, assuming they were both alighting in Melbourne. Outside her window stood Catherine's parents and her sister, Frances, with happy faces to send her off. They determined there would be no tears, as the occasion was a joyous one after all. Soon the train guard's whistle cut through the din on the platform, farewelling parties stepped back, and with a small jerk, the train started forward. Catherine waved, her eyes scanning over her mother, her father and Frances, conveying her love in a glance as they disappeared from sight. In moments, the platform, and the security she knew were well behind her, and thus the next part of her life had begun.

For hour upon hour, Catherine watched the scenery, drifted to sleep, and woke with the sound of trolleys passing through and fellow passengers rising. She stretched her legs and walked the length of the carriage many times.

'Care to read a newspaper, Miss Tounselle?' Mr Kilsby asked. 'I have a few outdated copies I keep to do the puzzles. This one from a few days ago has a wonderful article on travel on the continent but includes a dreadful affair of a lady's brutal murder that you may wish to avoid reading.'

Catherine accepted with thanks and Mr Kilsby added, 'Mind you, the reporter is a lady. She must have quite the constitution and she had done a good job of it, although I suspect the editor had a hand in it.'

Catherine smiled and bit her tongue, refraining from offering her thoughts on the need for interference by the editor and men in general. She had heard of the dreadful discovery of a body some days ago, but had been too caught up in her preparations to read the newspaper. Catherine set about reading the story immediately, as much to prove a point that women were most capable but the details did shock her, Mr Kilsby was right. The writer, Lilly Lewis, had done an admirable job.

A DIABOLICAL MURDER
A CEMENTED BRIDE FOUND
A WOMAN'S BODY FOUND UNDER A HEARTHSTONE

by Lilly Lewis, reporter.
Additional research by Fergus Griffiths.

A murder enshrouded in mystery was brought to light by Detectives Harland Stone and Gilbert Payne from the Roma Street Police Headquarters.

At the start of the week, a report was made at the police station to the effect that a stench in the front parlour of a home was intolerable, and fears that a crime of a very diabolical character had been committed seemed to be beyond all possible doubt. The messenger was Mr James Blake, the owner of the house, who carries on business as a butcher in High Street. As the detectives were familiar with the address of the house in question, they made haste to investigate.

On arrival, Detective Stone immediately called for men and equipment to unearth the hearthstone, expecting to reveal decomposing human remains in the front room of the house in Windsor. After about an hour of work with a pick and shovel, the men removed the hearthstone. This done, they encountered a slate slab held in position by a compact mass of cement, and underneath lay the corpse of a woman in an advanced stage of decomposition.

Detective Harland Stone said, "The body lay at a depth of 18 inches and had been squeezed into a space about 18 inches wide by 2 feet 6 inches in length. The knees wore forced up over the abdomen, the left hand rested under the chin, the right arm was crossed over the body, and in the skull displayed a large crack." The detective added that it appeared, "the hand had been placed there in the process of self-defence."

City Coroner, Dr Tavish McGregor described the woman as "slight but well nourished, presumably about 30 years of age." There were no articles of clothing beyond a chemise of which were observable. Detective Stone said, "it was evident that the body had been placed in the hole and the liquid mortar poured upon it, as the imprint of the toes was clearly visible." The body as soon as it was extricated was removed to the morgue, where it now lies.

The property owner, Mr Blake stated that about a week before Christmas a man called on his agent, Mr Connor, seeking a vacant house. Mr Connor said he had not many properties available, but among them, he mentioned this property in Windsor. The man said he would look at it, and accordingly got the key and went over it. On the next day, he came back to Mr Connor and said the house suited him, and he would rent it. He did not say for what term he would take it, but he paid a week's rent in advance. The keys were handed over to him and he entered into possession.

Mr Blake had the opportunity to meet his new tenant who introduced himself as Mr Zachariah Beaming. He described Mr Beaming as about 45 years of age, of medium stature and sturdy build. The man had a very fair moustache and a short beard. In conversation with Mr Blake, the man said he was an engineer's toolmaker and that he had noticed that the walls were full of nail holes, but added that that was a defect which could be easily remedied, as he would mend them with cement, he being a practical man. Two or three evenings later the tenant was seen carrying a bag of cement with which he purposed to repair the holes in the walls. On the same day, he further stated that he was expecting the arrival of a sister, with whom he had arranged to keep his house.

Mr Alfred Spedding, who resides next door states that on one occasion he saw some luggage arrive. "There were one or two trunks and a hamper." On another occasion, Mr Spedding saw the man leave the house in the company of a lady. Mr Spedding said, "It was in the evening, and as the pair were rather smartly dressed, my wife and I presumed they were about to pay a visit to the theatre. The lady was dressed in black; she was about 5 feet 6 inches in height, of slight build, and had dark brown hair." Detective Stone confirms this description corresponds with that of the murdered woman.

Having been informed that his tenant would not be returning, Mr Blake entered the house two days ago and found nothing beyond a stale loaf of bread, an empty brandy bottle, and a tin of condensed milk. In all the grates were the ashes of destroyed papers. Detective Stone is urgently seeking the tenant, Mr Zachariah Beaming, to assist with his inquiries but suggests the public not approach him as it is reasonable to assume that Mr Beaming, seems beyond all possible doubt to have been the murderer.

Catherine looked up after reading the sordid tale of the woman found under the hearthstone and realised she had been holding her breath while reading.

'My goodness, Mr Kilsby, what a frightful tale,' she gasped.

'Indeed, young lady, and what a rotter that Mr Zachariah Beaming is... although I tell tales out of school as the police only seek him to assist with their investigation at this stage. I shall not cast aspersions on his character.'

'No, but it is looking like he may be the guilty party.' She took a shaky breath and added, 'it makes one wonder how well we really know anyone these days.'

'I am sure if vexed we are all capable of anger, but one must control those impulses and be a better person, a Christian person. My dear wife and I – God rest her soul – met at a dance but we enjoyed a lengthy engagement and attended church together with our families, there was no doubt of our character before being wed.'

'That is sage advice,' she said, aware that her concerns were born from not knowing Major Williams very well at all.

'We do not know if this Mr Beaming and the poor woman are even wed... she has not been identified yet,' Mr Kilsby pointed out.

'How dreadful to meet your death at the hands of a person you trusted and loved,' Catherine said and sighed before offering a little of herself, keen to hear Mr Kilsby's opinion. 'Mr Kilsby I must confess that I am travelling to see my betrothed, Major Williams. We are to wed and settle in Albany, but I have known him for the shortest time.'

'A man who has served is a man of character indeed, putting King and country before all others.'

'I am sure you are right, Mr Kilsby, thank you.' His words gave her great comfort but nevertheless, she read the story again feeling most distressed for the poor lady under the hearthstone, and in truth, a little frightened.

The journey was not wholly unpleasant but Catherine was much relieved after the constant rocking, stops and starts, to see the Melbourne train station come into view. She had not seen a newspaper for the last 24 hours and had plenty of time to ponder on the terrible murder and wonder if the police had caught Mr Beaming. Catherine had not been able to communicate with her family at home or with her fiancé about her well-being, and no doubt they worried for her. She would amend that on checking into the hotel.

Rising with stiff joints and a wobble in her walk, as did most of the passengers, she bid Mr Kilsby well and thanked him for his company. No sooner had Catherine checked into the hotel recommended by her sister, than the desk clerk handed her a telegram.

'This is marked urgent and for you, Miss Tounselle. It arrived this morning. I hope all is well.' The young lady handed it over and Catherine thanked her, not reading it until she was inside her room with the door closed.

She hurriedly opened it, fearful that her mother's health had suddenly declined or that it was from Zachariah telling her not to come when she was over halfway on her journey. But it was from her sister, Frances and read only: "For God's sake, go no further."

Chapter 23

RANDOLPH ASTIN OF *The Economic Undertaker*, dressed in his light grey suit that made him look particularly handsome and respectable for a senior man, opened the mail and as always placed it in piles – correspondence to reply to, cheques to bank, thank you notes for support during a time of confusion and grieving. He found one addressed to Julius and noticed the beautiful handwriting. A quick inhale of the envelope told him the paper was scented and no doubt one of Julius's admirers, but the back of the envelope proved him wrong... possibly it was a matter of business. The correspondence was from Miss Violet Forrester.

No sooner had he put the letter aside, Julius arrived looking uncustomarily a little worse for wear. He closed the door behind him quietly on entering and saw the raised eyebrow his grandfather gave him.

'Do not say it, I know,' Julius said. 'At least I'm only meeting the dead today.'

'You won't receive my censure, lad,' Randolph said. 'I am the first to tell you to have a little fun now and then. Mind you, if you start appearing bleary-eyed and smelling like a brewery every day it might be a different matter.'

'I take full responsibility for letting Bennett lead me astray. I was quite ready to go at midnight when Harland left. Tavish will also be the worse for wear today at the morgue.'

Ambrose barged in and seeing his brother, laughed. 'If you look that bad, I wonder how your best friend fares.'

'Shh,' Julius said and winced. 'I am sure Bennet has had more practice at drinking than I have. And what happened to you?'

'Cousin and I went in search of some female company,' Ambrose said and added nothing more.

'There's a letter for you, Julius.' Randolph passed his grandson the fragrant correspondence.

'A love letter?' Ambrose enquired. 'Don't tell me Miss Hannah Reed has given up dropping in on you and has now started corresponding. *You are my one true love, Julius, and I can think of no other. How tall and handsome you are, sigh.*'

'Ambrose, do shut up, my head will not take it,' Julius said in a restrained voice and earned a laugh from his brother. Randolph noted his grandson's surprised look at the name on the back of the envelope and his hurry to open it. Julius then muttered, 'Oh no.'

'What is it?' Ambrose asked and saw the small smile on his grandfather's face.

'Miss Forrester wishes to visit today and give me her decision on the business.'

'Well, that is a good thing, isn't it?' Ambrose asked, squeezing his brother's shoulder, and grabbing the letter from his fingers. He read aloud, '*Dear Mr Astin, may I call on you on the morrow at 9.30am if that is convenient to discuss your offer? If that is not suitable, I shall on arrival, make another time with Mr Astin senior and call again. Yours faithfully, Violet Forrester.*' He smelled the stationery before Julius snatched it back from him.

'Ambrose you are trying at the best of times, but do not push me today,' Julius snapped. He looked at his grandfather. 'I can't see Miss Forrester this morning, not like this.'

'I will cover for you,' Ambrose said. 'Tell me what you offered and I will be your business manager.'

Julius looked to his grandfather who came to his rescue.

'Ambrose, go and ensure the hearse is ready, your first collection is at the hospital, and please let Phoebe know we are expecting two bodies this morning. I will have the list ready for you on your return.'

Ambrose gave an exaggerated sigh and headed out the back.

'I hate for her to come out of her way,' Julius said, frowning at the letter.

'Go and see if Phoebe can help you freshen up and I will do the first collection with Ambrose so you can meet with Miss Forrester. Mrs Dobbs can mind the reception. You are not too bad,' Randolph said studying him and then he called out, 'Mrs Dobbs, we have a sore head, alcohol-induced.'

'Really?' Julius complained at his grandfather's raised voice and indiscretion.

'I have just the thing for young Ambrose,' she called back from the kitchen.

''Tis not Ambrose,' Randolph answered.

An audible gasp could be heard from the kitchen and Julius rolled his eyes as Randolph chuckled.

'Go and see Phoebe and then return for whatever Mrs Dobbs is preparing.'

Julius massaged his temples and groaned. 'I feel like I have gone a three-round bout in the ring. But it best not to delay Miss Forrester. Why did she have to come today?' he muttered.

Randolph watched as Julius gingerly took the stairs to Phoebe's office. He smiled, the lad was a little smitten, not that Julius would ever admit that.

Just as he finished preparing the list of collections for the day, Julius reappeared at the top of the stairs.

'That was quick and you don't look any better,' Randolph said, with a frown.

'I cannot see her today, I have decided. I don't want Miss Forrester to think I imbibe as a habit. Can you reschedule her visit for tomorrow morning?'

Randolph flicked the page of the diary and nodded. 'The same time tomorrow is better. I will ensure Ambrose is occupied and you are free.' He looked up and handed the list to Julius for today's clients. 'See Mrs Dobbs on your way out.'

Julius nodded his thanks and taking the list, went via the kitchen prepared to be fussed over and to down the elixir as punishment for his folly.

Dr Tavish McGregor vowed to not drink to excess again, as he did the last time he found himself with the same wretched hangover and thumping head. The early start did not help but he was quite behind with his workload and people kept dying. At least he did not have to be pleasant to anybody during a dissection and while the smell did not help his constitution, he warranted it was no more than he deserved. On finishing the autopsy, he cleaned the area and his tools at no great pace, finishing with thoroughly washing his hands. With a glance at the clock, hoping the hours were flying by so he could return home to sleep, he frowned to note it was only 9 o'clock. He donned a clean jacket and entered the adjoining room where bodies were stored.

It wasn't long before Detective Harland Stone entered his office, this time without his sidekick, Detective Payne, but accompanied by Bennet Martin.

Harland smiled on seeing Tavish looking as worse for wear as Bennet. 'Your red eyes match your hair,' he jested and then shook his head. 'You are a fine lot; I hate to think how Julius is managing in the hearse today.'

'At least he has grounds to look sad and solemn, as does Tavish,' Bennet pointed out, rubbing a hand over his face. 'I had two clients this morning who both required me to be charming.'

'Does that not come naturally?' Tavish teased him indicating a choice of tea or water and a chair, the latter of which they accepted.

'Surprisingly no,' Bennet replied and once seated, downed the glass of water offered in three large gulps.

'To business, boys,' Tavish said. 'Were you not bringing in the aunt of the cemented bride to identify her?' Tavish saw Harland wince at the title. 'You can blame Miss Lewis for that title.'

'Actually, I suggested it to her, so I apologise,' Bennet said not looking at all repentant. 'She did a splendid job of that story though.'

'I agree,' Tavish said. 'I only hope the young lady's family overseas never see the newspaper; it is a distressing report.'

Harland sighed. 'I cannot help but think of that poor young lady, new to the country with so few friends, defending herself against that monster, and a mother across the sea knowing she will not see her daughter again.'

'That is very sentimental of you,' Tavish said and studied the rugged-looking detective. 'Perhaps you are feeling homesick yourself?'

'I am from Melbourne so not so far should I wish to see my family,' Harland said. 'Not like the distance between Australia and the mother country as you both have experienced.'

'But I do not miss it, or my father,' Bennet assured them.

'Is he still pressing you to return and take up your family duty as the only son and heir?' Tavish asked with a chuckle.

'He includes a few lines reminding me of my duty with every letter that my mother sends. He is annoyed that I have chosen to work as a private investigator when I could have joined the police force and worked my way up to detective like himself.' Bennet sighed.

'I would not have picked you for a policeman,' Harland said and added hurriedly, 'not saying you would not make a good go of it, but – '

'You are right though. I prefer to do my art. I simply investigate minor matters to supplement my living. I had not expected to be appointed to such a big case as this. The small matters allow me time to paint.'

'Ah, the painting,' Tavish said and smiled. 'You are very talented, Bennet. Are you still painting portraits of Miss Astin that she will never see?'

Bennet's eyes shot to Harland and back to Tavish, he flushed slightly. 'Well, she is most beautiful and extraordinary. I paint many ladies including those works commissioned of me.' He shuffled uncomfortably.

'They are a handsome family the Astins, but I suspect the ladies like the more rugged types, like myself and Harland, especially red-haired Scottish men such as myself,' Tavish joked stroking his facial hair, and the men laughed at his antics.

Harland sobered. 'To the case again, and the identification of the deceased lady...'

'Yes,' Bennet broke in. 'I met with the aunt, Miss Stubbings, and she is staying in town with a friend for a week. But to get back to your original question, Tavish, which was lost in my foggy head, she is a mature lady of gentle sensibilities. I fear the state of the deceased might be too much for her.'

Tavish nodded. 'What say I see if Miss Astin can do a little minor repair on the deceased's face, and make the deceased presentable for a viewing?'

'My thoughts exactly,' Harland said. 'But we need to do so in haste. I need her identified so that the family is not in limbo. I have heard from my overseas colleagues that since the discovery of Mrs Beaming and her four children, Rainhill is experiencing a wave of visitors.' He sighed. 'People are odd.'

Bennet agreed. 'I hear enough from my mother to keep me abreast of the news—'

Tavish interrupted, 'But you would not have received mail correspondence yet?'

'No, she telegrams regularly between letter writing – I am sure the telegraph operator hides when he sees her coming – and she tells me that the public is mortified and interest is at a frenzy.'

Harland groaned. 'I fear we should expect the same here when we manage to catch Beaming.'

'He will be publicly lynched, I am sure,' Bennet said. 'Mother said extra rail services had been scheduled so the curious could descend on Rainhill and shuffle past the house, which they are doing in long, winding lines. She has sent me the newspapers by mail.'

'A lynching is what he deserves,' Harland said.

'No argument from me,' Tavish agreed. 'If you can get Miss Astin's consent to prepare the deceased, I shall organise for the body to be sent this afternoon when our deliveries go out... unless Julius can pick it up sooner.'

'I don't think he'll be doing anything in a hurry today.' Bennet chuckled.

'In your current state, all three of you are a detriment to my investigation, I should arrest the lot of you,' Harland jested.

'A day in the cells with just bread and water would be much appreciated,' Tavish said and sighed as another body arrived. He indicated to the two men carrying the stretcher where to put it.

Harland rose. 'Thank you for the reprieve, gents, I must get back to it. Bennet, will you see your client – Miss Stubbings – and advise we will try to set up a viewing tomorrow? I shall swing by now and see if Miss Astin can prioritise the job and if Mr Astin senior can send a vehicle to collect the body urgently. Do you have a rate that I should pay them for police work?' he asked Tavish.

'Yes, that part is under control... we have an account, they know the rate and will apply it,' Tavish said. 'I shall have the body ready for collection.'

'Good. Thank you, gents. I hope the day is not too demanding of you both.' Harland tipped his hat, and with a smile departed.

Tavish looked at Bennet. 'Hair of the dog?'

'Thought you'd never ask.'

Chapter 24

AMBROSE CAST A LOOK at his brother sitting in the driver's seat of the carriage and leapt up on the same side forcing his brother across the seat and taking the reins from him.

'I shall drive today, Julius. You do your best not to be sick in the vehicle.'

'I assure you; I am not feeling that unwell. Although, your driving may contribute to it,' he shot back but surrendered the reins nevertheless.

'So, you are not meeting Miss Forrester?' Ambrose asked as they pulled out of the yard.

'Tomorrow at this time.'

'I can't imagine why she would not accept the offer for herself and her brother,' Ambrose mused.

'She was very keen to accept the apprenticeship for Tom and believed he would feel the same. But understandably, she has her own clients and is concerned that if she begins work in the new business and it fails, or they don't follow her, she will be destitute.'

Ambrose snapped to look at his brother. 'You would not let that happen.'

'Of course not, but she does not want charity any more than we did in that situation years ago.'

'Oh. I guess that is understandable.'

Ambrose turned the vehicle out onto the street and joined the flow of other traps of all sizes. 'It is a beautiful April day.' Turning his face to the sun and then back to the street ahead. 'Is it not?'

'Yes.'

Ambrose grinned. 'Do you like her?'

Julius sighed. 'Do slow down, we are a hearse, not a racing carriage, and I like people to see our business emblem. We are supposed to look dignified.'

'You look like a corpse. But it is not business you are thinking of, the motion is making you ill no matter what the speed,' Ambrose added.

'There is that,' Julius said, rubbing a hand over his forehead and conceding the argument which he rarely did. Ambrose did not push the subject of Miss Forrester.

They drove through the city and suddenly Julius grabbed Ambrose's arm. 'Stop!'

'What is it?' He looked around, panicking that something had fallen from the back or he had unknowingly run over someone.

'Pull over.'

Ambrose did as his brother ordered, searching in the direction that Julius was looking in and saw the back of a woman as she disappeared into a jewellery store down the parallel street. It was a respectable area with a range of stores from pawn shops to ladies' accessories.

'What is it?'

'Just wait,' Julius ordered him. 'Do not draw attention to us.'

'That is often difficult,' Ambrose said with a smile and a dip of his hat to a young lady passing who smiled at him and blushed prettily.

That sat in silence for a few minutes, Julius's gaze never wavering.

'How long are we waiting here for and whom are we waiting on?' Ambrose asked. 'I'm sure they are expecting us at the hospital.'

'Just a moment more,' Julius said, never taking his eyes from the street and then he leapt down from the carriage, grabbed the edge and momentarily braced, closing his eyes until he settled.

'No sudden movements, huh?' Ambrose smiled; he was no stranger to imbibing.

'Yes, most helpful,' Julius grumbled. 'Wait here for me please, I won't be long.'

Ambrose frowned watching as his brother stopped on the corner and deeming the area all clear, raced down the street and entered the shop where the lady had just exited. He was in there no more than five minutes when he returned, and slipped a small package into his coat pocket. Julius levered himself back up next to Ambrose.

'Thank you, continue.'

Ambrose started the horses forward and asked, 'Who was that woman?'

'It was Miss Forrester. I suspect she stopped to do business there on the way to our office.'

'But you did not speak with her?'

'No. I shall see her tomorrow.'

They rode in silence for a short while before Ambrose spoke again. 'Are you not going to tell me what you purchased?'

'No.' Julius sighed. 'Can you be discreet?'

'Of course,' Ambrose said with a look that said he was most insulted and then smiled on seeing his brother's disbelief. 'I promise you, I shall not utter a word, as tempted as I may be.'

Julius hesitated. 'Miss Forrester was undertaking business in a pawn shop. She sold her grandmother's pearls. I believe they were very sentimental to her.'

'And you bought them back for her?'

'Yes.'

'Julius, what a kind heart you are,' Ambrose said and grinned. 'But if she does not like charity, how will you present them?'

'I don't know yet. Maybe a bonus for work well done if she takes the job,' he mused. 'But her very act of selling the pearls says to me she will not accept the offered position... Miss Forrester would not need the money if she came into my employ.'

'She might need it to tie her over,' Ambrose suggested, and Julius nodded considering the truth in that.

'You could give her the pearls as a gift to a sweetheart,' Ambrose teased and laughed at the expression his brother sent his way.

'I made an error in that regard.'

'Do tell.'

Julius frowned, opened his mouth to say something and then changed his mind.

'Tell me, Brother.'

'When I called to discuss the business proposition, I took with me a hamper with some provisions.'

Ambrose waited for more but no further explanation was forthcoming.

'I fail to see how that is an error. I would think it was a great kindness, especially knowing how they live.'

Julius's jaw tightened as he grimaced, then added, 'She did not wish to have charity and I said I would have brought flowers but knowing she had so many in the house from mourners...' He left the sentence unfinished.

Ambrose was still confused and then the inference dawned on him. 'Oh. I see. She thought you might have come to court her and offer her a job as well, leaving her with little choice either way.'

'Yes.'

'What shall you do about it then because I imagine you wish to court her?'

Julius exhaled. 'I shall do nothing. Miss Forrester made it abundantly clear she did not wish to be put in a compromising situation, so I am her employer first and foremost. As I said, I shall give the pearls to her as a bonus perhaps in due course.'

'Well, that is most frustrating, I was hoping for something new to tease you with as I watched you write poetry and swoon.' He nudged his brother and smiled.

'Seriously, not today.' Julius groaned.

'Nevertheless, it was thoughtful of you to buy the pearls. Miss Forrester will be working right next door every day, and Grandpa and Phoebe will be pleased.'

'Not a word,' Julius threatened.

'Not even to them?' Ambrose looked bereft.

Julius rolled his eyes. 'I suspect you will accidentally tell them anyway, so only them, no one else.'

'On my honour,' Ambrose said and steered the horse and carriage into the hospital grounds looking like the cat that swallowed the cream.

Violet had done the unthinkable, sold her grandmother's pearls, but practicality demanded it, and it best to look after the living, namely her brother, Tom. As the beautiful black pearls left her hand, her fingers brushed the smooth surface and she prayed her grandmother would forgive her. Violet calculated that if she accepted the offer with Mr Astin, she may not be paid for a month or so, and with the days not worked during the mourning period and funeral expenses, her funds were short on supply. There was rent to pay, food to buy and living to be done.

'Do not dwell on it further,' she whispered to herself, 'the deed is done.'

Violet turned in the direction of *The Economic Undertaker* and walked at a comfortable pace, she was early for the 9.30am appointment. She took a deep breath and prepared herself to meet with Mr Julius Astin who, she had to admit, unsettled her. He had a way of looking at her as if he saw inside, under her skin, what she was thinking, and in all honesty, Violet was not comfortable with being in his employ. Would he be demanding? Would she look up to find him present and gazing at her? It would be most unsettling and what if she did not meet his standards or his deadlines? Was Julius Astin prone to anger?

But, Violet conceded, it was a very good offer and she would be a fool to turn it down. Tom was keen to take on the apprenticeship and the very thought of him gainfully occupied brought her much relief. She then could not but help laugh at herself and her inflated opinion of her own importance. Julius Astin was a wealthy, handsome and successful businessman and no doubt well-practised in the romantic arts. She blushed at the thought. *He is not interested in me. Accept the role, be grateful, and work hard.*

She regretted the walk was coming to an end on such a fine April day, but the front of the store came into view. Violet studied the small shop next to it with the curtains drawn… that was likely to be the location of the dress stores she would manage.

Miss Violet Forrester, Manageress. Imagine!

It was neat with large glass windows that would allow for a display of the best garments. Gathering herself, Violet pushed open the door to the funeral business and entered the room for the second time – the last time had been to organise her grandmother's funeral and she could remember little of the visit in her heightened state of distress. The reception area felt different, warmer, and not as terrifying as it did that day.

Behind the desk, she recognised the senior man with a striking resemblance to the two Astin brothers that had tended her grandmother's funeral.

'Miss Forrester? Randolph Astin at your service,' he said with a small bow.

Violet smiled at the charming man with the gift of relaxing the most stressed of visitors.

'Mr Astin, it is a pleasure to see you again, this time under less duress.'

'Indeed. I hope your grandmother's service was dignified and to your satisfaction?'

'Thank you, it was perfect and Mr Astin, that is, both Mr Astins, were very kind,' she said.

'I am pleased,' he said and came around from behind the desk. 'I am sorry to have inconvenienced you, but my grandson, Julius, had a prior appointment. He hoped to reschedule for this time tomorrow if that was to your liking?'

'Of course,' Violet said and felt deflated. She had been mentally preparing for the meeting all evening, and would now have another night of anxiety and waiting.

'However, as you are here, would you do me and my granddaughter, Phoebe, the honour of having morning tea with us?' He held up his hands. 'You do not need to declare if you intend to take the position or not, but should you do so, we will see each other regularly as business neighbours and no doubt share a cup of tea on many occasions.'

She smiled. 'Thank you, Mr Astin, as I intended to be out for an hour, I have nothing pressing and would enjoy that.'

'Excellent.' He rang a small bell and ushered her into the kitchen, undertaking the introduction to the kindly housekeeper, Mrs Dobbs.

'I hope you don't mind having tea in the kitchen, dear,' Mrs Dobbs said. 'It is cosy and comfortable.' She indicated a seat around the table and Randolph sat once Violet was seated.

'Not at all, Mrs Dobbs. In fact, when Mr Astin called on me to speak of his business proposition, I'm afraid he was subjected to my kitchen table as well,' she said and laughed.

'The heart of every home,' Mrs Dobbs said with a smile.

Violet's attention was drawn by a slim, blonde young lady coming toward them. Her hair was down, loosely tied back off her shoulders and her dress was fitted but uncorseted. She was beautiful.

'This is my granddaughter, Phoebe.'

'Miss Astin,' Violet said studying her with curiosity and noting Phoebe Astin's surprised look on her face before the young mortician schooled herself to offer a warm greeting.

'It is lovely to meet you, Miss Forrester. May I offer my sincere condolences on the loss of your grandmother? I hope we were able to provide some support and consolation.' Phoebe took a seat opposite Violet and thanked Mrs Dobbs as a cup and saucer were placed before her. 'Forgive me, but I was startled to see you are not in mourning dress.'

Violet smiled and looked at Randolph. 'Your grandfather did not blink an eye.'

'Years of practice at being shocked,' he joked. 'Julius, Ambrose and even Phoebe have turned my hair this grey colour.' The ladies laughed at his jest and accepted a chocolate slice from the plate he offered. 'Mrs Dobbs made these so I am glad you did not turn down the invitation, Miss Forrester, or we might not have been allowed to have them without a guest.'

Mrs Dobbs coloured with delight. 'He makes me out to be such a taskmaster, but as if I could keep him and the boys from them.'

'How delicious!' Violet said taking a smile bite and relishing it. 'And I best explain about my mourning clothes. My grandmother's last wishes were that my brother and I were not to wear them. We have had several years of death in a row and she hated to see young people in black.'

'I could not agree more,' Randolph said. 'An eminently sensible woman, and not wearing black does not reflect the grief you will feel.'

'Not for a moment, Mr Astin, and thank you for your understanding.' She looked at her mauve dress. 'It does not sit easily with me though, and I occasionally fall back to wearing black, my neighbours expect it too.'

'I understand and, in your situation, I would want to honour her wishes too. Besides...' Phoebe leaned in as if discussing a great secret, 'the black dresses can be so hot and itchy.'

Violet raised an eyebrow and looked skyward as she thought. 'I shall make note of that... I wonder if it can be overcome with design and fabric choice.'

Phoebe grinned. 'Ah, my brother is right to speak so highly of you.'

'Does he?' Violet asked surprised turning her eyes to Phoebe. 'He is yet to see my work but that is kind.'

'I believe the dress you wore on the day was quite striking. Did you make the dress you are wearing now? It is exceptional.'

'I did, thank you,' Violet said and smiled as she brushed her hands along the skirt of her dress. 'It is an inexpensive fabric but I have spent more on the trimmings, hoping to disguise that.'

'It is beautiful. Julius has had this vision for a business for some time, hasn't he, Grandpa? But the lease becoming available next door has prompted him into action.'

'Yes, at the rate we are going, if we hire the grim reaper, we'll have the industry sewn up,' Randolph said.

Violet laughed. 'Indeed. Coffins, hearse wagons, funerals, mourning rooms and soon mourning clothes. Most industrious. I am sure a reaper could be hired for the right price.'

Randolph laughed. 'Please don't suggest that to Julius.'

Violet beamed but did not hide her surprised expression. Julius Astin was a mystery to her and her trepidation was evident.

'Grandfather is joking, I assure you, Miss Forrester,' Phoebe said and gave her grandfather a scolding look which made him laugh longer. 'My eldest brother is a very kind and loyal man, and is not completely focussed on business.'

'He has been very kind to me,' Violet agreed. 'He is very serious though, especially compared to the younger Mr Astin who engaged me in conversation on the way to the cemetery.'

Randolph nodded. 'Ambrose has a cheery outlook on life, while Julius saw a tragedy happen at an impressionable age and feels his duty to the family most profoundly. I would like to ease his mind, lighten his load, maybe in time a good woman will do that for him.'

Violet smiled and blushed slightly. 'Now you are sounding like my grandmother, Mr Astin.'

Phoebe laughed. 'Be warned, Miss Forrester, should you take the position, Grandpa and Mrs Dobbs will do their best to ensure every eligible and respectable gentleman crosses your path. I am constantly astounded by their ingenuity in doing so when I work downstairs in a funeral parlour.'

Randolph and Mrs Dobbs laughed, enjoying the jest at their expense.

'We care for our family and our extended work family, Miss Forrester,' Randolph said kindly. 'I do hope you and your brother will join us. I assure you of our best intentions at all times for the people in our business.'

'Thank you, Mr Astin. I am surprised you do not have people wishing to work here just for Mrs Dobbs baking!' She finished the slice and daintily wiped her mouth with the napkin provided.

'Will you take a slice home for your brother, dear?' Mrs Dobbs asked, beaming and rising to wrap a piece.

'Oh, he would love that, Mrs Dobbs, thank you,' Violet said. 'I will have no choice but to take the position once he takes a bite.'

'Make it two then,' Randolph said, making her laugh.

Violet looked to Phoebe. 'I admire that you break with convention, Miss Astin. If you will forgive me for being so bold, but you are very striking and I imagine not conforming is not easy.'

'No, not always,' Phoebe agreed and took Violet's hand. 'But there is strength in numbers.'

'It is part of the reason we keep her downstairs,' Randolph added and gave Violet a wink, lest she should take him seriously, and she laughed again, enjoying the company of adults and some pleasant conversation, two things now missing from her home.

'Tomorrow then?' she confirmed.

'Julius will be at your disposal,' Randolph said and Violet did not miss the smile on Phoebe's face or the hope in Mr Astin senior's eyes.

Chapter 25

LIKE MANY, AND FOR reasons that seemed unwarranted, Detective Harland Stone braced himself on arrival at *The Economic Undertaker* just after 10 o'clock. It was not as if he were dying, or visiting the dead, or organising a burial, but the very nature of the business required some trepidation. He glanced back at his young partner, Gilbert Payne, whose features mirrored his own, but he gave him a small smile and confident nod going forward. The door opened and Harland stepped back; he bowed to an attractive lady in a mauve dress as she departed. He noticed she was not in mourning.

Harland slowly stepped into the entranceway and peered into the sober reception area to check it was clear. It was, then he heard the words, 'But he was buried alive, you can only imagine our surprise.'

Harland's eyes widened and Gilbert gasped behind him. Moving into the reception area, he glanced around the corner to see Randolph standing alone, arms crossed across his chest with a grin on his face.

Harland laughed and step aside allowing Gilbert to enter.

'Mr Astin, how many people have you horrified with that line?' he asked.

'Many, but the reaction is always the same.' Randolph laughed. 'Come in, Detectives.'

Gilbert glanced at the coffin display in the next room. 'I read that in England they are putting a latch inside the coffin for people who fear they will be buried alive, so they can get out.'

'Rightly so, Detective Payne, you are well-read,' Randolph said. 'We've had a few requests to do so here. It won't help you if there is six feet of dirt on top of you.'

Harland grimaced, closing the door behind him. 'I will ensure Tavish takes my organs out before I'm buried, just to be safe.'

'You can donate them to science if they want them,' Gilbert said looking at his boss.

'Are you implying my organs would be rejected, Detective Payne?' Harland asked with a small smile so his protégé did not take him in earnest.

'I'm sure they would want them,' Gilbert answered quickly.

Randolph chuckled. 'I believe you are the most sensible of the bunch this morning, Detective Stone, so your liver should be in reasonable condition.'

'I know my limitations,' Harland said. 'Besides I have a case on my hands at the moment that requires my full attention.'

'Indeed, that man, Beaming, must be stopped,' Randolph agreed. 'If it were my Phoebe that wed him, I would kill him with my bare hands.'

'Trust me, your sentiment is widely shared,' Harland said. 'Which is why I hoped to ask a favour of you and Miss Astin to prioritise a job for the police department?'

'We are at your service,' Randolph said. Harland explained what they needed.

'I will send the smaller trap and the two lads from the stable now. They know the routine and have collected bodies on numerous occasions when required,' Randoph assured him. 'Do you wish to brief Phoebe or have me do so? She is in her workroom.' He indicated the stairs and Harland thanked him, willing to speak with her.

'Perhaps you would like to inspect our coffins?' Randolph asked Gilbert whose eyes widened with interest.

'By all means,' Harland said permitting Gilbert with a nod. He wondered if Randolph Astin had a reason for allowing him time alone with his granddaughter. As he took the stairs to Phoebe's workroom, he thought of Bennet. He was not aware prior of the feelings Bennet harboured for Miss Astin. Most interesting, and he would be mindful now to ensure he did not overstep the mark with Miss Astin given his new friend's interest in her. He was grateful for the group that Tavish and Julius had welcomed him into and did not intend to ruffle feathers.

Harland could hear Phoebe talking as he came down the stairs. He was always a little in awe of Miss Astin. He had never met anyone quite like her and he had met many different types of ladies in the course of his work. She stopped speaking abruptly and her smile momentarily arrested him. Harland glanced around; her workroom was empty.

'Forgive the intrusion, Miss Astin, am I interrupting you?' he said removing his hat and running a hand through his hair.

'Not at all Detective Stone, you are most welcome. How are you this fine day?' she asked with a smile that indicated she knew of the activities the night prior.

'Somewhat better than your eldest brother I imagine,' Harland said and enjoyed Phoebe's delightful laugh.

'It is good for Julius to relax now and then. He always has the worries of the world on his shoulders. I imagine you are busy, what may I do for you?'

'Thank you.' He appreciated her consideration. 'You have been kept abreast of the case to date?'

'Indeed, from Lilly and Mr Martin. She is most grateful for your support,' Phoebe added and Harland accepted her praise with a brief nod.

'I am hoping to impose on you – an urgent job.'

'The lady from the hearthstone? You have a witness to identify her and she is not in a fit state to be seen?' Phoebe asked.

'Precisely, thank you.' He was relieved not to have to recount the story of the victim and how she came about her wounds. 'Her aunt is in town for a week to identify her but is a mature lady and may find the state of the victim distressing.'

'I can do the work immediately.' She glanced at the table where two bodies were covered with cloth. 'Neither of my clients is required for another few days.' She gave a small smile and looked into the corner. 'Although one is rather pushy.' As if remembering herself she straightened and hurried on. 'Forgive me, Detective, I get caught up in my work sometimes.'

'As do I, more times than not.' His look conveyed he had been accused of the very same before. They shared a moment of understanding as they studied each other with curiosity and then Harland remembered himself, gave a small bow and moved to the stairs. 'Your grandfather has kindly offered to collect the body now, so hopefully, she will be with you within the hour.'

'When done, I will have her moved to the mourning room and you may set up the viewing appointment for tomorrow morning if that is convenient?'

'That is what we hoped for and much appreciated,' Harland said. 'Good day, Miss Astin.'

'Detective,' she said with a nod.

Harland took the stairs, fully aware of the feelings she had stirred in him and suppressed them for revisiting later in the quiet of the night when he could focus on matters of a personal nature. He collected Gilbert and thanked Mr Astin senior, hurrying to follow up on any reports and sightings of the murderer at loose, Mr Zachariah Beaming.

'Time is of the essence, Gilbert.' They raced to the stop where Harland could see an omnibus approach. 'That was timely,' he said, and they hurried on. Once seated, Harland asked, 'What did you learn of the caskets?' He knew Gilbert would have stored away some information and he welcomed the distraction so his thoughts would not return to Miss Astin.

'It is a fascinating business; I am surprised more people do not consider it for a living. The Astin family has a cousin who makes the coffins and another who is a coffin trimmer – he does all the hinges and the lining. They choose timber based on price… anything from red cedar to ironbark but because they are *The Economic Undertaker*, it is usually an economical timber.'

'Makes sense,' Harland agreed.

Gilbert continued, 'Mr Astin said their business is evolving and more people are asking the family to do everything... to take the body, lay it out, present it for mourning and then bury it. They have a mourning room for the family to view the body in. It seems quite logical to do so and not have the body at home, especially in the warmer months. I remember my Uncle Fred was quite on the nose by the end.'

Harland couldn't help but laugh as they rode the omnibus back to the office. 'Forgive me, Gilbert, I should not make jest of that.'

'That is quite alright, Sir. Uncle Fred was a jolly man, I'm sure he would enjoy our mirth.'

Harland gave his protégé a smile. Gilbert wouldn't be to everyone's taste but he was growing fonder of the detailed young man whose skills might just be an asset to a less-detailed senior detective such as himself.

'Well, the information you gathered is very interesting,' Harland said and saw Gilbert's pleased look as if praise was rarely come by, and not knowing his family situation, perhaps he was a young man devoid of encouragement.

The men were no sooner back in the Roma Street Police Headquarters when the desk sergeant hurried into their office.

'Forget that paperwork, Detective Stone,' the middle-aged man said with a nod to the pile of sightings already received of Zachariah Beaming. 'This is the one.'

Harland stood eagerly and reached for the paper. 'Thank you, Sergeant.' He read aloud, 'It is from a Miss Catherine Tounselle in Melbourne. She was en route to meet her fiancé in Albany, Major Williams, and she believes him to be Zachariah Beaming. He is staying at the Albany Hotel in York Street!' He grinned at the sergeant and then at Gilbert. 'We have him, gents, we have him!'

Lilly and Fergus approached the editor's office with trepidation – everyone did – and as two of the youngest writers, they knew there were many others keen to step into their shoes and sit at their desks.

'Come, come, sit,' he said and they hurried their steps to do so. Mr Cowan studied the pair and Lilly studied him. Considering it was not yet noon, their editor was already dishevelled, the room smelt heavily of cigars, and Mr Cowan looked like he had eaten several journalists for breakfast. She braced.

He slammed his hand on the table making them both jump as he exclaimed, 'Excellent job, keep it coming.'

'Yes sir,' Lilly said and straightened. Her relief was evident and she cast a glance at Fergus who looked equally relieved that he lived to see another day and was not back on writing the shipping news.

Mr Cowan issued orders. 'I want more angles, all angles, and several stories a day. As current as you can, so we have something the opposition doesn't, you hear me?'

'Yes sir,' they both answered.

'I don't know what you're doing to charm the detective and I don't want to know, but keep it up, Lewis. Give me the ladies' perspective... talk to Beaming's victims, anyone who loved him, knew him, the neighbour, and get more of the horror of the man or his normality. Stay on the detective so the moment Beaming is found we are onto it. Get the illustrator drawing the ladies in his acquaintance or the man himself if you can find an image.'

'There is a family portrait too, if the detective will spare it.'

'Excellent. Get it, we'll run it,' Cowan said grinning which was a rare sight and as frightening as his serious countenance. 'Griffiths,' he turned his attention to Fergus, 'I want to know more about this Beaming character. Who is he, and where did he come from? What makes a man commit murder... was he damaged as a child or is he just evil? Got it?'

'Got it, sir,' Fergus said.

'Well get to it. Copy deadline by 4pm!' he snapped and they both raced out of the office, allowing each other a grin when out of his sight. They hurried back to their desks to confer.

'Thank you, Lilly, thank you for involving me,' Fergus gushed.

'You are welcome and you need not thank me again, it was I who was keen to work with you,' she assured him. 'Now, why don't you write of Beaming, while I visit the detective and get the names of any ladies in Beaming's life and call on them? I will collect the family portrait and get that to the illustrator as well.'

'Excellent. Take me with you to see the detective, if you will, and I will get a few lines from him on what he thinks of the character of Beaming and if he has seen his like before.'

'Yes, good idea,' Lilly said and they grabbed the necessities for their interviews and departed, knowing the envious eyes of the department were on them. Every journalist worth their salt wanted this story and the two youngsters had nabbed it. Now they just had to keep it, and Lilly hoped Fergus would not have grounds to regret being involved. Since she had a taste for real reporting, there was no going back to births, marriages and deaths... she would rather die!

Chapter 26

GILBERT WATCHED IN AWE and excitement as his superior, Harland Stone, set the wheels in motion to capture the villain that had murdered at least two women, four children and a man, and maybe more innocents. Gilbert marvelled at how – despite the excitement around him – Detective Stone remained calm and in control. The desk sergeant allocated a younger constable to take over his post and accompanied Harland to send the missives in morse code to the Albany post office for delivery to the local police station. Police officers and detectives milled around knowing that something was breaking and listened in on the exchange. Gilbert's eyes were huge, Harland's were not as he dictated the message.

'*Wanted for murder, Zachariah Beaming, staying at Albany Hotel in York Street possibly under the name Williams. Dangerous and unpredictable. Departure imminent to meet his fiancée, act quickly. Secure and arrange deportation to Brisbane for trial. Take assistance, public outcry expected. Please advise Detective Harland Stone by return message when suspect detained.*'

'That is sent, Detective,' the desk sergeant announced with great aplomb and many of the gathering men cheered and slapped Harland on the back. He thanked them and left Gilbert to wait on word back from Western Australia, while he took the stairs to update his superior before the press caught word of it. When he returned an hour later, the crowd was no longer around reception and the desk sergeant smiled at him.

'All done, Sir, Gilbert has the reply.'

Harland smiled and thanked the man. On arriving in his office, he found the first of the press had arrived.

'Word travels fast,' he said after a quick introduction to Fergus Griffiths who was in Lilly's company.

'Is there a breakthrough, Detective? Your partner would not say,' Lilly asked.

'Well done, Gilbert,' Harland said with a smile and accepting the telegram response from Gilbert, read it quickly and felt the weight fall off his shoulders. The man had been arrested. He returned his attention to Lilly and Fergus and said, 'Yes, Miss

Lewis, Mr Griffiths, there is a breakthrough and I cannot see the harm in you having the lead story.'

She gasped and sat immediately, pencil at the ready as Fergus hurried to join her, ready to ask his own questions. The room buzzed with the drama afoot! The next morning's newspaper would be magnificent indeed.

That evening the *Vexed Vixens* were gathered at Miss Emily Yalden's small townhouse in Bowen Hills on Montpelier Hill for their regular get-together and Phoebe raced in late, the last to arrive. Lilly had arrived just moments before her having filed her story including the portrait of Beaming and his family.

'My apologies, ladies,' she said, removing her hat and kissing each on the cheek. 'I had an urgent job to do for Detective Stone and I could not leave until I was satisfied it was done.'

'I too have just arrived,' Lilly assured her and then realised. 'Oh! You were working on the poor lady found under the hearthstone then!'

'I was indeed,' Phoebe said, accepting a cool glass of punch from Emily, and sitting beside Kate. 'An aunt is to identify her in the morning.'

'My heart aches for that poor deceased woman, and her mother. I cannot imagine the young lady's terror and loneliness,' Kate said placing her hand on her heart. 'Not to mention the task ahead for the poor aunt who has to identify her. What a ghastly chore.'

'Horrendous indeed! So we must never allow any of us to be separated or marry a man we have not researched thoroughly,' Lilly said. 'Although some men are terribly good at being bad without anyone knowing.' She could think of several in her workplace.

'Which reminds me, Lilly, I must congratulate you,' Emily said. 'Goodness, the front page, not once, not twice, but nearly every day. Your name emblazoned across the page – Lilly Lewis, reporter.'

Lilly grinned with delight; her eyes shone with excitement.

'You are amazing, your stories are amazing,' Kate agreed.

'I could not be prouder if I were blood-related,' Phoebe concurred and Lilly reached for her hand and held it, wishing it so that they were related, by marriage preferably and she was Mrs Julius Astin.

'Who is that Fergus person you are writing with?' Kate asked.

'He is married,' Lilly said and grinned knowing full well the intention of Kate's question.

'Oh, so boring,' Kate said with a sigh. 'Why do single men never come in to get their portraits done by me? It is always families.' She mused, 'Perhaps I should advertise that I do businessmen portraits... present yourself professionally.' She brightened at the thought.

'That is an excellent idea, Kate,' Emily said and then brought the discussion back on topic. 'Do you know what this Mr Beaming was like, Lilly? He was clearly a scoundrel but did he fool people?'

'It is timely you ask because that is one of the topics of our articles tomorrow.'

'I shall wait until then to read it in black and white,' Emily said pleased and turned her attention to Phoebe. 'Did you, um... speak with the young lady?'

Phoebe shook her head. 'Not all souls appear to me and she did not. I did my best work to honour her though. She was a handsome woman.'

'So terribly sad.' Kate sighed. 'Let's talk of something cheery.' She looked around the room tastefully decorated in shades of cream and pale blue. 'I so envy you having your own abode, Emily. I have been sorely tempted to sleep at my photographic studio some nights just for the chance to know the freedom of not living with my parents.'

'I do love it,' Emily said eyeing her surroundings, 'and it would not have been possible if my aunt had not bequeathed me a sum to buy it. For me, it was fortunate she had no children of her own. My mother has still not recovered from my moving out and not for the purposes of marrying.'

The girls chuckled at the thought as they moved to the table to enjoy the spread Emily had prepared for them.

'This looks wonderful, how you had time to do it is beyond me,' Phoebe said. 'So let us share the highlights of our week. Do tell us the latest happenings at Miss Emily Yalden's Deportment School for Young Ladies.'

Emily smiled. 'Well, this will cheer you up. A lady presented herself on my doorstep just this week to ask do I teach my students the wiles to acquire a husband. Mind you some schools do so, but not mine.'

'So, what did you say?' Phoebe asked.

'I said, "Madam, I am *Miss* Emily Yalden and if was teaching how to snare a husband, I am hardly the role model for it." I was sure her eyebrows were going to fly off her face she raised them so sharply.' The ladies were now well amused and Emily continued, 'She asked what on earth I teach them then as if there could be no more valuable lessons for a young lady than securing a husband! I said aside from deportment and ladylike behaviour, I taught how to manage your household, which of your cutlery you would use for various courses, how you will be judged by the company you keep, what perfumes not to wear to important functions for fear of overpowering the guests, and five interesting conversation starters. She said she would think about it.'

'Bravo you,' Lilly said and laughed. 'I must remember to mind the company I keep.' She teased giving them all a wary look as if sizing them up and enjoying their reactions. She turned to Kate. 'It will be hard for you to top your last effort having taken a photo of the Beaming family but what is news in your world, dear Kate?'

'I still cannot believe they were in my studio,' Kate said with her usual penchant for drama, 'but I do have a good tale. A lady returned with her family portrait that I had taken six months past at least and accused me of stealing her husband's watch.'

'Goodness, why?' Phoebe asked.

'Because he has lost it but was wearing it in the portrait so, after extensive searching, they determined my camera was able to steal goods from people while taking their image.' The ladies found humour in the very notion. Kate continued, 'If only that were true. A lady wore the most beautiful diamond necklace recently to a sitting and I could see myself in that.'

'What did you do about this accusation?' Phoebe asked.

'I told her she was ridiculous and that she should call the police if she truly believed it. I have not yet been arrested or questioned so perhaps she has decided not to pursue it.'

'I just hope she returns to apologise should they find it,' Emily said most indignantly on Kate's behalf.

'As do I. Tomorrow, I am photographing a dog, a rather handsome one. His eccentric owners want a portrait of the handsome hound.'

'Goodness, what lives we lead.' Emily chortled. 'Tomorrow I will be teaching young ladies how to drink tea daintily while sitting on a sofa, Kate is photographing a canine, Phoebe is hosting a viewing of the deceased, and Lilly is writing of scoundrels!'

They continued to laugh as they mused on their lives and shared the meal. And then, in a soft voice, Phoebe said, 'I think Julius is in love.'

All eyes snapped to look at her and questions were fired her way.

'With whom?' Lilly exclaimed.

'How do you know? Why do you think so?' Emily asked rationally.

'How did he meet her?' Lilly persisted, 'have you met her?'

'Has she a brother?' Kate asked.

The reality of the moment hit Lilly – her career had gone forward with leaps and bounds, but her love life had not. The rest of the conversation was lost to matters of the heart and Lilly was sure hers was breaking.

Chapter 27

AMBROSE ASTIN WAS AT work early the next morning, just on eight o'clock. It was not like him to arrive before the opening hour but with Harland bringing the aunt of the unidentified bride in to hopefully identify the woman, Phoebe assisting with the viewing, and Julius meeting with Miss Forrester, his grandfather had asked him to be on hand to hold the fort as needed. He sat in the kitchen enjoying a breakfast prepared by Mrs Dobbs who seemed to always be there no matter what time he came or went – not that he was complaining.

'I must say that young lady has done a very fine job of reporting that horrible story, I would not have the countenance for it,' she said, filling Ambrose's teacup and seeing the story that had his focus.

'She is wonderful, is she not?' Ambrose said, distracted and did not see the small knowing smile that Mrs Dobbs expressed behind his back. He raised the cup to his lips and drank as he read Lilly's account.

THE WINDSOR MURDER.
ARREST OF THE SUPPOSED MURDERER IN
WESTERN AUSTRALIA.
SUCCESSFUL WORK OF THE DETECTIVES.
IDENTITY CLEARLY ESTABLISHED. PRISONER DUE
IN BRISBANE SOON.
by Lilly Lewis and Fergus Griffiths.

The work of Detectives Harland Stone and Gilbert Payne in the investigation of the circumstances of the murder at Windsor has been sharp, able, and successful, with the arrest of Mr Zachariah Beaming in Western Australia and the prisoner en route to Brisbane.

They have now only to lay hands upon the mysterious male tenant of 57 Andrew Street to be able to place him in the dock, with a mass of evidence against him which can only have one result, and that one which should be eminently satisfactory to justice.

The discovery of a woman's body under the hearthstone in Windsor and the subsequent discovery of a woman and her four children under the hearthstone in Rainhill, UK, has been previously reported by this newspaper, and today, identification is expected of the Brisbane woman courtesy of a relative of the family who believes the victim to be her niece. The woman died from a blow that fractured the skull.

The character of the man

The man in question is of gentlemanly appearance and speaks with a British accent, more specifically of Lancashire origin. He is confirmed to be of 35 years of age, 5ft. 10 inches, stoutly built, with broad square shoulders, fair fresh complexion, fair hair, and considered attractive to the ladies.

He had successfully attained another fiancée, despite killing two women – the first his wife, and the second believing herself to be. The fiancée, Miss Catherine Tounselle, told this newspaper that "he showered me with love and affection, and even though I was in two minds about the relationship, I was never in any doubt of his feelings for me."

Detective Stone said the criminal was a "shrewd and callous man who gave no thought to the women who trusted him nor the children who relied on his protection."

It has also come to light that the accused has a police record for petty crimes including thieving and was alleged to have recently sold part of his murdered wife's jewellery and his tools to Messrs. McLean Bros. & Rigg. He also bought two diamond rings, omitting to pay for one which was valued at £35.

Arresting the alleged murderer

After determining the identity of the suspected murderer with assistance from Miss Anne Norris, a woman who declined Beaming's offer of marriage, Detectives Stone and Payne received word from Mr Beaming's fiancée that she was en route to meet him and advised of his location in Albany. He was soon to begin work as an engineer with a mining firm.

The detectives swiftly acted to secure his arrest and the accused will be brought to Brisbane by special conveyance for trial. Our Southern Cross correspondent telegraphed late yesterday afternoon to advise there was quite a sensation upon Mr Beaming's arrest and the accused almost received a public lynching. He faced a rowdy reception and was escorted by a policeman on each side, and additional police to keep the crowd at bay.

The manager of the hotel where Beaming was found in residence, informed us that the suspect was a very quiet and civil man, and the general impression is that he is one of the last who might be suspected of having a terrible crime on his conscience.

Detective Harland Stone appealed for calm on the pending arrival of the prisoner and assured citizens that the prisoner would receive the full extent of the law warranted to him.

Ambrose finished the article and his breakfast at about the same time and rising, said, 'Excellent.'

'Which one, dear?' Mrs Dobbs asked, taking his plate with a teasing smile.

'Both, Mrs Dobbs. Miss Lewis is such a brilliant writer, and you are such a magnificent cook.' He kissed her on the cheek making her chuckle. 'I don't know why you haven't been snapped up. If I was thirty years older...'

She laughed again. 'You would still be too young! Forty years older more like it, you young flatterer, but thank you, dear.'

'No, thank you, Mrs Dobbs. You brighten our day, and you make it much easier for us to do business.' He did not realise the impact his words had on her, but Mrs Dobbs's eyes teared up. Kind words were few and far between since the death of her husband and the work had given her purpose.

Ambrose turned hearing the back door open, and his grandfather entered.

'See there are benefits to arriving at work early, lad,' Randolph said seeing Mrs Dobbs cleaning up the breakfast dishes. 'Good morning, Mrs Dobbs.' He greeted her with a smile.

'Good morning, Mr Astin,' she replied and set about making him a cup of tea.

'Had I known,' Ambrose agreed.

'I like to see you men have a few good meals a day. Lord knows what you eat after hours, except for you, Mr Astin, of course,' she said referring to Randolph's wife and Ambrose's grandmother. 'I'm sure Mrs Astin looks after you very well.'

'She does, but she doesn't like me to have too many sweets. One of us is minding my figure and it is not me,' he jested. 'Thank goodness for you, Mrs Dobbs.' He nodded to the biscuit tin. Standing beside Ambrose at the table, he tapped the newspaper and added, 'That was an excellent story by Miss Lewis and her fellow journalist.'

'She is amazing,' Ambrose said and sighed, not seeing the exchanged looks between his grandfather and Mrs Dobbs. He followed his grandfather through to the front reception area.

'I have a meeting with a couple this morning to organise a funeral for their dearly departed,' Randolph said. 'Phoebe will be with the detective for the identification and Julius—'

'—will be staring with a lovelorn look at the lovely Miss Forrester,' Ambrose broke in.

Randolph smiled and tried to unsuccessfully reprimand his grandson. 'Now don't go teasing your brother, Ambrose, I think this might be important to him.'

'He expects nothing less than my teasing,' Ambrose protested and then softened. 'Don't worry Grandpa, there is nothing I want more than to see him happy, I promise you.'

Randolph gave him an affectionate look. 'As do I. I want to see all of you happy for that matter. She's quite special Miss Forrester.'

'They have a bit in common – they are both far too responsible and serious for their own good. Although I did meet her at a funeral, so Miss Forrester may not always be as sober.'

'True, and if you were the eldest as they both are, you might be as solemn as your brother,' Randolph said, opening the diary to confirm the day's appointments. They heard Phoebe arriving and after greeting them, she hurried downstairs to check again in the morning light on the lady she prepared for viewing.

With a glance at his timepiece, Randolph leant over and turned the sign on the door to "Open".

'Let the day begin,' Ambrose said theatrically and no sooner had he said the words than the door opened and Julius and Harland came in together and made their way down to see Phoebe. Next came Randolph's clients who he showed through to the meeting room and Mrs Dobbs prepared refreshments for them. Bennet entered moments later with a mature woman to identify the lady in question and was shown downstairs to Phoebe's room where Harland awaited.

Ambrose stood alone for a moment catching his breath from the whirlwind entries when Julius came up the stairs and with a glance to the clock, looked out of the curtains, searching the street.

'Are you feeling alright, brother?' Ambrose asked.

'Yes. And you?' Julius enquired with a look his brother's way.

'Fine. You are not nervous?'

Julius frowned at him. 'Why would I be?'

Ambrose gave a small shrug. 'Here she is now,' he said with a glance at the window and Julius stiffened and turned. Ambrose grinned. 'Oh, sorry it was not her after all. Lucky you are not the nervous type.'

Julius turned on his brother. 'Ambrose. Just once, please don't—' He stopped speaking and shook his head, looking to the outside.

Ambrose felt a tinge of guilt. 'Forgive me, Julius. You tend to whatever you need to do, and I will call you when Miss Forrester arrives. Have you got the keys for next door?'

Julius patted his jacket pocket. 'Yes.'

It was such a rare sight to see Julius slightly ruffled that Ambrose could not help but stare at his brother whose routine and mannerisms were usually so focused and deliberate.

'Right then. Well, your necktie is not quite straight.'

'Is it not?' he asked and studied Ambrose for a moment to see if the words were in jest. Satisfied with Ambrose's sincerity, he rushed off to repair it, leaving Ambrose smiling. It was perfectly straight but at least his brother had something to fidget with while he waited.

Chapter 28

VIOLET DECIDED TO WEAR her mourning clothes to her meeting with Mr Julius Astin. After all, she was visiting a place where mourning was expected and should clients be in attendance, it seemed a respectful gesture. It also allowed Julius to see her workmanship again and her mourning dress was exceptionally well made, she would have it no other way in her grandmother's honour.

As she neared *The Economic Undertaker*, right on time, she took a moment to consider the momentous nature of the day. To others, it might seem like any other ordinary day as they went about their business, but for the Forrester family – namely herself and Tom – it was a day that would mark their future. Tom would gain an apprenticeship and be taught a trade that would serve him well throughout his life, and she would be gainfully employed with a wage. Not surviving from dress to dress. Violet could not believe her good fortune and was wary of thinking too much about it until it was agreed upon and a certainty, lest pride should be her downfall or hope be hindered.

Approaching the shop, she felt a flutter of nerves; it had nothing to do with Julius Astin, she told herself, it was about her exciting future. She had to think of him as her superior, her employer, and nothing more. Otherwise, she risked losing it all or having her heart broken when he paraded other women before her – surely his future wife would regularly visit his work practice. She put her shoulders back and banished the thought.

This was a happy day and she was a most fortunate woman.

There was nothing more for it, she had arrived and pushing open the door, Violet relaxed at seeing the younger Astin brother behind the counter. His smile was infectious.

'Good morning, Mr Astin.'

'It is indeed, Miss Forrester, and I was up most early to enjoy it.'

'Were you now? That sounds as if it is not a regular habit?' she said closing the door behind her.

'Right you are. I am more of a night owl than a morning lark. And yourself?'

'I am the lark,' she said with a laugh.

'Then you and Julius will be in competition to see who arrives first at work. He finds joy in the dawn for some unbeknown reason.' As he spoke, Julius entered the room, his presence creating a shift in the air. Violet noticed for just a moment he looked as uncomfortable as she felt, perhaps even pleased to see her. Julius's eyes darted to his brother and then back to her, his expression shifted to that of calm and aloofness.

'Miss Forrester,' he said with a small bow and Violet reciprocated. His eyes travelled over her but respectfully as if he assessed her dress, her features, her thoughts, her soul.

'Well, you two run along and I'll manage everything here,' Ambrose said smiling from one to the other.

Julius addressed Violet. 'Miss Forrester, I know you have not accepted the role as such, but as our meeting room is occupied, I thought we might talk in the space I have leased.'

'Thank you, Mr Astin, I would like to see the space.' She bid Ambrose farewell and exited as Julius held the door open for her.

'Try not to burn the place down,' Julius said under his breath.

'From memory, that was you, was it not?' Ambrose shot back and Violet's startled expression told Julius she had heard it all.

'A small bonfire when we were children playing in Grandpa's shed, nothing important,' he assured her with a smile.

'Goodness, your poor grandparents!'

'Indeed.'

She walked beside him toward the shop next door, conscious of his height and strength. Those large hands that had wrapped around her waist and lifted her so easily into his carriage on the day of her grandmother's funeral, and his handsome face so perfectly groomed that she wanted to touch his cheek and inhale his scent. She stood back as he unlocked the door.

'If you will permit me to enter first in case there is anything untoward?' he said with a glance around.

'Of course,' she said and waited a moment on the doorstep until he returned for her and welcomed her in.

'Were you expecting something untoward?' she asked with a hint of humour in her voice and a raised eyebrow.

'Always.' Leaving the door open for propriety, he smiled at her before explaining, 'My detective friend has advised that several of the empty buildings have encouraged men intent on illegal activities to take up residence. I would hate for you to startle a man sleeping off his night's proclivities.'

'Heaven forbid,' she agreed and watched as he pulled open the curtains across the front windows allowing the light to stream in. She turned around to survey the room and found it quite lovely. The timber floors were in excellent condition, there was plenty of light from large floor-to-ceiling windows, and a beautiful counter with shelves of mahogany timber mounted behind it on the wall.

'My cousin has started outfitting it for me and tells me it will be ready to open in one month if... well...'

'Nothing untoward happens?' she finished his sentence.

'Precisely,' he said with a small smile. 'I work in the death industry, Miss Forrester, it is always unpredictable.'

'I imagine so,' Violet agreed. 'Your cousin has done marvellous work.' She ran her hand along the counter moving away from Julius.

'Lucian is very talented. Your brother would be engaged in similar work with him, there is a great deal of variety – from counters to coffins.'

'All good skills for the future,' Violet agreed. 'My father used to say if a man was good with his hands, he could always sustain himself in times of hardship.'

What am I saying? She blushed to realise how her words might be misconstrued but Julius did not allow her to feel uncomfortable, as she imagined Mr Ambrose Astin might have made much of the same situation.

'I could not agree more,' Julius continued as if her words held no innuendo. 'Not everyone is a brilliant scholar, but everyone can work hard and learn trades to sustain themselves and their family.'

Violet noticed it was then Julius's turn to look uncomfortable at the talk of providing for a family; they both appeared to be very good at expressing the innocuous in a fashion that made it not so.

He swallowed and continued, 'I was envisaging this small room might be turned into two fitting rooms.' He indicated to the left and then walked behind the counter to a door which he opened onto a large room. Violet followed. 'I thought this would be a good staff room for lunch and rest breaks, and the area near the door could be for storage.' He indicated one-third of the room.

'I think that would work splendidly,' Violet agreed and after a glance around, she walked back to the main room. 'This is a lovely space. I can see it looking most attractive with some tasteful fittings, obtained with very little outlay,' she added quickly lest he thinks she was a spendthrift.

He nodded and indicated a small table and two chairs near the window that looked as if they had been placed there temporarily during the planning phase. Several reams of paper and a pencil sat on top. He quickly grabbed a white handkerchief from his pocket and wiped the seat for Violet.

'Thank you,' she said taking a seat. 'My brother often takes pleasure in wearing black; he reminds me it is one of the colours that allow you to get dirtied without fear of ruining your clothes.'

'Yes, it has worked to Ambrose's advantage for years,' Julius joked as they both spoke of their brothers. Mrs Dobbs appeared in the window walking towards them with a tray. Finding the door open she stepped in.

'I thought the young lady might like a cup of tea as you discuss the future.'

'I am sorry, I should have thought to offer you tea,' Julius said rising and clearing the table so Mrs Dobbs could place the tray in front of them. 'Thank you, Mrs Dobbs. You have met Miss Forrester I believe?'

'I have, hello again, Miss Forrester, and do not fret, Julius, it is my job, dear, to remember tea,' she said with a kind smile. 'That mind of yours is full of many other important things.'

'Thank you, how kind,' Violet said.

'Shall I leave you to pour?' Mrs Dobbs asked.

'Of course, and thank you, Mrs Dobbs,' Violet said, taking it upon herself to pour their tea as Mrs Dobbs departed. 'Milk, sugar?'

'Just milk, thank you,' Julius said watching her pour.

'That is how I take mine too.' *Why did I say that? As if he cares how I take my tea!*

She tried harder. 'I hope this is not keeping you from your work, Mr Astin.' She had never felt so nervous pouring two cups of tea in her entire life. If only he could look elsewhere, the passing pedestrians perhaps.

'Not at all, Miss Forrester. This is, without doubt, my most important meeting today,' he said.

She finished pouring and putting the pot down, handed him a cup, their eyes meeting as he thanked her. She noticed he waited until she had sipped before he did so himself.

'Will you tell me of your decision now, Miss Forrester?'

Violet smiled and met his gaze. 'Mr Astin, I am very grateful and flattered by your offer.' She noticed the look of apprehension as if he was sure she was going to decline; she could not imagine what would make him think so. 'As for my brother, Tom, he is exceedingly excited at the thought of the apprenticeship, as am I, and I gratefully accept on his behalf.'

Julius smiled which nearly took her breath away at the beauty of him.

'That is good news,' he said. 'Lucian will be pleased as well, as he is in need of someone and time-poor to start interviews. If you accept the manageress role, you will see Tom coming and going here for a short time until the job is done,' he added.

'As to that, I am concerned that—' She hesitated as if searching for words.

'Miss Forrester, you need not be—'

She held up her hand. 'Forgive me for interrupting, Mr Astin, but please do not distress yourself. I am not concerned regarding matters of a personal nature if that is what you are thinking... I know we spoke of that.'

He nodded and let her speak.

'I am concerned that I have so little experience in managing anything but my own time, that I will not know how to do the role and will fail you.'

There, I've said it, she thought, feeling both annoyed at herself for admitting it and relieved at her honesty that should she fail, she had at least been open from the beginning of negotiations.

He appeared to consider her words and then Julius relaxed, his shoulders slumped slightly and he leaned forward.

'I do not share your concerns, Miss Forrester. The gown you are wearing is striking, my sister, Phoebe, said the same of your workmanship with the dress you wore yesterday.'

'Thank you.' Violet could not but smile with delight.

'Tell me,' Julius continued, 'have you met the delivery dates for your clients' orders?'

'I am proud to say every single one, even when pressed, I did not disappoint.'

'And have you ordered fabric, haberdashery items, itemised orders, and recorded client measurements?'

'It would be impossible to do the job without doing so, and I have always paid my suppliers on the monthly date when due.'

Julius nodded satisfied and continued, 'Have you taken over your grandmother's work as needed in her last days and on her death, and organised Tom to collect materials and deliver garments, as such managing them both?'

Violet thought on this for a moment. 'Yes, it is true, I have done that if you consider them to be staff.' He smiled and she marvelled at her increase in confidence. 'I think this is a job interview,' she said, challenging him.

'It is. A tough one would you not say?' Julius said and she laughed.

'Continue. I am stronger than I look,' Violet assured him.

'I imagine you are, Miss Forrester.'

She felt herself redden slightly at the compliment and then he continued with his barrage of questions.

'Have you good taste, in your opinion, that would allow you to contribute ideas to make this room a respectable and welcoming place of business – not so ostentatious that clients of lower means would be frightened to enter, but respectable enough for clients of higher standing to feel at home as well?'

"I believe so,' she said, her eyes twinkling with excitement. 'I have no examples to present you but I can imagine the lighting, fresh flowers, and select pieces of upholstered furniture that would be so tasteful, and less is better,' she said looking around with increasing confidence. She returned her attention to Julius to find him watching her with an unreadable expression

– was it admiration? Her throat felt dry in his presence, and he persisted, asking, 'Can you make mourning clothes at the varying stages of mourning, from black through to the lighter colours when appropriate for those wishing to purchase at different stages of grief?'

'Yes, we would cater for the full black dress for the first year-and-a-half of mourning, plus stock some tasteful grey and lavender gowns for the last six months of half-mourning. Some children's black mourning clothes would not go astray either,' she mused. 'Plus, we must have a range of weeping veils, caps, and bonnets. Oh, and black petticoats and stockings.' She flushed at the mention of the undergarments, but her intent being innocent, she looked up ill at ease, only to find Julius's expression of support and he continued immediately with his questions.

'Have you studied the latest fashion and emulated it?'

'I have indeed. Since you first made your offer, I have also studied the dress materials related to mourning wear. As we are right next door to *The Economic Undertaker*, I feel we need to specialise in very affordable mourning wear – fabrics like bombazine, trimmed with crepe. But we could also stock better quality silk for anyone wishing to have options. As you might have observed, I have embellished my designs a little, like your sister, Miss Astin, also favours, but I will keep this in check in your conservative business, I assure you. Unless of course someone should request the variation in design.'

'I have no further questions. I believe you have experience already in every aspect of my business, you have just not called yourself "manageress" and now you need just apply those talents here.' Julius raised his hands to indicate the surroundings. 'Will you accept my offer, Miss Forrester?'

Violet released a slow breath, feeling so much better and more comfortable with the job offered. 'Mr Astin, thank you, I will happily accept your offer.'

They smiled at each other with obvious delight before Violet looked away and Julius gathered himself.

'Miss Forrester, could you start as soon as possible, tomorrow, or at your earliest convenience? You will be able to put your interior design thoughts to my cousin and then purchase your starting stock. If you have a preferred fabric shop, I will have my bookkeeper set up an account there for you to order as needed and they can deliver. There is much to be done, and you will need to hire at least one assistant dressmaker, to begin with. It might be ideal to have a few dresses on hand from day one that can be fitted to clients.'

'I could not agree more, death comes suddenly sometimes and not all will have a mourning gown on order,' Violet said caught up in the excitement. 'I can start the day after tomorrow. That will give me time to finish my current orders.'

She realised that indicated how little work she currently had commissions for, but Julius had the good grace to ignore her comment and to appear delighted at her announcement.

'Excellent.' He sat back. 'My bookkeeper will manage the accounts and pay wages weekly. Just keep your cash box, orders and receipts and he will tally the rest, I will introduce you to him. And I shall have a key for you on your starting day.' He reached into his pocket and pulled out a folded sheet of paper. 'This is my contract and offer, I hope it is suitable. Lucian will provide apprentice papers to Tom for your perusal as his guardian.'

'Thank you.' Violet nodded, nervous at opening the offer and hoping after agreeing to take the job it would not be an amount that was less than what she was capable of earning in the security of her own surrounds. He presented a pen.

'I shall leave you momentarily to read this if you like, or would you prefer to take it and return it to me?'

'I shall read it now, thank you.'

Julius rose and went to the back room where Violet could hear him opening the back door to the lane behind where *The Economic Undertaker* kept their horses, hearses and carriages. She heard a man calling out and the timbre of Julius's voice as he called a reply.

Opening the paper, she admired the penmanship, although it may have been the bookkeeper's and not Julius Astin's fine hand. She nearly dropped the writing implement at the sight of the weekly wage he had allowed for the manageress, with her name beside it. There was no mistake, it was for her.

Was this an error? Surely manageresses did not earn this much.

She quickly read through the rest of the conditions and found it more than generous.

Was Julius Astin providing me with charity in the guise of a very large wage? Was everyone paid as generously?

Violet was annoyed she did not do her research beforehand and asked her neighbours if they knew of anyone in the industry and their earnings.

What to do now?

She heard the back door lock and his footsteps coming back into the room. He paused. 'Do you need longer, Miss Forrester?'

Violet shuffled the papers keeping the one of most concern on the top. 'Mr Astin, forgive my ignorance but this amount seems, well, rather exorbitant.' She saw his frown quickly reappear and she hurried on. 'Not that I am ungrateful, but I would prefer to be paid a fair wage for a fair day's work and not see you out of pocket.'

His countenance relaxed again. 'I assure you, Miss Astin, I will not be out of pocket, I expect this business to be a success. I also had nothing to do with the wage or contract. My bookkeeper manages that side of my business; I believe he does his benchmarking.'

'Of course,' she said feeling foolish. She studied him for a moment, and then hurriedly signed the document, and rose, returning it to him. 'Thank you, Mr Astin. I am grateful for this opportunity.'

'Thank you, Miss Forrester,' he said, his voice low and his tone belaying that he was the grateful party when Violet knew any number of women would have grabbed the opportunity with both hands. 'I was quite convinced you would decline my offer.'

Violet's eyes widened with surprise. 'I wonder whatever gave you that idea?'

'I can't imagine,' he said without any sign of amusement.

She studied him for just a moment expecting him to elaborate, her eyes drawn to his strong jaw and throat, the line of his black necktie. He spoke again and her eyes snapped to his.

'I am grateful for your trust in this burgeoning venture. I shall see you in two days and anticipate you will be ready to outfit the store with stock and staff?'

She could not help but smile. 'I am sure I will not sleep until then with the excitement and my mind ticking over with all there is to do.' Violet realised that drew one's mind to her boudoir and looked uncomfortable again. Words were so deceptive at times.

'Well, if you are working late hours already, I am sure you will earn that income you believe is too large,' he teased in a manner she would expect from his brother.

Violet laughed, pleased by his candour.

'May I see you to a hansom?'

'Thank you, I shall walk, it is a lovely day for it.'

'It is, but I am conscious you have client work to finish on time before starting so soon with the business. Allow me to send you home promptly so I can avail of your services without guilt. The advantage is mine.'

She could not afford a hansom and she was sure Julius Astin knew that. He had a way of getting his way and providing for her without removing her dignity. She gave a small nod of agreement and thanked him as they moved to the footpath and he raised a hand to call a cab and driver. Offering his hand, Julius settled her in the hansom cab. He paid the driver and with a brief nod, turned and moved back inside the business rather hurriedly, glancing down the sidewalk as he did.

When he was out of sight, Violet turned to see what drove him inside with such haste and saw a young lady and her mother arriving at *The Economic Undertaker*.

She smiled and sat back. Yes, it was inevitable that Julius Astin would be pursued by the mothers with eligible daughters, she could not begrudge him that. But for now, she was a store manageress and her first job was to shop!

Chapter 29

Phoebe Astin glanced at Detective Harland Stone standing rigid near the stairs as if he were on sentinel duty, as Bennet led the aunt of the victim down the staircase – or at least they hoped it was the victim's aunt. Failing that, the poor dead woman would remain unidentified until someone stepped forward to claim a missing relation. Phoebe did not often get the chance to study Harland Stone without herself being observed, but he was an interesting man. Handsome, refined of manners, but yet slightly rough in appearance, manly her grandmother would call it. He displayed no evident emotion, similar in that regard to her brother, Julius.

A glance at Bennet and then back to the detective confirmed he was not prone to excitement like Bennet, who seemed to be working hard at restraining his enthusiasm for the identification and letting his overseas clients know the outcome. Harland remained silent and collected. She wondered if he was like a duck – calm on the outside while paddling furiously below the surface. He must have sensed her studying him and turned her way. Phoebe smiled and quickly focussed on the lady on her bench covered in a material sheet.

'He is a handsome one isn't he,' Uncle Reggie said appearing nearby and startling Phoebe. She could not respond with the number of people – none of them family – entering her room and so she gave Uncle Reggie a scolding look which just made him laugh. 'He's the tall, silent type. I imagine he would know how to protect a lady,' Uncle Reggie continued to tease. 'How lovely you would look together, so contrasting. But you will break that other young man's heart who looks like he could be your sibling.' He sighed and Phoebe looked confused and turned to see who Uncle Reggie was looking at – it was Bennet, on the lower stair. She turned back to her ghostly uncle but he was gone.

Does Bennet have feelings for me? But does he not just visit here to see Julius?

There was no time to consider the matter further and she turned to greet Bennet and the mature lady before her who had turned quite pale at the thought of what lay ahead.

'Good morning, Mr Martin, and you must be Miss Stubbings, I am Miss Phoebe Astin. Perhaps you wish to sit a while and have a cup of tea before we proceed?' She saw Bennet's impatient expression but not a flinch from Harland who must have been busier than all of them.

Phoebe indicated a chair and Bennet led the woman there, assisting her to sit.

'That is most kind, Miss... forgive me, I missed your name.'

'Astin, Phoebe Astin. Understandable, I imagine you are quite distracted.'

'Quite so, Miss Astin, it is rather daunting to be here,' she said and with Bennet releasing her arm, she took a moment to look around.

'Of course,' Phoebe said, not unaccustomed to that reaction from visitors to her room or to herself when she was dressed in a less than formal manner. Today she had worn more conventional clothing, a long skirt and blouse, given the nature of the interview at hand. 'Have you been introduced to Detective Harland Stone?'

Harland moved closer, his hat in his hands and undertook formal introductions.

'I am grateful for you finding this young lady, whether it be my niece or someone else's child, Detective, so she can be buried in holy ground.'

'That is my desire too, Miss Stubbings,' Harland said. 'We would like to give this lady her name and a grave site where the family can visit.'

Miss Stubbings took a deep breath and turned to Phoebe. 'I think it is best if I make the identification first and then have a fortifying cup of tea afterwards. I'm sure the detective is pressed.'

'Take all the time you need, Madam,' Harland said.

Miss Stubbings thanked him, raised her head and put her shoulders back. 'Duty first, as my father would say.'

'That sounds rather like what my grandfather would say,' Phoebe assured her with a smile. 'Allow me to assist you, and then we will go upstairs to the guest room for tea, it is pleasant there and Mrs Dobbs does like to spoil visitors with her slices.' Phoebe did her best to normalise the occasion as best she could.

Miss Stubbings rose, assisted again by Bennet and with a smile to him and the detective added, 'Forgive me for being so silly. I assure you I have endured many challenges in life and am no wilting flower.'

Harland moved towards the body and spoke to distract and reassure the lady as she came to join him. 'Miss Stubbings, no apology is necessary. We all react to trying situations differently. I have discovered that my young partner likes to know what to expect and is better prepared to deal with it on arrival. For myself, I have found that the more time I have to prepare, my dread rises in equal measure.'

Phoebe was surprised at his sharing of himself to assist Miss Stubbings; she would store away this information and think on it later as to her own reaction under duress, but the aunt was much buoyed.

'Why, Detective, I think you are absolutely correct. I believe the thought of this morning has become larger in my mind than the moment it will take to undertake the task at hand. Thank you.'

Harland gave her a conspiratorial smile and standing side-by-side, they both looked to Phoebe, ready. Bennet joined Phoebe on the other side of the table ready to view the body which he had not seen, the written description supplied by the young woman's mother – the landlady – was the only vision he held. Phoebe slowly drew back the material covering the lady's face and she saw the detective's stance relax slightly. The victim's appearance was much improved. She was a handsome woman of young appearance.

Miss Stubbings clutched Harland's arm. 'Oh, that is her, my dear, dear, niece,' she said and nodded. She reached out with a gloved hand to touch the deceased's face and Phoebe was pleased the glove would mask the cold, stiff feeling of the skin.

Miss Stubbings looked across at Bennet and then to the detective beside her. 'It is her, Miss Eliza Stubbings or Mrs...'

'Mrs Zachariah Beaming or Mrs Zachariah Williams,' Bennet said. 'Let us remember her as Miss Eliza Stubbings.'

'Yes, I think that would be best,' Miss Stubbings said. 'Mr Martin, will you notify her parents?'

'Immediately and advise them of your formal identification,' Bennet said.

Phoebe covered Eliza Stubbings' face and marvelled at Harland's stillness when he must have been keen to depart with the identification in hand.

'Let us go have a cup of tea, Miss Stubbings,' Phoebe said. 'Detective Stone, Mr Martin, will you join us?'

Both men declined.

'Miss Stubbings, I will release the body of your niece now if you care to see to her funeral?' Harland informed her.

'Yes, thank you, Detective. I will.'

'Regretfully I will leave you and go notify the family immediately,' Bennet said. 'But I will return once I have sent the telegram and see you back to your hotel, Miss Stubbings.'

'Thank you, young man, but that is not necessary. I will walk. The fresh air and stroll will give me time to fully recover.'

'Thank you, Miss Stubbings,' Harland said and with a small bow, a grateful look to Phoebe, and a quick clip of Bennet's shoulder, he hurried up the stairs departing the party.

'Could you assist me with an economical but tasteful funeral?' the spinster aunt asked.

'That is what we do best. First, a cup of tea, then I shall ask Grandpa to give you our options – there are only three as simple is best – and do not worry, I will look after your niece. Be assured of that.'

'That is of great comfort,' Miss Stubbings said and looped her hand through Phoebe's arm to be led to tea.

They followed Bennet up the stairs and arriving in reception were nearly bowled over by Julius as he raced inside the office of *The Economic Undertaker*, slammed the door behind, and seeing them, doffed his hat to Miss Stubbings and continued at a great speed to the back door and out.

Ambrose stared surprised and Phoebe saw him gather himself to farewell Harland who left just as quickly through the front door, followed by Bennet. Mrs Reed and her daughter, Hannah, entered moments later, and behind Ambrose, the meeting room door opened and Randolph appeared with a young couple in mourning clothes. Everyone made way to allow them to pass as Randolph saw them to the door. Phoebe directed Miss Stubbings to a small room and Mrs Dobbs appeared.

'Tea is ready, I shall bring it straight in,' she said and disappeared again.

'Ambrose, please send Grandpa in when he is ready, and perhaps you can assist Mrs and Miss Reed,' Phoebe said with a nod of greeting their way. She gave Ambrose a small smile as she disappeared into the room with Miss Stubbings, musing how it was like central railway station for the traffic coming and going at *The Economic Undertaker* this morning.

Lilly Lewis all but leapt on Detective Harland Stone as he exited *The Economic Undertaker*. She had been waiting in a tea house across the street for some time, not wishing to intrude on the identification but watching the procession of people coming and going. She was keen to have the scoop if the lady was identified by the visiting relative. She had also had the unfortunate opportunity to witness Julius Astin showing a beautiful woman to the empty shop next door. Once they entered, she could see no further, until they came out and he put her in a cab and hurried back inside as if the sunlight was going to burn him. She laughed moments later when she saw why – a mother and daughter entering the premises.

But was this other woman his love interest or was it a business arrangement? Why could he not find her interesting and attractive? She was told she was a beauty, and surely her ambition was not a deterrent for a man like Julius Astin. After all, his own sister was different from most and had a profession.

'Detective Stone.' She stepped in front of him forcing Harland to a sudden stop. She saw his grimace but Lilly was quite used to that reaction. Men either seemed to grimace or swoon, there was no in-between measure.

'Miss Lewis,' he said with a curt nod. 'I must be off.'

'Of course. But could you tell me, did she identify her?'

'Yes.'

'Will you give me the victim's name, please? I shall try and get a comment from her relative later but would rather hear it from you and report of your successful outcome, again.' She gave him her best smile and Harland gave her a wry look.

'Miss Lewis, I am sure your charm works on most gentlemen, but unfortunately, you have encountered a hardened soul.'

'I doubt that Detective,' she flattered him. 'Besides, I have reported fairly as promised.'

'You have,' he conceded. He lifted a hand to hail a hansom. Lowering his voice he said, 'The deceased lady is Miss Eliza Stubbings or Mrs Zachariah Beaming or Mrs Zachariah Williams.'

Lilly hurriedly wrote down the name. 'May I travel with you back to the station? The newspaper is nearby and I can get a quote from you en route?'

He smiled. 'Miss Lewis, I believe they are nowhere near each other, but by all means, if you are that determined.' He offered his hand to assist her into the cab as it pulled over. With five brothers, she was not the type to need assistance having spent years playing and fighting with her siblings as if she were a boy, but no woman of sane mind would turn down the opportunity to be treated like a lady by a very handsome man. She waited until the detective was seated opposite and asked, 'Was it the English landlady's daughter?

'Yes.'

She asked a few questions, quickly wrote down the detective's quotes and looked up when finished.

'We are nearing the newspaper; you dropped me here first when you were in a hurry!' she said surprised.

'Yes. You have been most professional, Miss Lewis, thank you. A small detour will not delay me too much and your office was quite a walk from my work.'

She smiled. 'Thank you, Detective, that is most kind of you. The experience has been very rewarding for me professionally and personally. Thank you for trusting me.'

'Where is your partner, Fergus?' Harland asked.

Lilly looked a little sheepish. 'Waiting at the hotel of the lady who was here to identify the victim. We desired an interview whether the victim was known to her or not.'

Harland nodded. 'Of course. Miss Stubbings decided to walk back to the hotel after taking tea with Miss Astin. She was intending to arrange the funeral but I imagine she will not be too delayed.'

'And where is your partner?' Lilly asked.

'Coordinating manpower for the arrival of the accused,' he said and added, 'hopefully.'

Lilly hid her laugh at poor Detective Payne's expense. Changing the subject, she asked, 'Was that a business meeting for Mr Astin this morning... Julius Astin?'

'I could not say.'

'It was personal curiosity, not a professional question,' she clarified, should he think something amiss. 'I saw him entering the store next door that was available for lease.'

'Is that so? Perhaps they are expanding. Death is an industry that will not die out.'

Lilly groaned and he gave her an apologetic look.

'I do not know Julius that well as yet, I have only recently come into his acquaintance.'

'Of course, through Dr McGregor at the morgue?' Lilly asked.

'The very same. They are all involved in end-of-life work.' Harland looked to the outside. 'Here we are then.'

She thanked him, departing the hansom with a small skip down before assistance could be offered. He doffed his hat and the hansom pulled away. Lilly returned her thoughts to matters at hand and raced in to start her piece for tomorrow's newspaper.

Chapter 30

I T WAS A BLUSTERY, warm, but fine April day as Detective Harland Stone stood at the end of the platform where passengers regularly disembarked from ships and ferries. He was surrounded by police officers who valiantly tried to keep an angry, swelling crowd in control. Enraged men, and women in disbelief wielding umbrellas and bags of all sizes, were ready to take justice into their own hands. Despite his disgust of the man, the murderer – Zachariah Beaming – Harland wanted him to be tried and to be found guilty, for the families to have that satisfaction.

'Are you alright, Gilbert?' Harland asked over his shoulder as his young protégé's eyes darted nervously around.

'I am, Sir. I haven't seen a crowd this size since the last country fair but none of them was angry. Quite the opposite.'

'I imagine so.' Harland was amazed so many had arrived at the Dry Dock at South Brisbane to see the arrival of the man accused of murder. He raised his voice. 'Hold steady men.' Some of the younger constables looked fearfully at the burgeoning crowd and the anger radiating from them. 'The good people of our city are not here to harm us or hinder us getting this man to justice,' he said loudly enough that many of the people around nodded in agreement. Several called out, 'Absolutely right, Detective', 'Hear, hear,' and another yelled, 'Make sure you see him hanged' which got a rowdy reception.

He heard his words carried through the crowd, rippling like whispers. He wondered if they should have brought Beaming overland by train all the way instead of just from Perth to Adelaide, but he had thought that was risky as the rail could be delayed. The ship was the best option for the final leg of the journey and he saw the crew anchoring it ready for the passengers to exit, one very unwelcomed passenger in particular.

Harland glanced at the conveyance nearby ready for the delivery of Beaming from the ship to the gaol. In his heart, he did not believe the people would delay their efforts, but they certainly wanted to see the man capable of such brutal crimes against the innocent and the fairer sex and to let him know how they regarded him. After securing Beaming in prison, the next challenge would be the trial. He had heard that Beaming was going to offer a stubborn defence to the charge of murder with the able solicitors he had engaged. Harland could not imagine what that defence could possibly be – murder was murder and, in this case, there was no doubt of it.

Unless, of course, he will attempt to plead insanity.

The thought angered Harland even more. His eyes never stopped scanning his surroundings: the crowd, the ship, Gilbert, the constables, as he absorbed the scene looking for trouble to quell it and keep order. It was then he saw a hansom cab just on the fringe of the gathering and a lady and man standing on the seat where the driver normally sat. It was Miss Lilly Lewis and her reporter partner, Fergus Griffiths.

Good grief, this woman would go to any length to get a story.

He almost admired her for it if she were not in a situation that might turn dangerous. At last, the ship passengers began to disembark and Harland turned to the sea of black uniforms around him.

'Ready men,' he said loudly and then turned to the crowd, speaking as loudly as he could and hearing the hush descend as they leaned forward to catch his words.

'Ladies and gentlemen, please do not hinder our attempt to get this brutal man to justice. Miss Eliza Stubbings and Mrs Beaming's family deserve that.'

There were more nods, calls of agreement and support, but nevertheless, they surged forward to see the accused, and there he was, his hands restrained in front, being escorted off the ship. Small, ordinary, respectable looking. No monster, nothing that would say 'killer.' Harland heard the nearby comments.

'—is that him?'

'—that can't be him, he looks like any man.'

'—I'd like to bury him under the bloody hearthstone!'

With a nod to Gilbert, Harland and his partner stepped forward and accepted the man from the authorities. Harland checked Beaming's restraints and satisfied, Gilbert and Harland flanked each side of the man and started to walk him to the vehicle on hand.

'Good God,' Beaming said, eyes wide at the crowd before him. 'Do not let them near me.' He looked pleadingly at Harland.

'Your comfort is of no concern to me, Mr Beaming. If I had my way, I'd release you to them right this minute,' Harland hissed in the man's ear. 'But I wish to protect and keep you alive so you may face the full extent of the law.'

I could snap your life out in a moment, Harland thought, his anger rising, but he kept it in check, put his head down and pushed the man forward, Gilbert gripping on the other side, attempting the same. The police officers swarmed around the three men, and the crowd pressed into them, yelling and screaming abuse.

The shortest journey took the longest time, but Harland bundled the man into the van and secured the lock, standing back and taking a deep breath.

'Gilbert, you go ahead and prepare the officers at the gaol, I will ride with the driver. Men, begin to clear the way for us,' he said issuing orders and the constables moved in front of the carriage creating a path for its journey. He hoped that such a man would never be released again. As Harland settled into the seat beside the driver, he acknowledged Miss Lewis as he passed.

He could not help but reflect that his new case with his new department had been more dramatic than he could have ever imagined. Quite satisfying really and the first of many with young Gilbert Payne by his side. The young man acquitted himself well under pressure. Harland turned his attention to getting Zachariah Beaming to the cells.

Chapter 31

THE NEXT DAY, PHOEBE Astin's behaviour was quite out of the ordinary and her grandfather was pleased about it. Dressed in a slimline, dark navy dress with the smallest bit of cream lace around the neck and sleeves, she looked dignified and demure. Her hair was tied in her customary fashion with a lace strip of fabric at the back, and she had chosen a hat of matching colour for the outfit. It was tasteful and most becoming.

'Perhaps I should not go in case you get busy,' Phoebe said, looking from Julius to Ambrose and back to her grandfather.

'Nonsense, it is only one day, and you deserve a break,' Randolph said. 'It will do you good to step out and I like Miss Lewis, it pleases me to think of you two progressive young ladies taking on the world.'

Phoebe smiled delightedly. 'Thank you, Grandpa.' She saw her grandfather glance at Ambrose and Julius and they added their support.

'Go by all means,' Ambrose said. 'You are lucky Miss Lewis secured seats in the courtroom. Thousands are wishing to attend from what I hear on the streets.'

'The power of the press,' Randolph said. 'She does deserve it. The coverage has been excellent.'

'We will manage, Phoebe,' Julius assured her. 'The dead are not going anywhere and you are up to date. Should we get any requests, we will add a day to our delivery or showings.'

She smiled and exhaled with relief. 'Thank you all, I shall go then.'

'And report back, dear,' Mrs Dobbs said entering the room and the conversation. 'I imagine it will be a most passionate trial.'

The door of *The Economic Undertaker* opened and Lilly Lewis stuck her head in. 'Goodness! All the handsome Astin men in one place!'

Phoebe and Mrs Dobbs laughed, and Ambrose teased, 'Some more handsome than others.' Julius rewarded him with a grimace.

'I am ready,' Phoebe said. 'I don't wish to hold you up.'

The ladies were seen off with warnings to be careful, and departed, arriving at the courthouse well in time. Seated,

Phoebe could not believe the number of ladies present – clearly affronted by the attack on the two wives and children – and many were dressed so gaily; several even had opera glasses. Both Phoebe and Lilly had dressed sombrely for the occasion as appropriate.

'Have you been in a court hearing before?' Lilly asked.

'Never.'

Lilly nodded and explained the seating while they waited for the trial to begin. 'That is the witness box,' she said pointing to a seat that seemed to take centre stage.

'How frightening it must be to sit and face everyone to give evidence,' Phoebe said with a small shudder.

'I believe some enjoy the theatrics of it.' Lilly continued, 'In front of where the judge will sit is the barristers' table and at the other end is the counsel for the defence, which will be Beaming's team.'

Phoebe studied them and wondered how they must feel about defending such a man. 'Is it all press people sitting here behind the barristers?'

'Yes, three rows for us and the illustrators. It is the story of the year!'

Phoebe squeezed Lilly's hand and whispered, 'I know this trial is for a dastardly crime, but it is most fascinating. Thank you for letting me accompany you.'

'It is a pleasure. We were allocated two tickets and my editor was happy for me to see the story through. Fergus will attend tomorrow with me, but today he is outside, talking to the witnesses before they reach the stand,' Lilly said, with her pen and pad ready. 'I can't thank you enough, Phoebe.'

'But you have thanked me enough already,' Phoebe assured her. 'You did it all yourself, I did nothing but provide an introduction.' She pointed. 'Oh look, there is Detective Stone.'

They watched as Harland entered, took a seat in the gallery, and moments later the court was called to order. The prisoner was brought in and seated in the dock. He was the picture of misery. The judge arrived and Phoebe marvelled at the ceremony of it all. She could see out the court windows that a huge crowd had arrived outside, and inside the court, every seat was taken, the standing room packed with keen onlookers.

Throughout the morning of the trial, Lilly scribbled copious notes and Phoebe found the ladies' testimonies – which were up first – most interesting. She hoped Harland would be called to the stand today so she could see him in action as she would not be attending tomorrow.

Lilly nudged her and whispered, 'It is Miss Anne Norris's turn. This is the lady who tipped off the police initially and they ignored her. Not Detective Stone of course.'

'Of course,' Phoebe agreed, and she marvelled at Miss Norris's story, her courage and strength. She leaned forward with interest to hear the testimony.

'He knew what women wanted to hear from their lovers, what we needed to hear,' Miss Norris said with a hint of scandal; several women gasped and fanned themselves. 'Even though he exercised an amazing fascination over me, I refused his offer of marriage several times. Something about him frightened me... but I did not know then that he had children and wives strewn around the world.' She held the floor in her assertive and confident manner. 'When Zachariah spoke of how easy it would be to murder and hide the bodies in quick lime and bury them under the hearthstone in the—'

'Order,' the judge called banging his gavel on the timber block in front of him as the court audience reacted to Miss Norris's words. 'Continue please Miss Norris.'

'As I said, when Mr Beaming spoke of using quick lime and then I found a photo of a family including him hidden in a drawer, I immediately went to the police with my suspicions. I was not taken seriously until Detective Stone was given the case.'

Those in the court who knew the detective and most did from the media coverage Lilly and rival newspapers had provided, turned to look at him. Phoebe marvelled at his calm demeanour.

The prosecutor turned to the jury. 'We now know that the family in that photo was Mrs Beaming and the couple's four children, all found deceased and buried under the hearthstone in a house in England. Miss Norris, your common sense and sound intuition may have saved your life.' There was much murmuring and agreement amongst the ladies in the court gallery seats and looks of disgust directed at the accused.

Phoebe was surprised to see Miss Stubbings take to the stand on behalf of her niece, the deceased Miss Eliza Stubbings or the second Mrs Beaming. Phoebe was pleased someone was present to be the voice of Eliza whose funeral was on the morrow.

'My niece was a kind-hearted and obedient girl. She helped her mother in the management of tenants and that is where she met her husband and her fate,' Miss Stubbings said and dabbed her eyes with a white handkerchief trimmed with lace. 'She sailed to this country with him.' She gave Beaming an accusatory glance and turned from him. 'She sailed in good faith as his wife, but did not have the chance to enjoy married life, her new country or experience motherhood.'

The prosecutor turned to the jury. 'On Christmas Eve, Zachariah Beaming, shattered his new wife's skull and buried her, cementing Mrs Beaming or rather, Miss Stubbings as her family prefer the young lady to be known, under the hearthstone.' He raised his voice as the voices in the court rose with shock and horror.

When all was calm again, Miss Stubbings continued, fumbling in a small black purse and retrieving a letter that she unfolded. 'This man is not insane as he claims. He had the wit to send a letter home to Eliza's dear mother saying: "We have spent a happy Christmas. Eliza is the happiest woman ever seen. Fear not, she is most at home with me." That was sent after my poor niece was believed to be dead.' Miss Stubbings folded the note again and put it back in her purse.

Phoebe's hand went to her heart at the deception, as Lilly sat beside her furiously scribbling notes, including recording the reactions of the witnesses and jury. Phoebe was most impressed with her friend.

Next on the stand was the final love of Beaming's life, the woman who was unceremoniously being called "the uncemented bride", Miss Catherine Tounselle. Phoebe saw Miss Tounselle look to another woman seated in the court, who was similar enough in appearance to be her sister. Phoebe believed Miss Tounselle to be the luckiest woman alive as she gave her account to the packed courtroom.

'It was a whirlwind romance on the ship and I confess I enjoyed his company but did not love him. When we came to shore, he departed immediately and I was set to follow. I began to have my doubts but everyone told me love would grow and there was no doubting his affection for me. He gifted me many things which I have since learnt belonged to his dead wife.'

Gasps were heard and heads were shaking in the court as everyone regarded the criminal, Beaming, with disdain. Miss Tounselle continued, 'It was my sister who saved me with a telegram to the hotel midway on my journey telling me to go no further.' She looked to the lady Phoebe guessed earlier was a relation. 'I then hurried out to the street and bought a newspaper only to see the headline "Williams alias Beaming sought for murder". There was a portrait of the man I was going to meet. You can imagine my horror.'

'And how did your sister know of this to warn you if she had not met the man?' the prosecutor asked. 'As you said, he departed once the journey ended.'

'Because he was not able to meet my family before we were betrothed, he gifted me a portrait of himself in a gold frame, and a lock of his hair for me to keep on my person. My sister studied his portrait for some time, commenting on how dignified he appeared. The portrait in the frame was the image in the newspaper. He had cut his family out of it.'

There were mutterings throughout the court about how looks could be deceiving and that the man knew no shame. Then, the prosecutor addressed the jury. 'There is no end to this man's depravity, continue Miss Tounselle, and please tell the jury of this man's request after he was arrested in Albany.'

Miss Tounselle nodded, straightening her stance, and with a quick look at Zachariah Beaming then back to the prosecutor, she said, 'He wrote to me immediately after his arrest professing his innocence, and saying he knew nothing whatsoever about the charge and believed he would have no trouble in clearing himself.'

While the rumble of comments threatened to occasion the judge's ire again, Miss Tounselle opened a folded piece of paper in front of her. Phoebe thought about Lilly's earlier comment; Miss Tounselle did seem to be enjoying being the centre of attention. The young woman raised her voice and said, 'Major Williams, as I knew him by, wrote, "I know my dear Catherine that you could not believe me guilty of such a fearful crime and that is of great comfort to me," and he finished the letter by saying, "if you can send any part of the twenty pounds I sent you for your passage to my solicitor to help to pay for my defence I should be very grateful and please sell the five-stone ring I gave you for whatever you can get for it and send me the money. I will soon get you another." I have sent him nothing.'

The court erupted and the judge adjourned for lunch warning the gallery that he would have them removed if they could not conduct themselves appropriately. Phoebe was relieved to have the break and gather herself. She regularly saw unsavoury sights and heard tales of woe in her role, but the affrontery of this man was something to behold.

Outside of the courtroom, across town, Bennet Martin told his clerk and housekeeper not to disturb him for the afternoon and locking himself in his studio, Bennet passionately painted a new portrait of Miss Phoebe Astin in all her beauty. For days he had been caught up in his client's file with no creative break, now he could indulge. Bennet was a man not accustomed to being denied and soon, he would need to let her know of his intentions to court her and seek Mr Astin senior or Julius's blessing.

Several miles away in the general cemetery, Julius paid the gravediggers who had prepared the plot for Miss Eliza Stubbings's burial tomorrow. He looked down into the deep dirt hole and was saddened to think of another young life returning to the earth before reaching their potential. He thought of the last funeral he attended, for Miss Violet Forrester's grandmother, and the thought of Miss Forrester happily distracted him for the rest of the afternoon.

At the office, preparing the hearse, Ambrose Astin wished he was seated in court beside Miss Lilly Lewis in place of his sister. To see her in action, what a marvel, what an amazing and passionate lady she was. He was sure they were suited.

On their return to the courtroom for the afternoon session, Phoebe and Lilly braced themselves for further admissions – the list of witnesses was considerable, everyone from the man who sold Beaming the quick lime to shopkeepers who knew him by different aliases. The judge called for police evidence and Detective Harland Stone took the stand. Phoebe sat up with great interest. Lilly nudged her and they exchanged a smile.

'He is an interesting man,' Lilly said under her breath.

'Very interesting. He reminds me a little of Julius.'

'Yes, I see that in his stance,' Lilly agreed. 'But he is not as handsome.'

Harland's testimony did not get completed in the afternoon session and he would return to the stand tomorrow. In a matter of days when all witnesses had been presented, the jury took no time to convict Zachariah Beaming and give him the death sentence: he was to be hanged.

But there was still the matter of the death of private investigator, William Walker, and before Phoebe left court that afternoon, Detective Harland Stone secured the outcome she most desired for her recently deceased acquaintance. She clasped her hands in anticipation as Harland brought the matter of the private investigator before the court. Her movement drew Harland's eyes to her momentarily before he turned to address the presiding judge.

'Your honour, we have found evidence that Private Investigator, Mr William Walker, was brutally murdered by the defendant,' Harland said and stopped as the judge called for order at this new outrageous claim of another victim dead by the hand of Zachariah Beaming. Harland continued, 'Mr Walker was hired by Mrs Beaming's family in England when they feared for the whereabouts of their daughter and their four grandchildren. Taking on the case, Mr Walker visited the defendant and got too close to the truth. His skull was smashed by a blunt object and his body was deposited in the river.'

Again, the judge had to call for order and instructed Harland to continue. 'Your evidence, Detective?'

'We found the instrument used to kill Miss Eliza Stubbings or Mrs Beaming the second, buried with her under the hearthstone.' He hesitated knowing the admission to come would cause more disruption, 'A meat hammer.'

There were groans, hands went on hearts and much shaking of heads.

'Our government analyst believes it to be the very same object that killed Mr Walker. He also found hair on it which was visually compared to the victim's hair and judged to be identical in colour and length to Mr Walker's hair.'

Phoebe congratulated herself for cutting a sample before burying Mr Walker and providing the clue to the instrument itself.

Harland added, 'A witness has also confirmed a visit by Mr Walker to the residence of Beaming on the day of Mr Walker's death.'

And then, she saw the stately, kind gentleman – Mr Walker. He appeared next to Harland for no one else's eyes, removed his hat and bowed his thanks to Phoebe. Her hand went to her heart and tears formed in her eyes. And then he was gone just as quickly.

Her work was done.

THE END

Author's notes:

Thank you for reading the first book in the series of the Astin family set in Australia in 1890 – a spin-off from the Miss Hayward and the Detective series, volume 4, *The Mortician's Clue.* I hope you enjoyed it and the incorporated elements of real historic crime in the fabric of the story. The Astin family themselves are fictitious, but *The Economic Undertaker* was a real funeral business in Melbourne possibly around the late 20th century (1890). My journalist husband, who grew up in Melbourne, recalled seeing their faded painted name on the side of a building, but we haven't been able to find out too much more about them.

I am mindful that the crime I have based this on is a tragedy and hence my story is fictionalised, the names are changed, and I have endeavoured to be respectful to the real victims. I am pleased to report that in real life, the criminal also did not get away with it.

Zachariah Beaming was inspired by a true criminal, Frederick Deeming, who murdered his two wives and four children and buried the bodies under the hearthstone in England and Melbourne, Australia. On 23 May 1892, Deeming was hanged for his crime. He wrote an autobiography during his brief stint in gaol, and no doubt his perspective would have been interesting, but it was destroyed.

My Miss Anne Nolan was inspired by the very real Miss Annie Salter who declined the real Frederick Deeming's advances and whose investigation saved her life. She did share her concerns with a police confidant, but the police initially disregarded her suspicions as "unfounded fears of a nervous woman." The police later admitted it was her early suspicions that brought him to their attention when the net grew tighter. The lines in my book where Zachariah Beaming tells Anne that it would be easy to kill and hide a family were the actual words used by Frederick Deeming to Annie and reported in the media.

The murdered bride, *my* Miss Eliza Stubbings was based on Miss Emily Mather. As the story is in the public domain, I have used several of the actual news reports, amending them to change names and add a bit of Lilly Lewis influence (and yes, a stale loaf of bread, an empty brandy bottle, and a tin of condensed milk was all that Deeming left in the house). Oddly, I also toned it down as reporting in the past was much more graphic and factual which readers might find quite shocking today. For example, the description of Miss Mather's body when found was truly confronting and not included in this book. Miss Mather was murdered in 1891, so I have taken a little licence with the date as the book is set in 1890. She also resided in Melbourne but this book is set in Brisbane.

The owner of the house that the real Frederick Deeming was renting was a butcher and he alerted the police after taking a prospective tenant to the house that Deeming and his then-wife, Emily lived in. The smell from the front room was most unpleasant and suspecting the worst, he called the police and Emily's body was found in a shallow grave under the fireplace hearthstone. Interestingly, an old invitation in the name of Deeming's alias, 'Williams' was found in the house, thus alerting the police to the suspect and his name changes.

The telegram "For God's sake, go no further" was real and *my* Miss Catherine Tounselle was based on Miss Kate Rounsvelle, who survived Frederick Deeming, her fiancé. She did immediately acquire the newspaper after receiving the telegram and saw the headline, "Williams, alias Swanson, arrested at Southern Cross".

During the trial, there were three rows of seats allocated to the journalists, and ladies in the gallery did appear on the first day dressed brightly. The next day, it changed and the press reported, "On the second day, after certain severe comments in the press, there were fewer ladies, and they were all attired in sober black; one or two, however, stuck to their opera glasses and greatly annoyed Deeming by long and continual staring at him."

After his hanging, Frederick Deeming was buried in the prison yard of the Old Melbourne Gaol. The real victim, Emily Mather's grave is in Melbourne General Cemetery, Australia (see picture below).

This story of Frederick Deeming and his victims, what became of Annie Salter and the real uncemented bride, Kate Rounsvelle, is told as one of the 18-stories in the non-fiction book I co-wrote with journalist (and husband) Chris Adams – 'Grave Tales: True Crime.' It is available in ebook and paperback and is in Kindle Unlimited. The character of Mr William Walker, the private investigator, is fictitious.

Writing historical fiction is exciting for the opportunities it affords to include and research actual details and events of the time. We are so lucky to have TROVE (the National Library of Australia) and to be able to check facts and even lingo from the day. Often, I will use an expression and sadly, when I check the newspapers of 1890, it did not exist!

Telegrams between Britain and Australia were made possible in 1872 and letters from England could take from a month to four months to reach our shores depending on the ship and the weather.

Photographers in 1890 did have females amongst their ranks like Phoebe's friend, Kate. There were several impressive female photographers at the turn of the century and definitely some pioneering lady photographers in the 1890s including Harriet Pettifore Brims (1864-1939) – a commercial photographer in Queensland. Harriet had her own studio in Ingham and later in Mareeba in 1904. In 1914, she moved to Brisbane. Her work is a record of the people and places of our early days in Queensland.

Deportment schools, like that of Phoebe's other friend, Emily, existed and taught ladies the necessary skills required for acceptance in 1890 society.

As for burials and funeral houses, mourners often waited at the residence, hospital or even a hotel to follow the funeral cortege to the place of burial as featured in this story when Julius and Ambrose collected two corpses and waited as the mourners followed the hearse to the cemetery.

Hatched, matched and dispatched or rather births, deaths and marriage notices were listed in newspaper columns in the era (as they are today) and monthly statistics were often reported such as the following which appeared in a local 1890 newspaper: "The vital statistics for last month are available this morning... 17 males and 21 females were born, 12 males and 3 females died, and there were 11 marriages."

Thank you for reading *The Missing Brides*. Next... another volume with the Astin family – *The Fake Child*.

Emily Mather's grave in Melbourne General Cemetery.

With thanks:

My sincere thanks to **Mary Fuxa** who once again took on the role of beta reader and suffered through the early manuscript! Thank you, Mary – your observations were spot on and I hope I have done your suggestions justice.

And to **Crystal L. Wren** and **Penny Clarkson** for their proofing eyes and picking up my quirks, many thanks.

Finally, my grateful thanks to cover designer, Karri Klawiter – I thought a cover about a lady mortician would be too hard, but wow, look what Karri created. Thank you, ***Art by Karri***.

Also by Helen Goltz:

Miss Hayward & the Detective Series (historical mystery/ romance set in Australia):

Murder at the Freak Show

The Artist's Missing Muse

Mystery at the Asylum

The Mortician's Clue

Murder in Bridal Lane

The Clairvoyant's Glasses (paranormal/romance)

Volume 1 – A vision unexpected

Volume 2 – Time has a shadow

Volume 3 – Love has no bounds

Volume 4 – Fate comes to call.

The Jesse Clarke series (cosy mystery):

Death by Sugar

Death by Disguise

Death by Reunion

The Mitchell Parker series (crime thriller):

Mastermind

Graveyard of the Atlantic

The Fourth Reich

Writing as Jack Adams (mystery suspense):

Poster Girl (stand-alone)

The Delaney and Murphy childhood friends' series:

Asylum

Stalker

Cult

Hitched (coming late 2023).

About the Author:

After studying English Literature, Media, and Communications at universities in Queensland, Australia, and obtaining a Counselling Diploma, Helen Goltz has worked as a journalist, producer and marketer in print, TV, radio and public relations. She is published by Next Chapter, Wild Hearts Creative and Atlas Productions. Helen was born in Toowoomba and has made her home in Brisbane, Australia with her journalist husband, Chris, and Boxer dog, Baxter.

Connect with Helen:

STAY IN TOUCH FOR new releases and discount offers:

Website: www.helengoltz.com

BookBub: www.bookbub.com/authors/helen-goltz

Tiktok: www.tiktok.com/@authorhelengoltz

Facebook: www.facebook.com/HelenGoltz.Author

Twitter: https://twitter.com/HelenGwriter

Instagram: www.instagram.com/helengoltz1/

Ingram Content Group UK Ltd.
Milton Keynes UK
UKHW010928260423
420810UK00001B/170